PRAISE FOR

"Heuler continues to delight w[...]rn surrealism/magic realism – a cri[...]
Jeff VanderMeer, New York Times bestselling author

"Karen Heuler's The Splendid City is a wonderful fabulation, both humorous and contemplative, about the desperate state of US politics and society."
Jeffrey Ford, author of Big Dark Hole

"A thoroughly original and quirky novel. You'll find witches, cats, animatronic politicians and much more besides – plus sinister undertones combined with laugh-out-loud surrealism."
Liz Williams, author of Comet Weather

"Karen Heuler's soaring imagination is matched only by her integrity of vision and humanity. She's always a must read."
Paul Tremblay, author of The Cabin at the End of the World

"Satirical, and yet somehow more than just a satire, the joy of The Splendid City lies in the quirky and all-embracing exuberance of Heuler's imagination."
Brian Evenson, author of Song for the Unraveling of the World

"The Splendid City *is a splendid read indeed! How can anyone resist talking cats? I know I can't. This novel is so much fun and yet there is a deeper, darker story here… Heuler's excellent imagination and biting humor brings it all together.*
Ann VanderMeer, Award Winning Editor of The Big Book of Modern Fantasy

"Whimsical, satiric, and bursting with imagination, The Splendid City *is the novel we've all been waiting for from Karen Heuler."*
Nicholas Kaufmann, bestselling author of The Hungry Earth

Karen Heuler

THE SPLENDID CITY

ANGRY ROBOT

ANGRY ROBOT
An imprint of Watkins Media Ltd

Unit 11, Shepperton House
89 Shepperton Road
London N1 3DF
UK

angryrobotbooks.com
twitter.com/angryrobotbooks
Remember, we love you!

An Angry Robot paperback original, 2022

Cover by Kate Cromwell
Edited by Gemma Creffield and Claire Rushbrook
Set in Meridien

ISBN 978 0 85766 985 8
Ebook ISBN 978 0 85766 986 5

Printed and bound in the United Kingdom by TJ Books Ltd.

9 8 7 6 5 4 3 2

"Well, as everyone knows, once witchcraft gets started, there's no stopping it."
— *The Master and Margarita* by Mikhail Bulgakov

PART ONE

CHAPTER 1
Liberty

Betsy Bunderoo was used to seeing cats, but not ones who walked upright or spoke. She was standing at the bus stop, reading the notice that said the bus had been cancelled, permanently. Why? she wondered. Why don't they say? But these were the times – indefinite suspensions, removals, reversals, etc. Things suddenly were, and then just as suddenly, were not.

The structure is breaking down, she thought, and no surprise there. She felt a sort of grim satisfaction in it. So much had already changed since the election, why not this, too? Why should anything work when none of it made sense? The president did not want buses to run anywhere near the palace, and that was necessary, she supposed. She understood. But the larger problem was that the world was going crazy. No one could tolerate anyone who didn't agree with them.

"It's true," the big black cat said, nodding wisely. Ah! She had been muttering again, a bad habit that was growing on her.

The cat was wearing a bowtie and a fanny pack. "I'm finding it very hard to have a reasonable conversation these days. Everyone shouts sound bites and no one shouts facts."

"I wonder if there *are* any facts left," she said with a sigh. "I mean, everything is endlessly manipulated." If she'd had time, she would have wondered why she was having a conversation with a cat, but right then and there she felt it was best to be polite, because he was such a very *large* cat. And he sounded irritated.

"Things would be so much better if there were no internet," the cat said moodily. "Because it spreads everything too fast. People see crap, believe it, and act on it before there's a chance to respond. And there's never just one response. It branches out. Have you heard about those mushrooms whose underground roots spread out for miles in all directions? That's the internet for you."

"But mushroom roots aren't right or wrong," she said, frowning. "I don't think you've got quite the right kind of analogy there."

"Really?" he asked with a nasty, hissing kind of snarl, pulling off his fanny pack and rummaging through it quickly to pull out a gun. "Really?" he asked again. And shot her.

She clutched her upper arm. Blood ran through her clothes. The cat put the gun back in his pack and ran off.

Eleanor was going to be mad. A happy growl rose in his throat.

"How was your day?" Eleanor asked the cat when he walked in the door. She could see that he was miffed. He was always miffed.

"I shot someone again," he said, sighing. He had to agree it was becoming a nasty habit. "I do regret it."

"You always regret it." It was very hard not pointing out the cat's failures. She tried to make sure her face was neutral; it wasn't easy. She had pale skin, medium length brown hair, hazel eyes, and a face that gave away everything.

"Well, that just tells you about my character. I'm not actually the kind of person who goes around shooting people."

"And yet you do," she said. "Let's consider the circumstances.

No doubt they said something to annoy you. What was it?"

He frowned and shrugged his shoulders. "She contradicted my theory about the internet being like that huge mushroom root."

"Stan," Eleanor said firmly. "It's a bad analogy. Now, do you want to shoot me?"

Stan scowled. "I do." Of course he wanted to shoot her. Shooting people made him feel better, for a while. And it was certainly true that she could benefit from being put in her place every so often. She was bossy. Opinionated. He was the way he was because of *her*.

"Why not talk it out instead? You have the power of speech, so why not talk about things instead? Gloria will blame me if you continue to go around shooting people."

"I never kill them, you know," he said, his hairs rising.

"Try to be the kind of cat who never shoots them in the first place," she said. "You're just drawing attention to yourself."

The cat shrugged. "Who'll believe a cat shooting a woman anyway?"

"They're a nation of believers here," she said in disgust. "Read a newspaper once in a while."

Of course, his hands twitched at that. But he only allowed himself one shot a day.

They were walking down the street when a bell rang out, a familiar sound in the city, though it roved from district to district around the palace. People stopped and turned, waiting to see the messenger approach. The message could be good or bad. Once, a van had stopped a woman and then gave her the car that pulled up behind her. Then there was the time when a bunch of men got out of the van and grabbed a young man – a Latino, by the looks of him – and pulled him inside. An older man ran towards the van, but he was too late. They were gone.

The messengers were often on the news and were the most popular part of it, after the reported disasters in the rest of the country, and any attempts to overthrow the republic. Then the weather, updates about the president's latest triumph, and finally on to the messengers. People loved the giveaways and ignored the disappearances, which were generally explained as reunions. They were also fond of the whipped cream pies that hit people identified as tourists from the north.

"They'd better not hit me," Stan muttered. "I've got a gun."

Eleanor snorted. "*Everyone* here has a gun."

"My gun is better," he said with satisfaction. Eleanor could see no point in challenging that. Besides, she often carried a can of whipped cream with her in case anyone threw a pie. She might not be able to prevent it, but she was all for revenge.

Finally, Stan said, "There have been fewer messengers this week."

"That's a relief."

"Maybe. I was hoping they'd stop for me and give me a car."

"You can't drive a car."

"Why not?"

She scowled. "You're a cat." There were times when she thought that he just couldn't see himself as he was – but really, when had he ever?

"Which could change at any point, you know. All I have to do is hang in, and all *you* have to do is learn to be nice." He circled around himself in agitation for a moment. "But that's the flaw in my plan!" he growled.

"We're here because *you* were a jerk," Eleanor snapped. He always did it – he always had to bring things up, and bring things up!

"And yet *you're* here, too," he purred.

What could she say? He was right. They were each other's punishment. She couldn't get rid of him until she redeemed herself with Gloria. She hated to admit it, but she was shackled to the cat. "I'm here to find out what happened to Daria," she said. Gloria hadn't given *him* a mission, and she liked to point that out.

"You know that's not completely true," he said smoothly. "Gloria wanted to get rid of you before she heard about Daria. You went too far. You always go too far."

She wouldn't dignify that with an answer. She knew perfectly well that she and the cat were bound together until Gloria decided they'd learned their lessons. Luckily, she was also there to help find a missing witch, and that at least made it seem like Gloria respected her.

"I make the decisions," she said finally. "You're in charge of nothing."

The cat dropped to the floor in an elegant way and circled around her, pumping his tail up. "But to continue," he said, "I can say with all modesty that I *do* deserve a car. A convertible. Deep blue, I think."

"I suspect the van would decide to take you away instead," she scoffed. "And since no one cares what happens to the disappeared, I wouldn't care either." It wasn't a good look, she thought, saying things like that. But the cat was so annoying!

"I bet it's some kind of parking problem," the cat said philosophically. "Like getting towed."

"They don't tow people, they tow the cars."

"In other places, yes. But this makes more sense." He got a little jaunty, swaggering and swishing his tail.

He was like that, completely indifferent to what happened to others.

The bell was getting closer. She was determined to see what it was this time, to see up close. She and the cat had been in the city for three weeks now, adjusting and observing. Everyone had explanations for everything, but she wasn't going to fall for it. She would keep her New York City smarts for as long as she could. There could hardly be a good explanation for people being taken away.

A large tan van with side and rear doors rounded the corner.

There was a cheerful logo on the body, a smiling chicken with a frying pan. How typical, she thought: pretending animals were delighted to be killed and cooked. The van began to slow down, and some people stood still, watching, their heads swiveling as their anticipation built. Others, mostly Latinx, took corners, vanished into stores or up the stairs. And still the van moved along, ringing its merry bell.

In another era, it might be a siren, Eleanor thought, but it didn't matter. It was never ignored; everyone had their eyes on it. And then they could all see where it was heading – a young man, turning to stand and face it down, his legs spread out firm against the ground, his arms crossed, his head high, his eyes relentlessly watching it approach him, closer and closer.

How fierce he was! She could feel the tension rising in the air. Everyone contributed to it, as if they were a massed beating heart. The van's door opened, two arms reached out, grabbed him, and he was gone.

"Ooh, that was good," Stan said. "Neat and clean."

They heard a second bell, and almost immediately a car with the same logo came rushing down the street. This one had a sunroof, and a woman's torso stuck out of the roof and shouted, "They found my husband! They found my husband!" and she threw nougats at the crowd, who began to relax and grin.

These nougats were particularly popular right now. There were scarcities in a lot of items – milk, cheese, water, toilet paper – but nougats were everywhere and very cheap. Stan loved them, though Eleanor felt that he said this, and ate them, merely to irritate her. Cats didn't eat candy.

All around them, people were bending and picking up nougats, laughing and pointing out locations to other people. Some stuck them in their pockets and looked for more, others unwrapped them, threw the papers in the street, and began to chew blissfully. Some with open mouths, Eleanor noted in disgust. And the litter – these nougats were a disgrace.

"Put down that nougat," she said to the cat.

He popped it in his mouth and began to chew. "Leave him alone," a woman said. "Everyone likes nougat and why not enjoy it? We earned it."

"We did not earn nougats," Eleanor said through clenched teeth and the cat laughed.

"I have to put up with a lot!" he said. "This is my reward."

"As if you deserve a reward," she said. "You're arrogant and selfish."

The cat licked his paw once. "The problem is, you can't handle me. That's why we're both here. You've got a nasty temper."

She narrowed her eyes. "I *respond* to you; that's the problem. You set me off."

"Everything sets you off."

"No, it doesn't."

"Well then, every*one*."

"That's not true."

The cat snickered. "You don't imagine you're *good* with people, do you?"

Her face twisted a little and she had a brief fight with herself to get it back in order. "No, I know that," she said. She straightened her back and stepped forward, followed closely and carefully by the cat.

She hurried, but the car and the van had both raced down the street, making a turn onto President's Avenue, and were heading quickly towards the palace. Trying to chase them on foot was a fool's errand, she admitted. But tomorrow she was going to meet the local coven; perhaps they had information and could tell her what was going on. Maybe they would even give her some of her powers back. Any small amount of magic would irritate the cat, and that would be a gift.

They were only a few blocks away from what served as home, and they walked there together quickly at first. The cat soon dropped back to whack a nougat wrapper floating in the air, then rushed forward to toss it at Eleanor's feet.

Eleanor approached an old house with a small set of wooden steps that led up to a porch and front door. Ivy had crept up to wind its way along the railings and it had spread all over the front of the building, draping it in green.

Stan trotted forward to scoot in ahead of her. Eleanor was looking forward to some tea and maybe a piece of cake. Nothing for the cat though, who'd just had candy after all.

And he was getting fat.

But she believed he liked it.

She got the tea kettle and turned on the tap. Nothing happened. She turned it off and on again, even though that was ridiculous. Doing something twice wasn't magic. She sighed, thinking.

"It's Tuesday, isn't it?" she asked the cat, who was busy licking his tail.

"It is," the cat answered.

"Didn't we pay to have water on Tuesday? Did you forget to send the payment?"

The cat was offended and stroked his paw in annoyance. "You see why it makes no sense to put me in charge of paperwork? I have a philosophical indifference. It is not in my nature to be diligent. I am a free spirit! If there is no water, we will drink champagne!"

Typical behavior! That cat never got over his airs. It wouldn't really matter what kind of creature he was turned into, he'd always be lazy and selfish. She could see him as a boastful snake, a snide bird, a swaggering toad. He'd manage to turn it to his advantage no matter what. It was better to just ignore his moments of grandiosity because he got too much pleasure out of her annoyance. She had to admit she was annoyed too often.

She rummaged in her handbag on the table. "Go give this to the water man," Eleanor said, and handed the cat a twenty-dollar bill. "And get a receipt!" Fat chance of that, she thought, but she couldn't stop herself from giving him orders she knew he would ignore. At least he'd be out of the house for a while. Some days she just couldn't stand him.

Stan clutched the twenty-dollar bill in his paw for a block then tucked it into the pocket of his bowtie, which Eleanor had made specially for him to shut up his constant complaints. He strolled down the street, listening idly to the shouts not too far away in the distance. He liked to think of himself as an observer of the human condition, having recently been human himself. Having experienced life as both cat and man, he felt he had a unique width of perspective. Why go to work when mice were so abundant? Why wear ugly clothes when sleek black fur was so superior?

He took the long way around to the water office, thereby encountering the outskirts of the Tuesday parade. He saw signs that said, *Support Our Coal Workers* and others that said *Solar Power Isn't Power.* He could see some signs with business logos as well. Not merely the ever-present chicken with a frying pan, but also *Water Is Beautiful* signs, which had the virtue of not meaning much at all. The energy signs were propaganda; he was superior enough in his understanding of the world to know that. This week's march was therefore about energy, which made everyone feel good since it was a warm, pleasant day.

He turned a corner and ran into a line of people forming the end of the parade, or the side of the parade. He hurried up to join them, picking up a discarded sign that read, *You Don't Need Progress When You've Got Good Solutions.*

"What do you think of this sign?" Stan asked a marcher, once he had sidled into the middle of the crowd. It was moving slowly, and protestors waved to each other in delight.

His fellow marcher looked at it briefly and then shrugged. "A lot of words to carry. I prefer small signs." He waved his, which merely said, *We're Right.* "I think this covers just about everything, and it's easy to make."

"I've always felt very right as well," Stan said companionably.

The marcher frowned at him and moved away, and Stan quickly wandered back to the edge of the cheering crowd and sauntered off, heading for the water store.

There was a grumpy old man leaning over the counter as Stan entered the store. "No cats," he said without rancor.

Stan looked behind him, surprised. "Cats? I don't see any cats."

"You're a cat."

"My dear sir, I have a rare skin condition that makes me *look* like a cat. I am used to constant humiliation, to whispers and stares and the odd can of flung tuna, but I am not a cat."

The water man stared at him for a lengthy piece of time. "Okaaaay," he said, "as long as you're about to pay me for a water transaction. Otherwise, get lost."

"You see right through me! I do indeed want to pay for today's water." He handed over a piece of paper with an account number and an address. "We appear to have neglected to pay for today, though I believe you'll see the rest of the week is paid up."

The guy looked rapidly at his monitor, clicked a few keys, and said, "That will be one hundred dollars."

"For one day?"

"Reinstatement fee, update fee, penalty for lapse, plus, yes, forty dollars per day charge."

"That's ridiculous! It's always been twenty dollars a day!" Stan was about to say more but the fierce look on the guy's face stopped him.

"Rates went up. You want it or not?"

"I only have twenty." That was all Eleanor had given him; he was not about to touch his own money.

"Tell you what," and the old man suddenly got conspiratorial. "You give me the twenty, I'll give you, what, say, five hours of water?" He glanced at the screen again. "And five hours tomorrow. But from then on it's unfortunately double."

"Double!" Stan was shocked.

"Hard to find clean water these days. Liberals and illegals stealing it, y'know. Plus, lots of hands held out all along the way. But if you want clean water, we guarantee it. There's a black market for it, of course, I'm not saying there isn't, but what kind of water do you think you'd get from them? Huh?" The last word contained so much satisfaction that Stan stepped back a bit and then pushed his money across the counter.

"Five hours, then," Stan agreed. "And not a minute less. We just arrived from the East and we're not used to the water situation here." He gathered himself stiffly.

"Ah, Easterners," the old man said sharply. "And complaining already, when we all know that the reason for our lack of water is that you've been taking it from us for years." The man held up one of the local thin-print newspapers in proof and tapped it. "It's all right here. Land grabs and water grabs and court case after court case. It's good seeing some of you living with the results of your own greed. Maybe then you'll learn to think of others."

He bent his head and entered some numbers on to his computer keyboard, then nodded and looked up at Stan sternly. "Five hours. No more, no less. And don't think you can fill up your bathtub with water, either. We have ways of checking that." This threat worked a surprisingly large amount of time, the water clerk thought smugly, this impossible threat. It gave him a tremendous sense of power because mostly the customers believed him. In his estimation, the world was a sneaky place to begin with, and he liked the moment of surprise he saw in customers' eyes when he said this; he liked being the authority.

"We'll manage," Stan said. He wasn't feeling altogether satisfied with how this transaction had gone. He wasn't, it was true, good at monetary responsibilities. He was good at posturing and hissing and taking advantage of people. Getting them confused. Getting them annoyed. But he couldn't confuse or annoy the water person because they needed the water. If only Eleanor had kept a bit more of her powers! Though he knew perfectly well that she deserved not to have them. He knew that better than anyone.

Stan hurried back, avoiding the parades for the most part, but came across a string of people dressed in bright clothes with flowing colors. Half of them held signs that said *Horses tomorrow at 2* and the others said, *Camels tomorrow at 3*. One thing he did admire was that there was always something going on, despite the water shortage and the (possible) kidnapping of citizens. Eleanor took a more jaded view of that last one, though he liked the excitement of possibilities more than she did, it was true.

He decided to follow one of the women carrying the sign about camels.

"Hello," he said politely when he caught up with her. "Can one ride the camels?"

She stopped and looked him up and down. "No," she said with a sneer, "for the same reason that the camels can't ride you." And she started off marching straight down the street.

That was interesting. "And why can't the camels ride me?" he asked after her.

"Because there are no camels!" the woman shouted, and ran off.

This was exactly the kind of thing Stan loved. He was a student of absurdity and hated to think he might have missed this opportunity. He would walk a block towards the parade in case there were stragglers with interesting signs. Or anti-president agitators. They were rare and always filled with possibilities. He suspected they were hired, more often than not.

And he was in luck! It was only another two short blocks before he came upon what he believed was an actual agitator – moody, morose, holding a sign that said, *Is this the best we can do?* – a sign that might get him into trouble, depending on who was watching. He pulled up short. "My friend," he said, "as a completely neutral observer, I want to say that this kind of sign might anger some people for its moral ambiguity and lack of patriotism."

The man turned his sign so he could read it. "It's true," he agreed. "I understand that it's not acceptable, and yet I can't help myself. It must be a disease."

"It's not safe to have a disease in times like these."

The man shook his head sadly. "Of course," he agreed. "Of course."

"Put that sign down. Or better yet – give it to me," the cat said.

The man nodded and gave him the sign. Stan propped it next to a garbage can, turned around, and squirted it. That was one of the many things that made being a cat so pleasant.

And he gave himself credit for having intervened in that poor man's life. Perhaps he had saved him from a disastrous encounter. Eleanor needed to realize that he was underutilized. He sashayed a little, preening, because he was just so good at everything he did, then remembered that it was close to dinner time, and Eleanor had promised him a treat. Of course, he could get something for himself... in fact, now that he thought about it, he *would* get something for himself. There was bound to be a café or small restaurant that had exactly what he was hankering for – fish tacos. Possibly with a spicy mayonnaise and a lovely beer. Eleanor frowned on his drinking beer. "Cats don't drink beer," she had said, "so you're deliberately flaunting the fact that you aren't, at heart, a cat. And *that*, if you were more aware, is a dig at how you became a cat, which is a dig at me. I have apologized a million times, so there's no need to shove my face in it."

She was always annoying, of course. Always thinking she was better than he was. And therefore in charge. In charge of what, exactly? The water bills? He laughed at the water bills!

No need to let her ruin his life. He had done his errand, he had saved that stupid man with the sign, and he had shot only *one* person. And that not seriously. Besides, it was hours ago. It had been the kind of day that required a celebration, he was sure of it.

He paid more attention to his surroundings. There were a lot of small shops in this area, though it unfortunately appeared that most of them were closed. But then two blocks more and there was a café with some chairs on the street. It had an open-air counter with a cook behind it and a menu written in chalk. The first item was "Fish tacos" which delighted him. He strolled up and ordered two from a waiter cleaning a small table. "Are the tacos authentic?" he asked, without thinking.

"They're not really authentic tacos," the waiter assured him. "They're an American version of tacos, and therefore so much better than the authentic kind."

"Of course," Stan said magnanimously. "Americans are the only ones who understand Mexican cuisine."

"You're so right!" the cook said wholeheartedly from behind his counter. "Or any cuisine, when you come down to it. These tacos use pure American ingredients."

"Are the fish local?" Stan asked.

"Frozen! Pure American frozen fish!"

Stan liked how much attention the cook gave him. He decided he would even pay for his meal, though he had been intent on causing a commotion and escaping in the confusion, as usual. In a sudden fit of remorse, he decided now that he would *always* pay for his meals.

His tacos arrived promptly, beautifully prepared, with soft shells, some shredded cabbage and a salsa of fruit. "Wait," Stan said. "Is this a pineapple salsa?"

"Yes." The waiter looked alert.

"Aren't mangos in season? Why would you use pineapple? Aren't pineapples less American?" He forked his tacos into pieces – fish, cabbage, pineapple, cilantro, etc.

The waiter whisked it away. "I'm so sorry," he said. "Mango salsa! Of course! What was I thinking?"

Stan felt a mood coming over him. He had meant to be understanding; cooperative, nice. What had gone wrong? Was it his fault it had gone wrong? "And don't forget the ketchup!" he yelled to the retreating back. "This is how a good mood gets shattered," he muttered to himself piteously.

What the waiter finally came out with was actually pretty good, and the ketchup was a full bottle, which Stan used generously. Why were people always so snooty about ketchup? He loved it. He paused and made a note on his phone. He liked to pose provocative questions on his new social media startup, and he was sure ketchup would be a hot topic.

The waiter stood nervously nearby, refilling his beer when it reached halfway, over and over. Stan found the beer very good, clearly an American beer no matter what the label said. He paid, feeling kind and generous, and swayed his way down the street. He wondered how angry Eleanor would be if he stopped in a café and had a coffee and a cream tart as well. Surely the water would be back on by the time he got there, and she might not even notice he was late. Besides, he was very fond of cream tarts.

Eleanor tried the taps every few minutes and finally there was water. It was amazing how quickly they could turn it off and on, as if it was all computerized so recently. Perhaps it was, she considered. Although computers and bureaucracy didn't usually go well together, bureaucracies somehow changed the speed at which a computer could do its job. There had to be a reason why this worked so quickly, and of course it all had to do with money. Turn it off fast and you cow people into submission. Turn it on quickly and it depletes resentment. And the constant reminders about the water shortages made everyone uneasy and glad to have water at any cost. Or, almost any cost.

Eleanor didn't believe that the shortages were due to liberal misuse and theft of water rights by the East, as the president claimed. She didn't believe that whatever was wrong was because of the liberals. Gloria had laughed about that in their last conversation. "Pollution, agricultural runoff, fracking; storing mining residue in failing pools; damming rivers so that the wildlife and the rivers die. You can name a dozen culprits as to why the water's so bad, and it still won't explain why anyone has to buy clean water. Where does the clean water come from?"

Gloria was the one who had sent Eleanor to Liberty. Part of it was punishment, of course, because of the cat, but most of it was that Gloria wanted eyes everywhere. She wanted to know what was going on with the Liberty witches and why the coven was so small. And, of course, to find where the missing witch had gone.

The water had come back on more than an hour ago. Where was the cat?

The cat was licking his whiskers clean of cream, taking long luxurious swipes with his paw and then running his tongue along it. He felt very good about himself, which was true most of the time, but especially true at times like this. Eleanor believed in simple foods; he was more of a gourmand, notwithstanding the whole mouse thing.

He leaned back against his seat and glanced around with a superior, satisfied eye. He caught a touch of exasperation in a couple's conversation nearby and changed his seat after pretending the setting sun was in his eyes. He loved to eavesdrop. It was an art, and he was an artist. He also loved to take whatever provocative statements he heard and post them to Whispers, a kind of Twitter thread that paid out for the whisps with the highest engagement. He had been surprised to find that Liberty had nothing like this social network when he arrived, and so he had started it. That was one reason he actually enjoyed being here. It was technically an underdeveloped country. Eleanor might chafe at being here, but he loved it.

The tense couple held themselves politely apart, though the woman in particular was trying to appear casual and contained. It was clear that the discussion was well on its way to being an argument. The man leaned forward. "When you picture 'American,' what do you see?" he asked. "I mean, what's the image you have? I'll tell you what I have – it's a man in a field, working on his crops, standing tall to see his work. Or on a steel girder, or looking at his architectural plans, or on a commuter train, going home to his family. Or defending his country, in uniform. And none of them are Asian, or Arabic, or even black or Hispanic. They're white men."

The woman's smile was slow and chilling. "I think it's interesting, too, how it's always men you see when you think of Americans."

"Oh, don't do that. You know what I mean. When anyone says men, they include women in it."

Stan could hardly keep himself from cheering. He loved this kind of thing. "Really?" The woman's hand slowly curled itself up. "Do they ever say women and include men? Would you stand for that?"

"You're just deliberately turning it around. I mean only that when you say Africa, you think of blacks. When you say Puerto Rico, you see Puerto Ricans. When you say a country, you see the people who live in that country. And it's good. Why would you go to India or Africa if it was just like going to the suburbs? No difference? All I'm saying is that the differences matter, they have value, they have weight. And when I see America, I see, yes, a white, middle-class man, the picture of what this country was built for."

"When it was stolen from the Red Man, yes. Not the Red Woman, either, which again is very interesting."

The man groaned in annoyance. "This is an unpleasant part

of your personality. You're too stubborn. You're refusing to argue the merits of the case, you're just falling back on feminist crap. Feminist martyr crap."

"You know, they did tons of studies on what causes heart attacks and what to do to prevent them, to treat them. And you know what? They only studied white men. And it turns out the signs aren't even the same for men and for women. When women went to the ER they were turned away because the symptoms didn't match the symptoms for a man's heart attack. They went home with their heart attacks. Because whenever they studied something, they studied it with the male in mind. Whether it's medicine or, or – geography, apparently."

"Again, I see your point and that's a case to think about I'm sure, but it's not typical."

"It *is* typical. And it's time we did studies of all diseases but used only women. Let's see what happens then."

"That's stupid! That's just so stupid! How could it possibly be right, a study like that? How could it possibly be right if there are no men in it? Women and men are not the same."

"There! You see! You know that and you're not particularly enlightened. But medicine didn't know it. Isn't that amazing?"

"You have to start with the male," he said. "Of course you do. I mean, how could it possibly be valid if you started with women? Men don't have that whole menstrual thing, those hormones, they don't get pregnant, none of that stuff. Of course it wouldn't work. The baseline has to be male."

"Why?"

He spluttered. "You're doing it again. You're being stubborn. I don't know how to say it without getting you mad."

"Penises? Is that what you mean? It can't be valid if it doesn't include a penis?"

He sighed dramatically. "It really took you that long to get to it? Everyone knows it. The penis is the dynamic force of civilization. There, you wanted me to say it and now I did. If it doesn't have a penis, it can't matter. What else? Penises made the world the way it is."

"That's true," she said bitterly. "Look around you. Walls. Polluted water. Forced marches."

"Keep your voice down." They glanced quickly around the café, and their eyes settled, together, on the cat.

"What's that?" she whispered. Stan had excellent hearing; it was ridiculous how people thought he couldn't hear what they were saying. Maybe they thought he spoke a different language. He grinned and turned it into a yawn and then waved at the couple, whose enmity had been overcome by their uneasiness.

"It's a cat," the man said. "Or something like a cat."

Should I? Stan wondered and then shrugged. "I *am* a cat," he said grandly. That would unsettle them on so many levels. If the cat could talk, they would wonder, could it report their conversation? Their faces went through contortions trying to remember all the things they'd said.

"Let's go," the woman said. The man took out a credit card. "In cash," she hissed. "Cash!" They glanced again at Stan.

"I don't have enough," the man said, but the woman was already going through her pockets. She took out a bill and put it down. "Now," she said. "Let's go."

He nodded and they stood up quickly, keeping their eyes straight ahead as they passed Stan.

What a good day this has been, Stan thought with satisfaction, as he wrote down a question for his new and thriving Whispers feed: Which is more typical of the human race, a man or a woman? That would get them going! He really should reward himself. "A delicious cream tart. Should I have a second?" He considered, seriously, whether a second cream tart would be against his principles.

It would not.

* * *

A day or so later, Eleanor asked Stan, "Did you get the newspaper?" He had gone out for a leisurely stroll and come back smelling of cappuccino.

He tapped his fanny pack in response. "Amazing news today," he said. "It makes all my hairs stand on end." He took out the paper, looked at the headline and yes – his fur puffed up.

"You do that deliberately," Eleanor said. "I'm not impressed."

"Can *you* do it?"

"Why would I want to?" She shrugged. "What's in the paper?"

"The most marvelous thing," he murmured in a hushed voice. He did seem impressed. "Really. Look at this and tell me you're not thrilled!"

She opened it up and right there on the front page, a graphic read: *Treasure Hunt!*

She shrugged and put it down. "There was a treasure hunt last week, too. It was a goldfish. I think the clue read Living Gold, or something. Obvious, when you think about it."

"Read it." He gave her a sharp look, which wasn't unusual, but she could tell by the tone of his voice that he'd fallen for it, whatever it was. Get rich quick, no doubt.

No doubt.

She picked it up and noted the headline: *The Legend of the Grandiose Diamond Ring.*

Grandiose Diamond Ring? Was that supposed to be a brand? More likely just a made-up description to hook the readers. But it actually did look interesting, and little by little she dropped some of her disdain. She smiled. Oh, this would be good!

Lawrence Dean Wilcox, 95, owner of Meridian Investments, was born in 1869. He had properties in Texas, New York, the Riviera, and Colorado, along with two yachts and a railroad. His wife of fifty years, Enid, died two years before him and had no children. He was a lover of chess, golf, and riddles. He buried the bulk of his collection of gold and jewelry in

*the desert sometime before his death, fearing that it would
be lost in the stock market, and as he lay dying, he thought
out a series of clues and references that were difficult but not
impossible for any true treasure hunter. His servants often
heard him chuckling and laughing in glee as he worked on
them in the study. "He bequeathed us the first clue, which was
'Not in town.' Not much of a clue. Not much of a thank you."
The clues were to be revealed one hundred years after his
death, a date that came up two weeks ago. Now that the box
keeping the clues has been recovered, the grandson of his
original lawyer is releasing hints and suggestions, which he
said were pointless, but he is bound by law and custom to do
as directed.*

*His final note to his staff and lawyers claimed the treasure
is worth over a million dollars.*

"See?" Stan said. "Treasure." He began to sing gently in his
throat, his eyes half closed before opening wide again. "I'm
very good at puzzles," he said.

"Are you?" Eleanor was amused despite herself. Once you
knew one thing about this cat, you knew everything about this
cat – what motivated him, what he thought of himself, what
shiny thing would catch his eye. It was a terrible admission, but
she didn't think she'd ever known anyone as well as she knew
Stan – unwillingly, unhappily, and without release, at least until
she managed to redeem herself with Gloria. And speaking of
that, she had a meeting with Dolores, the local head witch, in an
hour. It would be best if Stan kept out of it. "You know, you *are*
good at puzzles," she said finally. "I think you stand a chance."
She managed to keep a straight face. He was so easy!

He lived for compliments. A compliment always overcame
any suspicion he had, and this did exactly that. He stretched
his front legs way out, and dipped his spine a little, trying to
ignore the belly that ruined that long cat form. "I do," he said.
"I really do."

CHAPTER 2

She was happy to see him leave soon after that, armed with his cellphone and a rubber-tipped pencil (a paw was a disadvantage with a touch phone), and she went off to meet Dolores, who had canceled their meeting a few times already.

The witch lived on the edge of the city, in a quiet residential area. She had a small front yard but a large, shaded backyard with an herb garden. A traditional witch, Eleanor thought.

Dolores looked tired and worried, and it wasn't long before she got to the point. One witch, Daria, had disappeared without a word of warning. "The problem is that I don't know what happened, and that concerns me," Dolores said. They sat under the shade of a tree, drinking tea, and Dolores' hands moved nervously, straightening things over and over again. She hesitated, staring off to the mountains, then looked back. "I assume she left willingly. But I don't *know* if she left willingly." She shook her head. "Sometimes I just worry that I didn't do enough to keep her with us. It was just the two of us for the last six months or so. The other witches drifted away, and I understand that. It's a difficult place to live, more because of the political situation than anything else. Two of them went to California. One of them converted to the president's party." She frowned. "I didn't expect that. It's a constant carnival for some of the population, and she liked that. But still," she said, "they told me where they were going and why. Daria never said anything."

"What's Daria's gift?"

"She's a water-witch," Dolores said. "Another thing that concerns me, because of the drought. She was incredibly good at finding water. Might someone have taken her so she could find water for them? I really didn't think anyone knew about her gift besides our coven. And, well, friends out in the desert. They believe in dowsers here, and most people try it out at some point. She has helped people before, just a few, and maybe word spread. I think it's actually illegal for anyone but the president to authorize a well, and wells cost a lot. Not everyone can pay those prices for water. They help each other, either by digging or by sharing. Small deliveries in the middle of the night, that kind of thing. Black-market water."

"Is the drought real?" Eleanor asked.

Dolores stared at her for a moment. "There was a river outside the city before; it's gone. I went there as a child, and I drove there last year. I went with Daria a few times. She would wade in and stand there, sometimes for hours. I never knew what to make of it. She'd just stand there and stare."

"At what?"

Dolores shrugged. "At the water. I thought a few times that it wasn't healthy, couldn't be healthy, to stare that long." She blinked. "Do you ever do that? Stare at something for hours, and then go back and do it again?"

"She must have loved it."

"I don't do it," Dolores continued. "Some water-witches can get obsessive, I've heard that. It made me uneasy, and I told her so and then she stared at me so long I had to catch my breath." She paused, thinking. "But that's not what you mean. I don't know where she is, I don't know why she left, and at least half the time, I just don't care."

That was unexpected. Dolores shot Eleanor a defiant look. Only moderately defiant.

"Gloria cares, though," she finally continued. "She reminds me that I've lost my coven, and there's a reason for it."

"Gloria can be direct."

"I think she's trying to get me to care about it more than I do." She sighed. "To care about all of it. There's the drought, of course, and the way it's been handled, and this, a missing witch."

Eleanor made sympathetic noises. "I don't really know what I can offer. You know the territory; I don't. You know Daria; I don't. I want to help but I don't really see what I can do."

"Gloria said you were the right person. Everyone here has accepted this way of living, one way or another. Oh sure, people complain, but they won't do anything. Why do people just take it? You won't. That's what Gloria said about you. You're impatient and judgmental, and you act without thought of consequences. We need that here. None of this is acceptable. That's what Gloria said, anyway. And Gloria wants to know what happened to Daria."

Eleanor sat there, her mouth hanging open. That wasn't how she saw herself. Persistent, yes; curious, fair-minded but outraged by injustice. Things like that. Of course she had made mistakes; she wouldn't be here with that cat otherwise, even though Stan deserved more of the blame than she did. All the things Dolores had said about her really were the cat's fault. Yes, of course, she knew she wasn't entirely innocent. She was guilty of having been provoked and pushed.

She sat there, with those phrases spinning in her head, admitting that Dolores was exaggerating, but she wasn't making it all up. Eleanor *had* been impatient. She had been judgmental. She had acted without thought of consequences. She was here to learn her lesson. She knew that, but she had assumed Gloria knew she was fundamentally innocent.

She nodded, stiff-necked, but it was a nod, nonetheless. "All right," she said finally. "I agree. I will do my best to use my weapons wisely."

"Not wisely," Dolores said. "But well."

* * *

The cat was still out when she got home, which was always a good thing. She had considered all that Dolores had told her about Daria going missing, the dwindling number of witches, the carnival atmosphere of the government, and the arbitrary restrictions. But underneath it all, she was still annoyed. She was a nice person, really she was. Not perfect, certainly, but not the figure Gloria had presented to Dolores. Why wouldn't Gloria give her a better resumé?

She finally made a decision and walked out into the backyard, a place with thick bushes and a small brick shed. "Hey, Gloria," she said near the shed. She waited a moment, and then a voice said, "Eleanor. How nice to hear from you. Good news or bad?"

Gloria, the highest-ranking witch in the New York coven, had initiated Eleanor into witchhood little more than a year ago. Gloria had skills with distance hearing, which simply required Eleanor to establish a specific location. Gloria could make herself visible, in a ghostly sort of way, which is what she did then. She was old and heavy and used a walker. Her skin was dark, and her voice was educated and just a little imperious.

"I have a question," Eleanor said. She sat on one of the chairs she had put near the spot. Gloria's apparition sat on a chair as well, at her end of the discussion. "I just met Dolores, who told me I was impatient and judgmental. That's what you told her. My question is, actually: what the hell! You know what he did, you know I was in the right and he was in the wrong – how could you betray me this way? I thought you liked me!" She heard the yip in her voice, the sound of a little girl in a schoolyard. She straightened up. "Sorry. What I mean to say is that I'm disappointed with your description of me, and I feel it's unfair. I'm not perfect. God knows. But you know what he did, and you suggest that I'm at fault?"

"We all react," Gloria said smoothly, settling back in her chair and clasping her hands loosely. She was no saint herself. "The real question is how well we've learned to control how we react. You know you didn't do well on that score. Stan certainly needed to be taught a lesson, but did you choose the right lesson? You transformed him. Which means you used your powers when there were alternatives, and in so doing you exposed the community. I wouldn't think Stan is the kind of person who should learn anything specific about witches – do you?" She waited for Eleanor's reply.

"Well. No. I've already admitted that."

"So, you were impatient and you acted thoughtlessly. Agreed?"

"I get it, I get it. I know what you're saying. But it was a mistake, not a plan."

"You reveal yourself when you don't have time to plan," Gloria said patiently. "You have strengths and perhaps you could consider that sometimes stubbornness is also fortitude, impatience is also righteousness. What good would moderation do in all circumstances? The world is not moderate. Quick to react may be a good thing when what you face is swift as well. Why did I send you there? Of course I wanted to get you away from your routines, and I wanted you and Stan to have to face the consequences of your actions, but I also needed someone in Liberty who would be unpredictable, resourceful, and who had a new approach. There's been a fracture in our community that needs to be repaired. Everyone else has been a witch long enough to consolidate their responses; you haven't. You'll try anything. I don't know a bigger advantage right now. What Dolores has described to me about the breakup of the coven is appalling. That's why I wanted you there. The fact that a witch is still missing makes me even more convinced that you're the right person in the right place."

That was better, Eleanor thought. A mixed kind of message, but better. She would do all she could to be impatient and unpredictable. She could be a jerk better than anyone she knew.

Well, except Stan.

And where was he?

The beautiful thing about being a cat was that it was easy to be ignored. Stan could drop down on all fours and look like a normal but very large cat, or he could stand up, pluck at his bowtie, straighten his fanny pack and pass for human. Not an average human, and occasionally he got into tiffs with people who objected to his claim that he was, but it was usually good enough. There was a lesson in that. He supposed that whatever spell Eleanor had cast on him actually changed perceptions (well, yes, he still felt human, so it was perception), and had different effects on different people. Some fell for it totally, some stared and shrugged, and some got furious. This, he felt, must be a general statement about humankind. After all, look how many people loved the local president, which made no sense. The water situation, for one, didn't call up the amount of irritation he would have expected, though he admitted that he was charmed by the nougats and the parades and the constant surprises. In fact, maybe he didn't care about the water situation at all, really. He liked beer, and there was plenty of beer. If he needed a bath, he gave himself a bath. He stopped to consider whether the president himself was also a cat, because so many of the attributes of this society were completely acceptable to cats. Hmm. Would people vote for a cat? It was an intriguing thought.

Perhaps it was simply the way he was living now, but he hadn't run into any real cats since his change. He wondered if he could communicate with one if he did. He had the appearance of a cat and the opinions of a man. Which one would dominate if he tried to strike up a conversation with a fellow feline? It was worth a shot, simply out of a spirit for adventure. He puffed up a little. He knew no one who was more adventurous than he was. No one more likely to obtain valuable information, to figure out obscure clues (though granted, he knew nothing about geography or his new environment), or more willing to lie, cheat, steal, and mock to get his way. He was proud of his mockery; it was a sign of intelligence and superiority.

Stan assumed that the best place to find stray cats would be near eating establishments, especially those purveying fish. Did cats catch fish in the wild? He would have to look that up; it seemed unlikely. Most cats he'd met stayed away from water, and that meant by extension, they stayed away from fish. What a strange thing then that cat food contained so much fish!

He looked around. Why, here was his favorite café again, with the marvelous fish tacos. Maybe he should eat one or two, then pull out some of the fish and save it in case he met a cat, as an enticement.

He signaled for the waiter and added a beer to his fish taco order. What a splendid day it was turning out to be. He looked around, hoping for a couple going through a divorce, or a father disciplining a child, but was disappointed. No one else was there. He ate alone, drank alone, saw no cats, and kept the merest smallest crumble of fish in case he ran into one.

As he left, he heard the peal of the messenger, and hurried towards it. He could hear it getting closer, and as he raced to see it, a man turned the corner, his face contorted with the effort of running. He held a crunched piece of paper in his hand, but then as he passed the cat, the man shoved it at him. Just to get rid of it, Stan thought, but he speared it with his claws and curled it in his paw. It would be fun to see what it was. The messenger van squealed to a stop, grabbed the running man, shoved him inside, and then left.

This was exciting, and Stan loved excitement. He patted the paper into his fanny pack. No one had followed the man or the van down the street; it had happened almost invisibly. Well, he and the running man had seen each other, of course, but aside from that no one else had noticed. As a cat, he was often mistakenly overlooked. This very human trait of ignoring the nonhuman made them so vulnerable! They missed a lot by thinking they were the only important species around. Still, of course, he *was* human, and a true cat *would* have been unimportant – they had always been unimportant to *him* in any case.

He got a block further with all these ruminations before he realized he hadn't read the sheet the man had thrown at him. He stopped, took it out of his fanny pack, unfolded it, and automatically ate the last little piece of fish he'd been saving. The sheet had four columns of type, so it was a newspaper. Indeed, it contained an article discussing the water situation, another detailing an upcoming parade, and then a small bit about the treasure hunt. This was circled in a broad felt pen, and there was an exclamation mark next to it with a handwritten notation: *Mark/Tuesday night 7:30/ Vancampen 214/ knows about the gold.*

Stan's heart raced and stopped, and then raced again. The treasure! It had to be the treasure! He marveled at his luck, at the sheer audacity of being in the right place at the right time. He was such an exceptional cat!

This called for a celebration and a beer, or perhaps two more would hit the spot. He took a turn down an alley, realized his mistake and found a tavern with outside seating. There he slaked his thirst a bit more than he usually did. It got dark and he appreciated that, and then the tavern closed, and he blinked and took a wobbly step home.

He had had too much to drink; it happened now and then. Stan wobbled around the city, sometimes on two legs, sometimes on four, having a good time imagining himself in all sorts of surprising situations where he, of course, got the better of everyone else.

He napped for a while when the beer made him stumble over a branch – of course, the branch was on the tree. He had fallen out of a tree! That was funny. His head was extremely unclear in a very pleasant way.

He got up, licked a paw experimentally, and decided to see if any café was open. A nice taco would probably clear up this sort of seasick motion he was feeling. And perhaps there would be a good argument he could overhear. Or even cause.

But it was very late. He took out his phone and saw that it was close to midnight. This town didn't stay open into the night – no doubt there was a law about it. About everyone having to be asleep before midnight. The witching hour. He didn't want to get into the whole witch thing...

There was a nice, peaceful aspect to strolling around deserted streets that he began to appreciate. He thought he saw a few other cats, dashing away. It would be nice to meet another cat. Maybe. What a shame he had eaten that last bit of fish.

The lights around the palace were dimmed, which was surprising. Perhaps an economy measure? Since, ultimately, the citizens were paying for the castle's lights, it was a surprisingly thoughtful gesture from the president.

Stan was a little woozy, so he stopped and stared for a moment, which was when he saw something drop from an upper window in the castle into the moat. It wasn't a straight drop, either. He was impressed that the item could be controlled so well that it didn't smash on a lower parapet.

He leaned against a tree, attempting to analyze it. As a human, he hadn't liked water all that much. Never went to the beach, that kind of thing. Learned to swim just as a precaution – mere paddling, of course. Why was he thinking about swimming?

Ah. Of course. There was someone in the moat! A person – not a thing – had dropped down from the heights, and missed the parapet, and was now swimming? And swimming quickly. It was making him dizzy.

Perhaps he should cut his beer-drinking down. One less beer. Or maybe half of one less beer. No point in being ostentatious.

* * *

Eleanor was still smarting over the things Dolores had said about her, and she wasn't feeling generous about the cat (in truth, she was never feeling generous about the cat), so her eyes narrowed and her mouth frowned when he walked through the door after midnight, smelling of beer and humming in the language of cats. The bastard.

He stopped at her glare. "What?" he asked. "Didn't you have a good day?"

"I did not."

He shrugged. "I had a wonderful day. I saw a man being taken by the messengers, but he gave me an interesting note before he was gone, and I passed a parade consisting entirely of suspended umbrellas, which was interesting because you had to figure out how they did it. I figured it out very quickly, of course. There was a man on a tricycle with clear plastic bars like a cage all around him, and the umbrellas were mounted to all the bars. He was followed by an elephant with a big sign for "Upton Umbrellas" and holding an umbrella in its trunk. It was an advertising parade. It was very well done." He was talking a little too much, very obviously throwing in a diversion. She would know it was a diversion. But she wouldn't know what from, so he still held the upper hand.

Eleanor opened the pantry door, bent down, and picked up a cardboard box. Stan groaned. "Not the box. Not right now." But she ignored him, took a step into the next room, and put the box down. He had no choice. Try as he would to ignore it, it kept calling to him. Would he fit exactly? Would the fat around his middle spill over the sides? Would he tuck his feet in so neatly that he looked like a loaf still in its pan? Sitting in boxes was so comforting and life-affirming that he had to promise himself he would only sit in it for a moment, and then go about his business finding the treasure.

He stepped in and sat. There was no longer any reason to move anywhere else.

Eleanor looked at him with contempt. For all his superior airs, he still couldn't resist a box. How must that feel? Being unable to resist? Lured by one's own nature, abandoning reason? She was sure it felt like any other impulse, obsession, or quite frankly, kneejerk reaction. She knew a lot about those. She was often trapped by a reaction. Just as a cat was trapped by a box, presumably. It was just in their nature.

She felt a little mean, of course. But it was better than using the laser, which he always had to chase. He would scold her, insult her, and still he couldn't resist chasing it. Doing that to him had started to feel shameful and she had stopped. But the box – how could that be torture? It just kept him quiet for a while, and that was good for the peace of the entire universe, she was sure of it.

She left him there for the night. It was late but she felt so put upon, so sorely used, that she gathered her flying ointment and her broom, and stepped out to the backyard. There was a half-moon watching her in the sky, with one eye and half an astonished mouth. She rubbed the ointment on her hands and face, sat sidesaddle on the broom, and rose gently.

Thank God Gloria had given her permission to fly, though she was warned to do it rarely and only for a good reason. No joy-riding, in other words. Eleanor had been careful to obey, but this was an emergency. She felt twisted with anger and anxiety. The cat; always the cat. The horror of it was that the cat was still ruling her life, still pushing her around. She had once believed she was smart enough to avoid manipulation. Obviously, that wasn't true. She could not steal herself to be neutral or indifferent. She reacted too quickly. Her judgement was not always sound.

She felt locked in, oppressed, pushed around. How had she gotten to this point? Did it matter? What else would she have done with her life? Yes, she wanted to be free, uncaring, the way Stan was uncaring. Not necessarily *be* Stan, of course; he was obnoxious. But there was something about him that she reluctantly admired: how he didn't care, how his lack of it became a strength, how she wished she had that strength. She disliked him and yet was jealous of him.

She rose.

Liberty was a fairly low city, with only a few high-rises, and those in another section. She lifted the broom to a modest height, enough to look down on the streets and the buildings around them. From this distance – not really very high – it all looked calm and almost kind. Her shoulders relaxed.

The lighting was dim in the city, since almost everyone rose early and went to bed early. She was sure the weird talking heads prowling the streets kept an eye on any problems, so she had no desire to fly in their direction. Instead, she rose up and up, moving gradually to the outer edge of town, watching as all of it became small and improbable. She was part of the sky now, more connected to the stars and the clouds than to the earth. Her shoulders relaxed; her hands unclenched. She felt free and untouchable. What did her own failures matter at this height?

There was a breeze. She hovered, content to be in a place where the cat couldn't reach her. She saw birds flying – mockingbirds or swifts, she wasn't sure. There was a beautiful, piercing cry from one of them, answered by another. How gorgeous.

She tried to mimic the call. It wasn't a particularly good imitation, but after a pause, a bird far away on the air answered it. She did it again and she picked out the bird who was calling. It come closer, gently riding the breeze. She called again; again, it answered.

It flew around her, swooping, and she mimicked its movements, swooping when it did, rising, going in circles. It coasted on those wings. She leaned forward on her broom, just a bit, just enough, until she caught up to it, staying discreetly to its right. Other birds flew by, joining and then leaving them.

Once she got very close and reached out to touch it, holding her balance carefully, but it shifted away, eyes straight ahead, and continued the arc it had begun. It moved off and was gone, not once looking back.

Still, it felt as if she had touched it, or been touched by it. It felt like a natural magic.

Eleanor got up late the next day and found Stan in the kitchen eating cereal. He waited silently while she made the coffee. Neither said a word.

She was able to think more calmly about Dolores' comments from the day before. She didn't have a high opinion of herself, but she had always hoped that no one else saw the multitude of failures she carried around with her. That hope was an illusion; it was as visible as the cat's box addiction.

The witches were a fair and just group, and they had punished her. Rightly so – she should never forget that it was rightly so. And while she didn't know if she would be of any use whatsoever in Liberty, she wanted to be. There was a missing witch, and she hoped to find her, though her own gift was of little help. Monica would be much better; she was good at finding things. As for noticing what was wrong and doing anything whatsoever to fix it, she was in the dark. She wanted to believe that Gloria knew exactly what she was doing by sending her here, but indeed she might have, in effect, offered Eleanor a box she couldn't avoid sitting in.

Either way, if she was going to do anything at all, she would need a good map, because she had no understanding of the geography of Liberty. She looked for one online, but Google kept freezing or loading sites with odd names. What little she could find seemed to have a lot of variation in geographical formation, and it was hard to track any one thing from map to map. The areas around the mountains became vague or contradicted each other. Were there two mountain ranges or only one? Had there been a major river and two tributaries? Or merely a creek? She deleted the map with the creek; too many people had mentioned the river by now. She believed it had existed at one stage, and yet she couldn't find any two sites that had the same river in the same place, or even the same size.

Well, she was a believer in libraries, so she looked one up and went to leave, without saying a word to the cat, who looked at her with half-lidded eyes and flicked his tail. He was annoyed. Good. She hoped she annoyed him as much as he annoyed her. Or even more!

The library was only five blocks away, in a nicely ornate building with tall columns out front. Inside, she asked where she could find maps of the area, and the librarian looked pleased. "Oh good," she said. "So many people don't consult the reference section, but we happen to have a good one. Go over to the right, there, and you'll see an open area with tables and chairs. The books are on the shelves all around them."

Eleanor went forward eagerly, determined to find out exactly where that river was, and what the area around it looked like. Wooded? Desert? Flat? Rocky? She knew there were mountains, and rivers often flowed down from mountains. It would be good to get a picture of what this all looked like.

And yet her frustration mounted. Each book she opened contradicted the one she'd just looked at. She went through the shelves, searching for an older book, but everything she found had been printed in the past year. Some placed a river in three different spots, one had no river at all, and there were mountains that changed place, depending on which book she picked up. She went back to the librarian and told her she was looking for an older reference map, something older than three years.

"Oh, no," the librarian said. "We don't have the older maps. We've been given new books – much *better* books."

"But the books contradict each other."

"Books often do. You have to be open to different perspectives, really, if you're going to read books."

"But they're *reference* books. They should tell me the correct information, but they don't. Or rather, the information is contradictory. The river, for instance – where is the river?"

The librarian looked at her suspiciously. "Are you sure? Because I've been assured these are all the latest editions. The head librarian sent us an email about it."

"Yes, I'm sure. I Googled it (and why is Google so wonky these days?) and some maps show–"

"Let me interrupt you. I see the problem. Google is so inaccurate. Always getting hacked and there are some sick people out there who like to put up phishing sites and such. Have you heard of them? They mimic real sites, but they actually just want to steal your credit card and so on."

"Who needs a credit card to check a map?" Eleanor asked, getting flushed in the face.

"And you shouldn't use Google for exactly that reason. So many falsehoods. Use Wiggle. The president spent a year getting scientists to straighten out all the misinformation in Google, but you'll get much better information with its replacement, Wiggle."

Eleanor's jaw dropped. She had never even heard of Wiggle. Her opinion of the librarian slipped immediately (and she had always respected librarians), but she also found herself tempted to see what Wiggle was all about. All she really knew was that she couldn't find what she wanted. Maybe Dolores had a map or an old book; maybe that would be best. The librarian watched her leave.

She was stumped. Falsity and contradiction – in the library! She heard the librarian's voice in her head: "You have to be open to different perspectives." But surely there was some central order, some litmus test to determine the truth? They couldn't simply fill a building with all sorts of claims and call one of them the truth and leave it at that?

Though again she heard the librarian's voice: "There are all sorts of views!"

Ridiculous.

Eleanor marched back through the streets. Far off, she heard a messenger, but she didn't care. Messengers were as equivocal as the "facts" in that library. She looked up and saw a woman running and then turning a corner, followed by the van with the cheery chicken and its frying pan. The noise eventually dissolved.

And then, unexpectedly, there was a sidewalk newsstand with a large display of folding maps, the kind you used to buy when driving from place to place.

She stopped short and gawked; they were all knock-off maps: "Triple Way Guide to Southern Hills and Valley and Range," "Stand and Rally," "Finding Your Way to Liberty," and her favorite, "Drive Big or Go Home."

She opened a few and found differences between them. A sudden fit of perversity forced her to grab a handful of maps, pay for them hastily, and make her way home.

Once there, she spread out her maps, choosing different features and tracking them from map to map. It was difficult not to get sidetracked as the topography was slightly different on each map, but she began to feel the overall shape of the area. Enough to get started, anyway. She worked at it for a few hours, forgetting to wonder where the cat had gone.

Stan had a relaxed morning after Eleanor left. (She should go out more often, he thought. And stay out.) He took the laser from its hiding place and did his set of calisthenics – rolling the laser across the floor and following the red light as it hit the walls, the chair, the table, pouncing and leaping. It amused him that Eleanor felt guilty about the laser. He loved it. He had once done a dramatic sprawl and begged her to stop while he panted. She bought it. He had no respect for anyone he could fool.

A good long walk after all that pouncing would be perfect. He wandered over to the address on the paper he had received the day before, even though it was way too early. He saw a woman running, a long way down the block, and heard the messenger's blare, followed by cheers from the streets. No doubt another prize, then. He almost changed his direction to see what it was this time, but he could control himself when needed. Obviously, it wasn't for him, so what did it really matter?

He looked down at the note in his hand. He had a clue. This was a gift, after all. The universe was rewarding him, obviously. He began to hum as he strolled along.

The cat watched as a panel truck passed by with crates of bottled water. "Hmm," he said out loud to the people who were waiting for it to pass so they could cross the street. "Don't you wonder where they get that water from?"

"It's clean!" a pedestrian said dismissively. "Safe water bottled safely. The president said so."

"I hear he will only eat sandwiches wrapped in plastic," Stan said smoothly.

"So what?"

"Sandwiches in plastic and water in plastic," the cat said.

"You're an idiot," the pedestrian said as the light turned green. Stan watched him as he glared his way across the street.

The cat turned to a woman nearby, who had been listening.

"When I was a child there was water everywhere," Stan said. "I remember swimming in it, splashing in it, letting it run out of the spigot and fall to the ground."

The woman nodded. "It was that way when I was young, too."

"It's still that way everywhere else but here," he said cheerfully. "Why do you think that is?"

"He may be right," the woman said stiffly. "You could be an idiot. Are you an idiot?"

"I'm sure I'd be the last to know," the cat said, delighting himself so much that he didn't even reach for his gun.

* * *

He spent the rest of the walk thinking what he might need for the treasure hunt. Transportation was the obvious problem. How would he get around outside the city, since the first clue announced by the man's staff was that it was beyond the boundary? It was unfair that the messenger had already given away a car! He had never actually driven a car, having lived all his life in New York City, but it now seemed important. Manly. Competent and sexy. For a moment he saw himself in a convertible with a gorgeous cat sitting next to him.

What was happening to him?

His fur rose and he hissed at nothing in particular on the street. He was rattled. A female cat? He was a man! Or was he turning into a real cat? That shook him up. Was he no longer a man in a cat curse, but a man... who was now a cat? His fur continued rising stiffer than he'd ever known; his back was arching; his claws were extended.

He had to stop at a bar for a beer just to calm himself. A man down the end kept staring at him until he finally stood up, drank the last of his beer, and went down to face him. "What's your problem?" Stan snarled.

"You look like a cat," the man said calmly.

"You're insulting me."

"No. I like cats."

Furious, Stan turned around, sprayed him, and ran out of the bar. He could hear some exclamations behind him, but he had, in fact, left enough money to pay for his drink. And a small tip, if he remembered correctly. This was the second time he hadn't shot anyone! And Eleanor thought he had no control!

He cooled down on his way to the meeting. Perhaps he had been a little severe on that man. He was always able to control his own normal temper, but cats have an even quicker temper, and it sometimes got the better of him. He was a little sad now, about spraying that guy. But he had mistaken him for a cat! And it felt deliberate!

In another block he felt himself humming and realized that, while the beer hadn't calmed him down, getting angry had. In fact, he sauntered a little.

He was a very clever cat, and he had a particular ability to sense the heart of things. Eleanor was easy – she gave herself away constantly – but even ordinary people, whom he listened to at cafés and park benches, were easy to understand. Their emotions stood out, their desires and failures. Oh, it was so easy to be a superior cat! Though, of course, he had once been a superior man. A pity he hadn't taken advantage of that, done more with it, recognized his abilities and, who knew, maybe even become a politician? He could see the politicians here did whatever they liked, said whatever they liked; as long as they continued to shower the people with nougats, the people were fine with it.

He didn't know if other people had gotten the same clue for the treasure hunt that that man had thrust in his paw, and that worried him. He happened to be at the right spot when the note was passed, but when he considered the circumstances, he wondered if it was the *only* right spot. What if a number of people had been approached? He walked swiftly to the nearest newsstand and got copies of the two major newspapers. They often shared the front-page stories – a strange thing to do, if they were competitive, but there were shortages everywhere, so maybe reporters and printers were a part of it. No doubt there was no real problem with competition. The papers didn't even bother with an online site, he had noticed. Of course, internet sites went up and down, and it was entirely possible that the sites had to pay to remain up longer – just like with the water.

He sat on a bench and looked at the papers. The front pages were about a glitter parade near the presidential palace. The photos were grainy but the idea of it was very attractive. If only he'd known! He should try to stay informed, especially now that he was on a quest. There might be clues everywhere! He jumped up and ran back and forth in excitement.

But what did he really know about the treasure hunt? The first clue was from the help, who said they had been told the gold was not in town. Could they be trusted? Were they trying to steer everyone in the wrong direction? Maybe the clue *was* in town, and they didn't want anyone to know. But that was too obvious; everyone would figure out they were doing that, so in fact they *must* be telling the truth and assuming everyone would think they were lying.

Aha! He was a step ahead already!

But the note on the paper – he first had to make sure it wasn't written on all the papers; it wasn't. His scrap of paper alone had the information!

He arrived at a nondescript building, perhaps a secular church, and the open doors led to a basement. He went in and heard some voices downstairs. A stout woman who stood at the bottom of the stairs looked over his head and around and then down at him.

"That was insulting," he hissed.

"Just looking to make sure you weren't followed," she said, stepping back to let him in. "We have to respect privacy and secrecy, or we might as well give up right now, don't you think?"

He was mollified and nodded. "I got your address from a man who was running from the messenger. He thrust it in my hands."

She nodded. "Joe. He's our scout. My name is Effie, by the way. We sent him out to find treasure hunters. We want to band together and share our combined skills. After all – if we split a treasure six ways that's better than not having it at all because five other people were ahead of you."

"But I could be first," Stan said. "So that would be a loss."

Effie smirked. "I haven't met anyone yet who thinks they would be second. But consider this for a moment. If you can discuss it with six people, and see what they're thinking, and eliminate the places they've tried – why, that would be something, wouldn't it?"

He mulled it over. "I see," he said finally. "I get what you're saying. Of course, there's a problem in that I would be a fool to actually tell you anything I was thinking." He looked smug and stepped back a bit to see the effect this would have on her.

"Of course. That's obvious. So, what we're going to do is only discuss the places we've decided are *not* the treasure site. We have to bring back photos of where we've tried so we don't just throw in anything."

"What would keep me from showing you a photo where I did find it and saying it wasn't there?"

She looked at him steadily for a few moments.

"Oh, right," he said. "If I found it, I would cash it in. But maybe someone else wouldn't."

Again, she waited for him. "Right. We could figure it out because they'd stop looking."

She waited again.

"I'm in," he said finally.

There was a total of seven people when the last straggler arrived. Joe wasn't one of them, and no one knew where he was. Was he in or out? Had the messenger caught him and taken him? Did he have a brand-new clue and was he out tracking it down?

"It doesn't bother me, whatever he's doing," Effie said. "Look, this is all voluntary. You can leave, you can stay. If there's no advantage to you, of course, you'll leave. But the more we can share, the more information we each have and that, of course, helps us individually. And discussing it helps, too, because something someone says might spark something in your own head. It gets your gears turning."

Various people shifted and looked at the floor or straight

ahead, and one by one they nodded, considering it. Stan felt inordinately superior to them all. None of them seemed all that quick-witted. *He* was quick-witted, though. If he got any information from these guys, he would put it to use faster and with more insight than they would. He relaxed.

"What do you think about that statement that the gold is not in town?" he asked, eager to get them all going.

In fact, they had all pretty much followed his own line of thought, thinking at first that this was a coverup for the fact that it *was* in town. Then they decided that everyone would assume that the real answer was actually the opposite of the truth, and then all of them came around to believe that it was not, indeed, in town after all.

It was a little unpleasant to find that they were all as smart as he was – or he was as dumb as they were.

"I had the strangest day," Stan told Eleanor later. "I don't think anyone has had a stranger day."

"Mine's been interesting," she admitted.

"Remember that man who was running from the messengers and handed me an address last night? I went there today and found a bunch of people looking for the treasure as well, and we were supposed to share what we knew."

"Not your strong suit," Eleanor said.

"Exactly. I think it was disinformation. I think it means I'm getting close." He brightened up. "That makes more sense."

"Getting close?" Eleanor scoffed. "Have you even started looking?"

He looked insulted. "I have started looking. I spent most of the day looking."

"I smell beer on your breath."

He stiffened, his fur beginning to fluff. "I was thirsty!" he said. "You forgot to pay the water bill!"

She could feel her hands scrunching into fists, so she put

them on the table and leaned over. "You know you're in charge of the water bill. You agreed to it." She took a deep breath. "And, in fact, you don't do your share of anything. I'm sick of it."

"Aha!" He wished he had fingers – he would have snapped them. "Sharing! That kept coming up today and it must mean something! That's the problem with you, Eleanor, you don't know how to read the universe. If you did, we wouldn't be here. But what does sharing mean?" He cocked his head to the right. "The treasure's not in the city. People who want to share clues. People who keep track of the water. Sharing." Abruptly, he straightened his face and his fur and looked levelly at Eleanor. "Nothing. I can't come up with anything."

He thinks he knows something, she thought. He thinks he just had a revelation.

"You're no closer than you were," she said, just to irritate him.

He started racing back and forth, his tail held stiffly high, faster and faster.

"It's water!" he said, finally stopping and licking his paw. "That's the clue! I get a message, I follow the message and it's not about the message, it's about sharing and what do we share? Water!" He was so delighted with himself that he was overcome with energy and emptied out the things he carried in his bowtie – money, a cigarette lighter, his flip phone.

"Why do you have a lighter?"

He rolled his eyes. "For the ladies," he said. "I've always wanted to lean across a polished wood bar and flick my Bic at some beautiful babe. Can't do that without a lighter."

"I also had a run-in about water," Eleanor said. She paused for a moment. Why did she always end up *talking* to him? Having conversations? True, a cold silence towards someone you were living with made everything substantially more awkward. But why open up about what she'd been doing? Exactly how much did she want him to know about that?

He was not trustworthy. But being stuck with him in these conditions made sharing details in life almost unavoidable. She would try to be vague instead. "That missing witch is a water-witch – that's the water connection. I want to go out and look around and so I looked for some maps with rivers and topography on them."

"Ha!" Stan said, leaping up again and, she thought, getting ready for another race around the room. "Maps! Yes, maps! Where are the maps?"

She waved his excitement off. "Don't you want to hear what I have to say first? Can't you stop listening to yourself for a minute and listen to me?"

He stopped pacing and tilted his head towards her, but his eyes were elsewhere. "You know, I could be wrong. It's not about water. That's too obvious. The clue so far is *not* in town. And then there's water. I bet it continues. *Not* in water. Don't you think?" He licked his right paw once, then put it down. "I don't think it's water at all."

He was so obvious. Hadn't he once been more subtle? He was afraid she would make use of his clue. He was afraid he had given something away, when she was sure it wasn't a clue at all. In this place, anything could mean anything, and everyone believed anything, and it was damn hard to get even simple things verified.

"I believe you're right," she said smoothly. He lowered his lids and considered what this meant, this sudden capitulation.

"I mean it," she said, seeing his suspicions. "I don't care where the treasure is. That's not my job. I need to find the missing witch."

"And do whatever you need to do to release me," he added smoothly.

CHAPTER 3

Once again, the president walked through the city, stopping people and shaking their hands and asking about their ordinary lives. It thrilled most of them. Imagine getting a snapshot of yourself next to the president, him shaking your hand and grinning, or even holding your baby up, or in one case, bending down to pet the dog? What an amazing man!

"He's a wonderful man. So homely, so sincere. And look what he's done for us!" Eleanor nodded politely at the store clerk who was staring out his window to the president and his bodyguards and the carefully selected citizens who were allowed to go up to him and chat.

She wasn't really interested, and she was about to turn back when she saw… the cat!

"Just a loaf of bread," she said quickly. "Would you slice it? I have to step out and talk to someone. Be right back." People in Liberty prided themselves on being neighborly, so the man was stuck. He took a loaf and turned to the slicer.

She stepped out of the store and sidled through the line of onlookers.

"It's about the…" and here Stan leaned in close to the president and finished the sentence. Eleanor already knew how that sentence would end, how any sentence right now would end. Stan only had one thing on his mind.

The president shook his head. "Wish I could help," he said. "I really do. I'm all in favor of treasure. There's nothing like wealth to prove one's intelligence."

"Or luck," she muttered.

"But no matter what, you'll always have Liberty," the man said famously. She'd heard that statement a thousand times already and couldn't understand the bright smiles that always greeted it. It was a stupid catchphrase, that was all.

The cat bowed very nicely and took off. The president looked around and grinned. His bodyguard moved people out of the way, and he walked on.

She had to admit that it seemed like a nice thing to do – walk among the populace, bend down to the common folk. She had to grudgingly admire it, but of course there were the messengers taking people away, and the whole business with the water, and all those daily parades – which she really couldn't imagine were entirely voluntary, though she hadn't come across anyone complaining.

Someone should be complaining.

She went back inside, paid for her bread, and started wondering what the cat had been up to. Did he really think the president had a clue and would just give it to him? Of course he did. He was opportunistic. He had seen the president and wondered if the president was a walking clue. After all, a total stranger running by him had shoved a clue in his paw; nothing would surprise him.

Narcissist.

Well, of course the president was a narcissist as well. There were animatronic president's heads scattered throughout the city, all of them eager to talk to any pedestrian who had nothing better to do. She had yet to talk to any of them, and as she turned down a street, she saw a pickup truck swapping out old heads and replacing them with newer ones. It was a bit surprising. The used heads were all grinning, and their eyes seemed to be watching her.

She tried to imagine this scene in New York City, but in Manhattan, it could only happen ironically. She went back home, avoiding as much of the procession as possible. She wanted to have another look at the maps before meeting with Dolores.

Surely there had been six maps? Yet she could only find five.

She mentally went through the whole day with the library and the strangely convenient kiosk selling maps. Yes, there were six maps. Now there were only five. And a cat who was looking for treasure, she reminded herself. Why hadn't she hidden all the maps?

Something in her psychology always sabotaged her own efforts.

There was nothing to do but go ahead with what she had. She sat down and opened the maps on the kitchen table. Of course there could be something in the missing map that managed to explain all the other maps, but there was no point in punishing herself by not paying attention to what she had. She had five maps.

She straightened the maps out, and quarter by quarter, she compared all of them.

What she found was that the imaging of the mountains always looked the same, but the mountains themselves moved in relation to rivers and lakes. The lakes and rivers appeared or disappeared. She looked at configurations and altitudes, and began to assemble a composite starting with the mountains as the fixed point. Water flowed downhill, which made her put the largest lake and largest river south and west of the mountains. She backtracked when she remembered that someone had said there was a dam. Where would a dam go? She made a quick study of the topography looking for a basin in the mountain. She thought she found one, and then she re-pinpointed a river from that. That would be overflow but it would also probably be the original riverbed. You didn't put a dam where the water wasn't flowing.

There were no towns noted on the map within about seventy-five miles of the mountains. She suspected that this was mostly desert, and that whatever dwellings there were, were isolated cabins. Not worth naming.

If she were a person who yearned for water, whose qualities made water the pole toward which she was pulled, where would she go?

"Has anyone gone to the old riverbed?" she asked Dolores when they met again.

"It's close to fifty miles long," Dolores mused. "And the river wandered all over the place, including through a desert. A very strange sight to see. You'd be lost in the sands, nothing but sagebrush and cactus, dying for a drink, and then in the distance there'd be – a sailboat! People didn't believe it. At least two people died thinking it was a mirage."

A sailboat? Was that a standard mirage? "We could fly over it, just to see. And there's a dam?"

Dolores nodded. "The dam's still there."

"We should look at it."

"Sure. By the way, the closer you get to the mountains, the more guards and drones there are. The president has told us that there is indeed water theft, and it's coming from foreign terrorists, from Oregon, I believe. And he hated doing it – he had tears in his eyes – but he had no choice but to safeguard it."

"I hope you're kidding?" Eleanor asked.

Dolores shrugged. "You're new here. This has been going on for some time. He takes things away, and weeps for our misery. He would do anything to avoid this, but terrorists, liberals, socialists. The words change occasionally, but basically, he is forced to do these things in order to save us. People nod solemnly and clasp their hands as he explains that the water rates are going up because the Democrats have diverted the rivers; that we have to pay for Wiggle because Google is nothing but propaganda filled with false information; that we march to show our love for the Republic and the president voluntarily, and God loves it because marching improves our health."

"Is it? Is it voluntary?"

Dolores shrugged. "A lot of people like it, as far as I can tell. And yes, people are healthier. Or at least, the ones who march. There's a counter-march occasionally, usually at night. To prove we're open-minded."

Eleanor looked away for a moment, thinking. "But they're not really counter-protestors, are they?"

"No." Dolores grinned. "I mean, there's no proof. But they chant the weirdest things. 'Down with justice!' 'We'll come and get you!' Things like that. It gets reported on the next night's news, and then the reporters do their cross talk and say, 'Can you believe it? If it were up to me, I'd hang them.' And the other will say, 'But that's what makes us a democracy, John. We disagree with their vicious ideas, but we let them live. You can bet the president keeps an eye on them.'"

"It does seem a little clumsy, though. Who would believe it?"

"People here believe those are real protests. They eat it up and feel virtuous. Because they're 'threatened' by 'outsiders.' And that makes them heroic."

She shook her head and returned to her original question about the local geography. "I have a bunch of maps, but they don't agree on where things are in relationship to each other..."

"A new map every six months," Dolores said, nodding. "As the mapmakers correct the false information we have been subject to."

"The original maps have disappeared."

"Death to misinformation!"

"We could take brooms and see for ourselves?"

Dolores pursed her lips and shrugged. "There are so many drones. If we're out for very long, we'd be caught. But I do know someone who might help." Her chin sank thoughtfully on her chest. "Hector used to prospect for gold, as a pastime. Found nuggets once or twice but I doubt they even paid for tools and gas. Still, if you love something, it doesn't have to make you rich, does it?"

"No."

She raised her head and smiled. "Good. In fact, I think it would be a good idea to go visit him and chat. Give me a minute and I'll call." She got up and looked around the room. "Ah," she said, spying her phone. She got it and moved out of the room to make her call, though Eleanor could hear some of the conversation. "Doing some research. Yes. I mentioned prospectors but it's not all about you. It's about locations and geography and maps. Yes, maps. You have some of the original maps, don't you? Can we see? Yes, I'll bring cake."

In the old days, she would have heard the phone being hung up, a very satisfying sound. In fact, on those days (which always came) when she wanted to slam the phone down to indicate her absolute hatred of and contempt for the person she'd been speaking to, it was criminally disappointing not to be able to slam it. She wondered if there was an app for that slamming sound; she should make a note to find one or invent one.

Dolores returned, looking satisfied. "Can we go now? All we have to do is bring a cake. Hector loves sweet things but won't bake. I also like sweet things, and I also don't bake. I don't suppose you have a fresh-baked cake waiting at home?"

She laughed and admitted she didn't.

They went into town, but the baker only had chocolate cake, since there'd been a run on vanilla extract and the stores were empty. "Sadly, Hector is allergic to chocolate," Dolores told Eleanor. "We'll have to come back tomorrow."

"I don't know what the point of people hoarding vanilla is," the baker grumbled. "What can you do with vanilla? It makes no sense." She shook her head. "What has the world come to?"

Dolores sighed in sympathy. "My," she said soothingly, "perhaps you should tell the president. Sounds like a conspiracy to me."

The baker shifted a pile of flattened boxes to the side, then pushed them back again, obviously agitated. "The president has better things to do than worry about vanilla."

"Hmm. I wonder." Dolores turned to Eleanor. "I think I remember that vanilla is an ingredient in some homemade bombs?" She turned back to the baker and shook her head woefully. "It's truly a sad world we live in."

They walked out of the store sighing and looking sad. "Don't laugh until we get a block away," Dolores said under her breath. "I come here often enough. I wonder if she'll start Wiggling that combo, bombs and vanilla."

It was entirely possible that they were acting like East Coast liberals, being superior and dismissive, but Eleanor loved it.

Vanilla bombs!

The beautiful thing about being a cat was that you could so easily manipulate people, Stan thought. He was sitting in the sun on a low wall in the park. There were benches to his left and right, and people who came, chatted, and left. This was a perfect life, for Stan loved nothing more than eavesdropping. And he had an absolute faith in his ability to draw conclusions from what he overheard. He used them to make money in his Whispers thread which, granted, was still brand-new and didn't yet have sponsors. But it would.

Nothing happened for a long time, though, until an older man sat next to him. The man went over a list he took out of his pocket. He held it tightly up to his face. Near-sighted, Stan assumed. But whatever he was looking at probably wasn't that interesting. The man looked dutiful, Stan thought, exactly the kind of man with no imagination. Unlike himself.

The man's phone rang, and Stan began to lick his left paw, which allowed him to move just a little bit closer so he could hear. The one-sided conversation was disjointed but it mostly consisted of the man saying he would get things, "as agreed," and be home, "as agreed."

It meant nothing; it had no content. Unimportant people talking about unimportant things. The place was full of that. The man left, and Stan looked over at the paper he had left behind. There was something circled on it, and he pounced.

It was an ad. It said, "What are you looking for?"

Of course the ad was about cars, but that was irrelevant. Stan was looking for something; this man was a clue all on its own; the clue was meant for Stan. His mind locked onto the list:

Road trip

Hertz

Shovel

Wellmade

Dessert

He closed his eyes briefly in bliss. His heart beat faster, fur rising in anticipation. Which word was the clue? Were all of the words the clue? He opened his eyes again and considered.

Yes, of course, searching for the treasure involved a road trip.

He wondered if Hertz would rent him a car; he did have a license, but the photo wouldn't match his current appearance. And it was hard to grasp a steering wheel without thumbs, though he was sure he could figure that out.

Of course he would need a shovel.

He knew nothing about Wellmade.

"Dessert" was probably supposed to be "Desert." People often misspelled those two. He never did.

He took out a small notebook from his bowtie and wrote down all the words. Not that he was likely to forget any of them; still, it was proper procedure to write things down. It helped the brain consolidate all its information and shake it together to make sense.

A thought occurred to him, and he took out the map he had stolen from Eleanor and unfolded it. The day was bright and sunny, and by going behind the bushes, he could open the map without attracting attention. His question to himself was whether anything else on the list made sense in terms of the map. He looked for deserts and found an area that could indeed be desert, though oddly enough the map didn't identify the area as such. But there were no towns in various parts of the map, and that indicated inhospitable conditions. Deserts were inhospitable.

And then he saw it. He froze for a moment, his mouth open. He couldn't believe his luck, or his intelligence, or in fact his genius. His eyes rolled back and then rolled forward. He growled in delight.

In the middle of the desert, just off to the right, was a single small word: Madewell.

Dolores had an old Volvo, a very sturdy car with lots of discarded paper coffee cups ("I never buy anything with Styrofoam") and paper bags in it ("I recycle, when it's not greasy, sorry for the mess"), which felt like it had no padding anywhere. But it ran well. Eleanor had taken the subway one stop (which was the end of the line, and as close as she could get) to another bakery to get the day's cake (strawberry) and then walked down the streets, past a presidential truck throwing out free ice cream bars, and then to a bus that took her a few miles out of the city. Dolores would have driven to get her, but it happened to be a festival day, and the streets were closed to traffic.

No witch in her right mind would ride a broom in the daytime, though Eleanor wondered if it would surprise anyone, as used to spectacle and surprise as they were. Still, as Dolores kept telling her, there were drones and cameras everywhere, and they would have to be careful. The car rattled past thinning residential areas to smaller industrial areas and then out to the desert with its creosote and cacti sprinkled next to the rocks. It was fairly flat at first but there were more and more rocks and then small hills, and then irregular shelves of rock and shallow canyons. The rocks grew bigger, the mounds turned into hills, the overall color of brown got broken down into the greens of yucca, agave, with the occasional deer or small animal leaping or looking at them.

She had not been out in the desert yet, so it surprised her to see so much growing. Had she thought there would be sand? She had thought there would be sand. Instead, she found a strangely vibrant and varied landscape.

The road twisted for no particular reason, and Dolores took a wide side road off the main one and slowed down after a few miles.

"That's the river," she said sadly, looking fixedly ahead, and Eleanor felt a small sharp shock in her gut, though she'd never seen the river and therefore couldn't mourn it. But there was a wide, depressed area ahead of them, trailing like an enormous snake from left to right, a slightly darker shade than the land outside it – the "dry" land. It looked so wide and forlorn and *meaningful* somehow, as if it were a lesson, an example of the dangers of the future. She saw that there was indeed a small trickle of water at the center, and birds and some kind of animal drinking at it, but these just intensified the awful wastefulness. Those poor animals reminded her of vultures around carrion.

"It's awful," she said.

Without further comment, Dolores started the car up again, turned around, and continued heading towards the mountains, which seemed as far away as ever.

"I forgot," Dolores said at one point. "What's your power?"

"I can stop and start things – push/pull."

"Gloria said you were being punished. Did she take that power away?" Dolores wasn't being insulting; she was curious.

Eleanor felt her face flush. She hated being reminded of her sins. "My punishment is that I can't transform anything. And I stopped being shown more magic. So I'm kind of half a witch." She almost said, "half-wit witch," but luckily stopped herself.

"You can fly."

"I can fly. It's all up to Gloria, really. Her rules."

"She always had a lot of rules," Dolores said, and Eleanor wondered what she meant. Was there a story there?

"It's nice here," Eleanor said, looking around. "The colors are good. Browns and tans and greens. And if you look closely, you can see there's a lot of life. Bugs. Lizards. Some birds over there." She gestured vaguely.

Dolores followed her gesture and kept glancing at the birds. "I like birds," she said thoughtfully. "But those aren't birds. They're drones."

"Drones?" Eleanor asked. "What are they looking for?" They were coming closer, fast and low. It felt like they had eyes.

"Traitors. I think they're looking for traitors."

Eleanor drew in her breath. "Dolores! You don't mean *us*, do you?"

"Do you feel like a traitor?"

How would that feel? How would she know? It was probably a trick of perspective – she would see someone as a traitor who would in turn see her as a traitor. Or she might not notice that someone saw her as a traitor at all. "I'm just helping to search for a missing witch," she said finally. "Nothing in that sentence sounds criminal to me. Or did you mean they're looking for other people who are traitors?"

"Just for fun, let me ask you a question: How do you feel about this system of government?"

"I'm new here. I'm still figuring it out." Of course it was a strange kind of government. And of course a lot looked suspicious. Those messengers. The water. The hallucinogenic daily social life.

Dolores fell silent and Eleanor wondered if that was significant. Could drones hear their conversation? Eleanor didn't know enough about it, and looking at Dolores' serious face, it was possible that she simply wanted quiet in order to think.

The drones moved off, and the car continued forward, exactly at the same speed.

"Were you just trying to spook me, or did that mean anything?"

"I'm sure you know what drones are used for," Dolores said. "Their purpose is obvious: they're watching us. And by us, I mean just about everybody. They keep track of marches and meetings, to see who runs into whom. Surveillance. That makes sense in the city, but what's out here?" She looked around.

"They seemed to be meeting other drones and heading to the mountains," Eleanor said helpfully, only to be met with a frown of contempt. "As you know," she added.

"Did you bring one of your maps? Mark it down." She waited for Eleanor to open the map and slowed down, her head moving back and forth from the road to the map. She stuck her hand out and pointed. "We're here, roughly."

Eleanor marked the map and looked around. "The mountains are so far away. And the river is dry. There's not really anything out here for the drones to look at, is there?"

"Is that a fact?" Dolores said moodily.

Eleanor sighed. This whole place seemed to be hiding some vague mystery, with constant distractions to keep people from figuring it out. She wanted to know more, to be certain of more, but Dolores wasn't helping. "I can't get a handle on this place. All the parades. The cheerfulness seems mindless. The marches seem pointless. Am I missing something?"

"We're all missing something," Dolores said. Her eyes were still sweeping the sky for more drones. "Just be careful. Don't say anything dangerous. There are bugs everywhere. Outside, in the open air, keep your head down so there's no lip-reading. That's the only way to go."

"Oh, it doesn't seem that bad."

Dolores' steady, slightly disdainful look made a flush spread across Eleanor's face. "I'm new here," she said defensively.

"I'm grateful for everything you tell me. I haven't seen what you've seen. It doesn't make sense to me yet."

"Forget about sense. As for the drones, you just have to learn to notice them and then avoid them. Sometimes I don't see any for weeks, and then I see them constantly. And I start to wonder: are they following me? What did I do? It's impossible not to be paranoid. Although they haven't bothered me on the ground; they haven't pulled me into a van, so it may only be my imagination. The best thing to do is to act normally and don't wave." She looked quickly at her passenger. "You strike me as someone who would wave."

That shut Eleanor up for the rest of the ride as she considered: was she someone who would wave? Was that a bad thing? Did she *want* to be someone who would wave but she wasn't, and Dolores was mocking her?

It preoccupied her in both directions of the journey, because when they got to Hector's, he wasn't home.

Dolores sighed in exasperation. "He does that. He thinks he's a free spirit, and half the time that just means he's incredibly rude. Oh well, I don't think this cake is going to take too many trips back and forth; let's split it and each take half home. We'll try again tomorrow. Will that work?"

"Sure," Eleanor said. "I'll take the cake home to the cat. He loves cake."

"But I don't think strawberry is good for cats."

"Even better," she said.

CHAPTER 4

Eleanor had quickly gotten used to seeing the president's animatronic heads in various places all over the city. They were out in the open in the parks and plazas, and she came upon them near churches, stores, ATMs. She had asked a perfect stranger what they were for, and been given an odd, appraising look and a quick, "New in town?"

"Yes."

"This is our president."

"I understand. But why heads? Why so many?"

"He loves us and he's everywhere for us. He's always available when we need him. It's a great comfort and solace. I don't know if he'll listen to *you*, though. As an outsider, I mean." The stranger started to walk off and then turned. "I hope not," he said. "He's ours."

She saw people walk up to the heads, huddle close, and whisper. Like a confessional, she thought. She saw a woman step back from a head halfway down the block and felt a tug of curiosity. Was there a man behind the machine? Was it a recording? How did it work? She approached it and stood, waiting.

"What do you want?" the head said amiably. "Is there anything you would change?" The head sat on a platter ruffled with green silk. The face was an idealized version of the president's face – smoother, friendlier (though of course the president always seemed to be friendly). His eyes blinked and changed focus and followed her if she moved; it was uncanny.

She looked at the head skeptically, trying to analyze why it had such a bland expression yet provoked such an annoying reaction. It blinked its eyes and its gaze followed her as she circled it. "All right," she said finally. "Hello."

It nodded. "How are you?"

"Fine, thanks." She rolled her eyes at herself. Really, should she thank a computer or recording or whatever this was?

"Are you better than you were?"

The question unexpectedly stunned her. Was she better? She was not at peace with herself, certainly, but she was going forward. She had done something she shouldn't have done, even if it was to a person who deserved it. That was confusing. Was she saying that the action was itself justified, but she was not justified in doing it? That kept spinning out in different directions because, looked at objectively, if the action was right, then the actor was right in doing it, wasn't that so? How could the action be right and the actor be wrong?

Still, she admitted, logically or not, that she shouldn't have done it.

Would she do it again, if pushed that far? She hoped that she had improved, gotten better, had more control over her temper, her responses. Her instinct. Her instincts sometimes lashed out, and it was confusing that Dolores had said that this impulsiveness, wrongness, was something she hoped to use in order to find Daria. So, in that case, a wrong action would lead to a right end. And she wasn't like that all the time, anyway. She had made one mistake, one huge mistake. Though it was also true that she had always avoided people because they annoyed her. They were not like she was, and they had always noticed she was not like they were.

Was she any better now?

The head was patient. The head allowed her to think.

She was looking for Daria. She was living with the cat and hadn't killed him or thrown him across the room. In fact, they went their separate ways and had made a kind of accommodation with each other. That was something.

She recognized that what she had done to the cat was wrong. She should have done something that didn't jeopardize the witches.

She straightened up her head. "Yes, I'm better. Not perfect, but better." She felt relieved that she could say it.

"I knew it!" the head said. "I've done all I could to improve the life of the people I serve. And I'm gratified to know that I have helped you, in whatever way I could."

"You didn't help me!" she snapped. "I helped myself."

"We all work together under my administration to improve the people's lives, working together to get rid of greed and hypocrisy. Greed is your ruin! Give to my campaign as a token of your dedication to the abolition of greed! Will you give a small donation now to spearhead our campaign for a greater Liberty?"

The head grinned and waited for her answer. A small shelf came out with a touchscreen for a credit card. After two minutes of silence, it discreetly withdrew. The head made no mention of it, but instead continued, "Our greatness relies on our ability to move forward together in humility and loyalty. Of course, not everyone is loyal, and that's a danger to our democracy. Maybe you know people who are struggling with this and you would like to do something to help them move forward with you, and with us?"

A moment's pause.

"The best thing you can do to help them is to tell us who they are. We'll reach out to them. We'll send specialists to help them love our great democracy. Sometimes people just need a little kindness to discover how great we can be together. They're probably unhappy, too. Don't they seem unfulfilled? Tell us. Tell us and we'll help them."

She stepped back. She was horrified. A little bit of light lit up the head's left eye. Was it a flash or was it a reflection? She looked around. It was a bright day; there were cars and birds and anything could have made a shadow or a reflection.

But she felt uneasy. Terribly uneasy. She stepped back and then stepped away.

"Remember we love you!" the head called out.

"Oh, the heads," Dolores said. "Yes, I would steer clear of them. They're all over the place now, and some of them even sing snappy tunes to get your attention. Did it ask for a donation? They all do. And did it want to help you with your life or ask you to turn someone in? I wouldn't give out any names, of course, but I don't really think they do anything. I've never heard from anyone who *has* mentioned someone." She paused. "I suppose that would be true if someone felt guilty because the person they mentioned disappeared." She frowned; her head lowered. She looked up with something like shock on her face. "That couldn't be Daria, could it? Could someone have mentioned her?"

"Why would they? Did she go around criticizing the president? Did she have enemies?"

"Not exactly," Dolores said. "In fact, she liked the president. She thought he was interesting. But if that annoyed someone, they could have told the head that she needed 'help,' couldn't they?"

"How long has she been gone?"

"Close to a year."

"A year!" Eleanor was shocked. "And you're just starting to look now?"

"Well, she said she was going away for a while. That could have been a way of saying she was finished with the coven. Being polite about it."

"Was she that polite?"

Dolores laughed. "Never. But I didn't want to confront her. She drained my energy. I figured, fine, let her work out whatever she needed to work out."

"But a year!"

"Exactly," Dolores said calmly. "Witches have come and gone before. The general rule is that you have to withdraw formally before you leave. She didn't. So I began to worry."

Eleanor accepted this. She couldn't imagine Gloria adopting such rules. There certainly had been a formal way in. "But she could have been hurt or sick or something."

"I went to her house a number of times," Dolores said. "Just checking on things. Everything was in order. Nothing looked out of place. There were clothes and shoes and even a smelly container of milk, which I got rid of. But her plants never needed watering." She looked as if this was significant.

"Then maybe everything's fine," Eleanor said, not knowing what else to say. They seemed to have a strange conversational rhythm going, taking turns at deciding whether to worry or not.

"What really bothers me is that she was absolutely fascinated with the heads."

Eleanor's eyebrows rose. "What fascinated her about them?"

Dolores sighed. "I have no idea. The heads were strange and interesting at first. But I saw her a few times in front of a head, leaning in, and it looked like she was actually in deep conversation with it. I don't know why it alarmed me, but it did. I told her to be careful, that it could be a trick. The messengers were beginning to take people at that time, though the first few they took came back and claimed they had gone to a banquet. I'm sure that was all for show. But she didn't listen to me."

"I'm so sorry," Eleanor said.

"There was still unlimited water at that point, though they were starting to talk about a drought on the news. When the news was the news, I mean." Here she snorted, rolling her eyes. "And not just propaganda. Telling us we're so much better than everyone else, and so much better *off*.

"She told me that the heads were harmless and she was just discussing everyday things, that the heads wanted to know her opinion about parades and whether there should be a pet Olympics, things like that. Circuses. I should have done more."

"What did the other witches say? Were they still here then?"

"They agreed with me," she said after a pause, "and of course no one could stop Daria if she wanted to do something. A strong personality."

"I understand that. She went after what she wanted. Actually, I think I admire that."

"Don't. I think there was a kind of intoxication for her in being a witch. Or maybe specifically in being a water-witch. She *desired* water, in fact. I mean, even when she found water, she wouldn't stop at that, but would keep looking for more. I spoke to her about the dangers of obsession, but she wouldn't hear it. She said she loved searching for water and would continue doing it. It's hard to argue with someone who says that. Should I tell her to stop finding water because she loves it? This is mostly desert here; it's not like we're in danger of flooding. But it struck me as unhealthy.

"I steered her to people who were looking to put in wells, that sort of thing, and she was happy to help them, which is important out here. But helping wasn't important to her. She kept going out to the desert and the mountains, and she would mark her findings. Rocks, sticks, spray paint, building a kind of map of where the water was. She didn't mind if the wind swept away some of her markings. What mattered was the internal map she was building of the water routes underground. At least, that's what I thought. She wasn't particularly interested in communicating, she would laugh and wave me off. And I'm not happy with people laughing and waving me off, so I asked her about it less and less."

"It sounds like she's been creating a mental world of some

kind. Visualizing it. That the usual world mattered less to her than the world she could see, the secret waterways."

Dolores nodded. "Yes, I assume it wouldn't be as interesting if it weren't secret. But I could be wrong, of course. At any rate, she became reclusive – which meant that she was gone a lot and I didn't know what she was doing." She shook her head sadly. "She could have been one of those people who have secret families in different places, and she was off visiting one of them."

"But she had no family here?"

"I was the closest she came to having family. And I wasn't much." She said this with regret. "I fly once or twice a week, hoping to see her out in the desert."

"I would still like us to fly together," Eleanor said. "I need to get a better idea of the landscape, and you know what to look for; I don't."

"We could try again with Hector. We'll just have to bring more cake."

Stan desperately needed to get to Madewell. He was good at recognizing clues no matter where they came from, and "Wellmade" on the list obviously referred to "Madewell." He felt an inexhaustible exhilaration when he considered his own talents. It occurred to him that indeed, he might as well admit it, his life up till then had been petty. He shrugged mentally and sighed mentally. He had settled and settled and settled, when he should have looked around and found the vista that was meant for him. This Liberty was bizarre and offbeat. It had a tilt to it, and he loved that about it. Nothing like New York with its snobs and its exclusivity of talent. He hadn't gotten far there because he didn't know the right people, that was all. And he was too sui generis to ever know the right people.

His eyes were half closed with satisfaction. For a moment, he almost decided against looking for the treasure, because he felt, in a fitting burst of enthusiasm, that he had already found it, and it was himself.

But sanity asserted itself in an instant. Now that he admitted his own value, he also admitted that he needed lots of things in life, and they all required money. The difficulties he was having with his private account (hidden from Eleanor) were unnerving.

How to get out to the desert, though? It was too far to walk. He was annoyed that the messenger hadn't given him a car, because he was sure he could figure out a way to drive it. And how to get gas and fill the tank. He was good at figuring things out. It was hard having so much talent and no way to use it.

He passed by a messenger giving someone a new vacuum cleaner (really?) and also ignored a hand-puppet face-off in a tent on the avenue, which was obviously intended for children anyway and nothing that he could respect himself for mocking.

"Psst!" a voice whispered to him as he stood on a corner waiting for the light to change or a parade to pass by, and he turned to see a head smiling at him. He had noticed the heads before, of course, and noticed people talking to them, but he was not much for carnivals or circuses (perhaps out of a feeling that he would fit in too well), so he had ignored them.

If the head had had hands, however, it would have been gesturing to him to come over and whisper.

He went over. The head smiled in appreciation.

"What can I help you with?" the head asked.

"I'm debating how to get out to a place called Madewell."

"In the desert?" the head asked.

"You know it?"

"I do indeed. It's a very small place, however. The subway doesn't go there yet."

Stan laughed. "The subway doesn't go anywhere, really."

The head blinked, apparently annoyed. "Many people are grateful that it's being built. It's a vast improvement that we have done out of love for the people. Still, you can take a bus most of the way."

"What does 'most of the way' actually mean?"

"You'd walk about a mile or more. Through the desert."

There was a pause.

"You're looking for the treasure, aren't you?" The head sounded both sympathetic and insinuating. One eye blinked. "You're not the first to ask about Madewell." There was a conspiratorial grin. "I've been there; it's not what you think."

Stan's heart leapt, though he couldn't say whether it was from horror or joy. He was right about the clue! And other people had also been right! "It's there?" he whispered. "Tell me where it is!"

There was a whirring and a kind of blanking of the head's face. "We all work together under my administration to improve the people's lives," the head said stoically. "Working together to get rid of greed and hypocrisy. Greed is your ruin! Give to my campaign as a token of your dedication to the abolition of greed! Will you send a small donation now to spearhead our campaign for a greater Liberty and finish the great subway system to make all our lives better?"

Stan was annoyed. *He* was the one who should be getting handouts. The head went on to ask if Stan wanted to "help" someone by turning them in, and for a brief heady moment he considered Eleanor. But she might still come in handy, and he doubted he could fool Gloria if Eleanor disappeared.

But the bus might be all the information he needed. As for walking in the desert, he would fill a number of bottles of water from home. Which reminded him: was he supposed to have paid the water bill? Or had Eleanor finally learned it was better to keep things like that on her own to-do list? And, speaking of Eleanor, what was she up to?

He continued to make his way back home, even indulging in a two-stop subway ride, just to remind himself that the subway did indeed exist. There were various theoretical subway entrances along the main street – President's Avenue – but most of them were just rectangles of cast iron placed on the sidewalk with empty station signs. At least one of the stations did not have cast iron but instead had plaster painted black. The color had run in the rain.

The functioning stations were clean and well-lit, and the train was small and very, very bright. Someone had placed all the lighting for a much longer train into the one subway car available. He went two stops and got out.

There was a kiosk and a subway map at the station. He spent a minute moodily studying the dotted lines that indicated the future stations. There was intention here, all right, but it was hard to know what it actually meant. Should he ask his Whisper followers what a subway system this short indicated about the government? He paused for a moment, listening, while the train idled (the train's engineer was walking from the front of the car to the back of the car because it was going to reverse directions and go two stops the other way). No matter how hard he listened, however, he could not hear drilling or any sounds that indicated the line was being extended.

He hurried upstairs. He was still at least five blocks away from his home, and he hoped to get there while Eleanor was out and about on her own errands. He needed to assemble filled water bottles, food packages, charge his phone and get some small change for the bus. He would use the GPS on his phone, and did he need sunscreen or a hat?

The water was on! He hastily filled three plastic bottles with water and put them in the freezer, as he had read somewhere that frozen water was the best thing to take if you were going into the desert. Where would he have read that? He felt a little dubious. That kind of reading was not his usual fare. He liked stories about rogues and geniuses – people like him, who had learned how to read and dupe ordinary folks, for fun and profit. That was how he would think from this point on – no more small plans. He would find the treasure, be financially independent, and get away from Eleanor! He really disliked her. He would become the most important person in the city, by means he hadn't discovered yet, but there was time. Money and adulation (as one would automatically receive by finding the treasure) was the first step. Everything would fall into place after that. He could feel all those eyes on him, envious, admiring, whatever.

And oh, he would no longer be a cat!

He paused for a moment. It had taken him a long time to get to that, hadn't it? Of course, it went without saying that Gloria would realize how ridiculous it was to keep him as a cat when Eleanor was at fault, first, last and always. It was amazing to him that Gloria hadn't seen that from the start. She had never seen him for what he truly was, of course, just as Eleanor didn't and the world in general didn't. He wasn't sure that the head valued him at all, but he thought there were some promising indications that it did. Very congenial, the head. Almost conspiratorial. The whole subway thing was stupid, but he supposed that sometimes politicians had to say things like that because the voters needed a bit of bread and butter and jam.

He would like some bread and butter and jam, actually. He found butter and jam in the fridge, which was a little surprising, but no bread that he could see. Eleanor had a habit of hiding things high up, however, so he stood there, looking at the upper cupboards with longing and irritation. Then, with a mighty leap (awkward, actually, but no one saw him), he was up on the counter and steadying himself with one foot on the stovetop. He didn't realize that he had actually turned the burner on as he reached up and opened one cabinet after the other. He was disappointed. He turned and saw the lit burner. Had he done that? How interesting. He had never actually tried cooking before. He jumped down and looked in the freezer to see if there was anything interesting there, and wonder of wonders, there were fish sticks! Next to his bottles of water. He hadn't even looked, since he never cooked.

Well, this was better. He could simply put the frozen fish

sticks and water in his fanny pack, and the sticks would keep the water cold, and eventually the heat would warm the fish sticks. This was an extraordinary plan!

He turned off the burner because he was a civilized cat, and Eleanor was a tenant after all. A fire wouldn't be as devastating as it would to an owner, for instance.

He put everything in his fanny pack; it was a tight fit with the food and water. But he also wanted to bring a pillowcase, in case he needed to find shelter or stay overnight. A pillowcase could be any number of things. Bedding, cloak, bandage, flag. Stan was resourceful that way.

He checked the clock. Hmmm. It was actually quite close to sunset. It would be stupid to leave just then. He should look at his map; he should study the location. He put back the fish sticks and water.

There was an hour of daylight left and a cream bun and cappuccino at a café sounded perfect. He strolled out along the streets and found that the heads he passed all made a psst! sound at him, which was annoying. But then he thought it might be significant, so he stopped at the next head.

"Finally!" the head said. "I've been trying to reach you about a clue."

"A clue!" He was so startled that his claws came out.

"It's an odd clue," the head said. "Remember that meeting you went to?"

Huh. The heads knew about that? He would think about it later.

"Well, some of them are having a meeting again tonight," the head said. "But it's all in code."

"In code?"

"They might be talking about politics. It doesn't matter. There's another clue there."

"Are you sure?" he asked, wondering whether he really understood what he'd been told, but at that point the head asked for money, followed by a request to turn in someone who needed "help." He once again fought down the urge to mention Eleanor, and went back to the basement where the other treasure hunters had met.

It was a different group of people. Entirely different. There were four short rows of chairs and then a kind of podium up front, and behind that podium a man was confessing. "Twelve years free," he said to the group. "I was a socialist for my twenties, then a democrat for the next twenty years or so. Until I came here and saw what this life was all about. That New York drug had me under its thumb, I finally realized. The truth is here. The real people are here."

There was a smattering of applause.

"Thank you," he said. A man who'd been sitting at the front got up and asked if there were any other new members who wanted to introduce themselves. Stan looked quickly along the rows, hoping there was one, just to make sure he understood what the theme of the evening was.

"Hi, I'm Cathy." A woman stepped quickly to the front. "I just relocated here, basically because I couldn't live the way I had been living." She lowered her head for a moment, took a breath, and looked up again. "I was a phone banker. I called people to get funding. And I was good. I was really good. I'm so ashamed." She hung her head again.

"It's all right, Cathy," a few people murmured, and one other person said, "Use your powers for good, Cathy. The president needs you."

"I plan on doing that," she said. "I'm going to volunteer any way I can."

Oho, Stan thought. This is a group that has seen the light and it is the president. Well, fine, I like the man myself. He raised his paw.

"I just moved here from New York," he said, "where I was a pawn in the capitalist machine." He paused to look at his audience and saw nothing like recognition. "For the elites. You know, snobs." There were a few nods. This was harder than he thought. "I made some mistakes, by believing in the system. Now I'm here, to learn." That seemed safe enough.

As he moved to go back to his seat, however, a rough voice asked, "Learn what?"

He looked quickly around the room, at a loss. He shrugged. "How to be a better person." He paused. "The best person. How to be the best person."

The man with the rough voice nodded. "No point in being average," he said. "The world is full of average. If you want to be better, that means you're average now."

"Here we go," a woman sighed. She looked at Stan and said, "It's not worth it. It's never worth it."

"My name's Jem," the man said. "Not Jim. Jem. And I've spent half my life getting better, and half my life *being* better. I have achieved." He said this sentence with great solemnity, setting his head back a little so he could look down on Stan. "And you know what? I understand the world now. I see how it fits together. Can you say that?"

Stan lowered his eyelids. "I can say it. Anyone can *say* it."

Jem nodded in understanding. "You think I'm boasting, and I don't know what I'm talking about. But here's what I've learned: everything that happens, happens for a reason." He beamed while Stan groaned.

Control yourself, Stan told himself. "Is that so?" he asked between gritted teeth. "How do you know?"

"The president said it, and I thought about it, and it makes sense."

A few other people nodded. "He says it all the time," one man agreed, but Stan didn't know whether that meant the president said it all the time, or this man did.

"Listen," Stan said, exasperated. "I get that you love the president. I admire him, I truly do, but he's just a man. Why do you love him so much?"

"He loves *us*," a woman said. "Let's start there. He's always checking with us, do we want this, do we want that, he tries to make our days better by making us happier. I've never enjoyed walking down the street as much as I do now. Messengers! Parades! People smiling and waving! It's wonderful, a new life!"

"I agree," another woman said. "I've had a hard time and I'm not rich now by any means, but I feel that I'm being looked after. I know some people don't like all the surveillance, but I have to ask, what are you hiding? What are you afraid of?"

Other people nodded. "It's true. He tells us all the time how much he loves us, and those heads and the animatronics – always asking us what we want. I mean what we individually want. The polls tell him in general."

"Those polls were a great idea."

"Polls?" Stan asked. "I only got here a few weeks ago. What are the polls?"

Someone clapped in delight. "The beginning of the month, we get a letter in the mail or an email – our choice – asking us what the month's goal is. Transportation, groceries, health care, whatever we want–"

"Well, it's usually just three choices."

"It used to be *no* choices!"

"And is the next month better?" Stan asked.

They looked at him.

"How much can you do in a month? The point is that he asks us. No one took the time before. No one ever asked my opinion." This came from a scrawny woman in a large cardigan. No wonder.

"He cares. That's what's so good about him," another man agreed. "He keeps the oil prices down."

"Don't you produce oil here?"

"Proud of it!"

He wasn't going to point out that cheap oil from your own faucet was no big deal. Speaking of faucets...

"Great about the oil, but what about the water? I've never been to a place with rationed water like this. Not in the United States."

At once everyone got prickly, a few of them starting to mutter and mill around.

"New Yorkers," the man said. "Came here in droves, scouted our water sources and did a land grab or something. Stole it. The president was so apologetic – said he'd always tried to keep an open mind about Easterners, but this just goes to show." He shook his head.

"It really does," another woman said meanly. "If I ever get a hold of one of those monsters, it won't be a good day for them."

Suddenly Stan noticed that all eyes were on him, and a few of the taller men had taken a step towards him.

"I was there on the president's business," Stan said hastily. "Before he became president, when he was still a – still a…" He drew a blank.

Luckily, Cathy said, "Builder. He was a contractor. Made houses for the poor."

"Well, not always for the poor. That's not how capitalism works," Jem said. "He did make some houses for the underprivileged, but they didn't appreciate it. Sued him for poor materials or something. When they had *no* materials before!"

"Unbelievable."

"You said you were in New York on the president's business?"

"Before he was president, yes, when he was expanding his business. You know, capitalism. Then I needed to escape capitalism, so I came here."

"We have capitalism here."

He panted slightly. "New York capitalism. Not ours."

There were significant nods all around. "They're not like us, are they?"

"No," Stan said, pulling himself together. "They believe anything they're told. We only believe the truth." He puffed himself up a little. It hadn't taken more than five minutes before he had managed to figure out the kinds of spin that would appeal to them. "No one ever asked me what I wanted, come to think of it. It was always what to do to get the other guy to shut up. I had to play along with that and never ask what anyone wanted, only what all of us needed." Was that too much? Too tricky?

Jem nodded, his face opening up in friendliness. "They want to tell us what to do. But here, why here, we want to figure out what we want to do!"

Stan checked – the man wasn't being ironic. "And what do you want to do?" he asked, out of a completely selfish curiosity.

"He wants to find the treasure and start a horse farm," Cathy said, grinning. "Although he never had a horse in his life."

"I've ridden them," Jem said in defense. "I like the way they smell and the way they snort. What's wrong with trying something you've never done before?"

"Well, he's right about that," Stan said. "Nobody wants to get stuck with last year's wishes."

Cathy turned to Jem. "What *was* last year's wish again? Silver mining in the mountains?"

"Gold," Jem said. "Though historically, there's been both silver and gold."

"Jem Makewell's Gold Mine," a man said, making it sound sonorous.

Stan bolted upright. "Your name's *Makewell*?"

Once again, he felt a multitude of stares on him. He saluted lazily. "It's a lovely name," he said. "I've met Makewells before and they were always smart, ambitious people."

Cathy laughed. "But rich? Were any of them rich?"

Jem pointed at Cathy. "Gold digger," he said.

"Oh, Jem," she said sadly. "Give it up. Just give it up."

"We're not getting much business done here," the man up front said. "I was thinking we should hold a rally or parade or something. Maybe a yard sale? To be more visible as an organization. We won't get much done with twelve members."

The woman next to Cathy indicated Stan. "What about him? He'd make thirteen."

"My dear madam," Stan said with an attempt at integrity –
or, to be honest, an effort to avoid being signed up. "I have to
admit I'm here under false pretenses. I thought this meeting
was about the treasure."

Everyone laughed and looked around. "That's you, Jem,"
they said, nudging him or winking at him. "This guy is here
for you."

Jem laughed. "I hear it!" he said and turned to Stan. "Let's
you and me go out for a drink, then," he said, standing and
straightening his shirt, which had ridden up to his waist.

"Perhaps we could grab a bite to eat as well?" Stan asked.
"Do you like tacos?"

"I like tacos," Jem said.

"Who doesn't like tacos?" a voice yelled as they headed for
the door.

Jem nodded. "Should we take your car or mine?"

Stan cleared his throat a little. "Actually, I don't have a car."
His paws twitched a little. He desperately wanted a car—or at
least a good explanation for not having one!

"Huh. That must make it hard to go out searching. Or do
you have a partner?"

"No partner," Stan said. "Not that I wouldn't like one. I mean,
I'm happy to work with someone, if it looked like the right thing
to do." He wasn't really sure he was happy to do that, but why
not feel things out? Why not see what was on the table?

Jem nodded. "That's what I was thinking, too. I get that
sharing our searches might narrow our searches, because who
can be trusted – that's what I don't know. I could see holding
back on what I know just to keep someone else from getting
ahead of me, you know?"

"You want to get the info, not give the info," Stan said wisely.

"Exactly! Why buy the cow when you can get the milk for
free?"

That was a stumper! Jem must have one of those brains with
curious pathways. But Stan wasn't really interested in how

the man had gotten from a treasure hunt to a cow. Instead, he said, "Well, I don't have a car and you do, so you would be interesting to me. How can I be interesting to you? I'm not a fool. If it doesn't work both ways, then it won't help both of us."

"I'm going to level with you. I have a criminal record. I once stole some credit cards. I was a kid. But the point is that I think we can get some info from the president, from the heads, but they know who I am and won't deal with me. So, what I really need is a partner with a clean record. Do you have a clean record?"

"I do," Stan said virtuously. He may have done some dubious things, but he'd never been caught. Because he was smart.

"I personally believe it's in the mountains," Jem said. "Makes sense. Things happen in mountains."

"Things happen in deserts," Stan answered.

Jem ignored him. "If you were going to bury something, it would be behind a rock, wouldn't it?"

Stan's fur was beginning to rise. "Why?"

"Because that's where gold and silver and precious metals are found. Huh? Like to like. All that mining. And I think jewels, too. Like to like." He repeated it with such satisfaction that Stan began to wonder if he'd hooked up with someone a little light in the brains department. Think about that, he told himself. Why was that a bad thing?

"You might be right," Stan said generously. "I do sense a theme."

They decided to skip the tacos and instead made a date to go to the mountains fresh and early the next day. Stan felt amazingly light and hopeful as he began his walk back home. He wasn't tired and didn't feel like going home – Eleanor might be there, and he didn't want his delightful mood to be shattered – so he walked on, and found himself drawn to the lights of the palace. He stood on the drawbridge looking up. Would this someday be his? He felt it would be. He was well on his way.

He heard a splash below him and saw a swimmer in the dimmer atmosphere of the moat. Stroke, stroke, stroke. The swimmer moved on, alone, folding in and out of the water. Was this a thing, then? People swimming in the moat at night? He turned around and treated himself to another cappuccino. One of the beauties of being a cat was that caffeine didn't bother him. He could sleep anywhere he chose, anytime he chose. There were certain advantages, he mused, that would never have occurred to him, and most people wouldn't even have recognized.

He'd found Makewell, yes, as the universe had suggested. How interesting that it turned out to be a man!

CHAPTER 5

Dolores said there were lone people out in the desert and the hills, and they tended to check in on each other and share information. Maybe someone had seen Daria, and Hector had heard about it.

Eleanor picked up a vanilla cake on her walk over to Dolores' house. Dolores had an extra broom – actually, a garden rake – and they hung the cake box from the prongs of the rake, which Eleanor used.

The desert was bumpy, with hillocks and ravines and brush and stunted trees. They were flying low, and Eleanor noticed new odors in the air. Dolores identified creosote bushes and the heated-rock smell of some of the hillocks. Some flower was blooming. Every so often she could swear she smelled water. Was it the memory of a river? The ocean smelled of salt, and this wasn't the ocean. It perhaps wasn't even a smell, but a change in humidity, an omission of the smell of brush and rock.

"Look over there," Dolores said, pointing, and she rode over to a small circle of rocks. "I think Daria did that," she said. She flew in a curve then, pointing out another set of rocks, and then another. "I found these last month. She was marking something, I'm sure. You can see they're starting to be moved by animals. Come on, I'll show you another." They flew over the scrub for a while until the rocks started becoming larger, sometimes nestling against each other. "I don't think that tree belongs there," Dolores said, indicating a single deciduous tree among the rocks. "I think Daria planted it."

The vegetation in the desert tended to be low and thin-leaved, yet there was indeed one tree that looked like an oak – not that Eleanor knew it was an oak – but with wide, flat, normal leaves. It stood alone.

"I think she planted it there because there's an underground stream below it, and the tree can get more water than if it was moved ten feet away. That's why it's so hard to figure out where she might be – she knew the world around us in a different way."

They split up for a while, and Eleanor now saw the desert in a different way, too, recognizing that it held information in how the rocks lay, the kinds of vegetation that could thrive there, and how a mound of sand made sense in one spot but not in another. What had been foreign to her became familiar.

She was enjoying it, glancing up occasionally to see where Dolores was, looking ahead to see patterns from a distance, shifting her weight to get more comfortable, when she noticed, far off, two dots coming towards her.

She changed her direction and flew over to Dolores, who looked up and nodded. "Let's fly low. Those are drones. They want to see what we're doing, and I hate to give them anything to think about."

They turned and dipped and flew on, looking over a shoulder as the drones kept up with them. "An escort," Dolores said bitterly. "I can never stay out for very long without an escort."

"Do they ever catch up with you? And who do they belong to?"

"I saw a bit of drone footage on the news once. All our TV stations are state-owned, no matter what they say. And they get their footage from the drones, so they're state-owned, too. I believe it's the president, or the president's government, or whatever is behind what happens in the city."

"The city is so strange," Eleanor said. "Everyone seems to love the parades, the nougats, all the animatronic heads. They even love the messengers. I don't. I've seen them take a few people, just like that, out of sight, out of mind."

"Yeah," Dolores said. "No one knows how many have been taken, and there's an occasional question whether everyone comes back. But there's no proof that they don't. And no one wants to upset a good thing, you know. There are so many giveaways and interesting, unexpected things. It's like Christmas and your birthday could come at any time. It makes you look forward to the new day. Even I will admit that, and I'm very suspicious. The news is filtered, the taxes are high, you've given up on the expectation of privacy because they know everything about you, or so it seems. But in the end, this might be the day the president gives you a million dollars. Because that's been verified; he does that sometimes. And there's trumpets and ticker tape and marching bands, and it's wonderfully exciting. Who wouldn't love it?"

Eleanor shook her head. "There's always *someone* who doesn't love it."

She nodded. "There's a group of people who say their loved ones got messengered and never came back. The president says that's a lie. There are people who don't make enough money to have water every day. The president says it's a lie. If you complain too much, you are taken outside the city and left there. After you're given a makeover, of course: hair, clothes, exercise program. They get money, or so we're told, so they can go wherever they like. As far as we know."

It sounded like a winning strategy. "How do the heads all communicate?"

"You mean with each other or with the people?"

"It just strikes me as strange. It's very sophisticated. I passed by and they each continued a sentence with me, just started with one head and continued wherever I went."

"Just electronics. Someone is monitoring them. Spying is a good business in Liberty."

After about an hour, they veered generally to the right and flew lower. Eleanor saw the cabin and they landed next to it.

A few dogs barked at them, and a voice inside the cabin yelled at them to shut up. The dogs still wagged their tails, but their mouths resumed silent panting. They sniffed the broom and rake, circled around the women, and followed them happily to the front door, where a small man stood watching.

"Hector," Dolores said. "This is my friend, Eleanor. She's a witch. From the East."

They looked at each other for a moment, and then Hector nodded. "Fine by me. I appreciate witches. They have weird ideas, some of them, but nothing harmful. What's your weird idea?" He looked steadily at Eleanor.

"I don't know. I wouldn't think it was weird, would I? I mean, how would I know it was weird?"

"Good point. What kind of cake? Eat inside or out?"

"Out, I think. I want to look at the sky."

"Drones watching you? And you didn't blow them away?" He smirked.

Dolores laughed politely. "I was tired," she said.

Eleanor felt a little jolt of embarrassment. She had never asked what Dolores' power was. In fact, she had been thinking that she wasn't very witchlike at all. Because she had lost track of Daria? Because she didn't seem to care? She had not gotten past being judgmental at all, had she? "You can bring up a wind?" she asked finally.

"I'm not as good at it as I used to be, and it's hardly protection against the drones. They film you once they see you. It's better if you stay out of their eye. Everything here is a camera," she said. "In the heads of all the presidents, on the streets, in all the parades. Everywhere."

"But not here," Hector said. "I scramble most everything. Just throw out junk data and it's like going through a snowstorm for the eyes and ears. That's what I call the drones," he said, nodding to Eleanor. "So we're good, here. Unless, of course, they've got new designs. Do they have new designs?" He shrugged. "What do I know? I am a hermit, out in the wilderness and of no importance whatsoever."

"I still don't understand," Eleanor admitted. "What are they looking for? Why all these eyes?"

"They're hiding something. And if you were hiding something, wouldn't you want to know if anyone figured it out?" Hector asked. He had a squint in his eye that made him look a little doubtful. His voice was also doubtful.

"It's the water," Dolores said. "It has to be. Why this drought? Where are they getting the water they sell to us? I've lived here all my life, and yes, there have been droughts, but we've had the normal amount of rain, and still there's no water."

Dolores and Hector contemplated each other for a minute. "It's all right," Dolores said. "She's helping me find Daria. You can speak freely."

"I have a well," Hector said. "Daria found the water, and I dug, and the well is perfectly fine. Not one hundred feet deep, even. Normal water table for around here."

They looked at Eleanor expectantly and she couldn't figure out why. "I don't know what that means," she finally admitted.

"If the water table's normal, where is the drought?" Dolores said. "The underground water hasn't disappeared. It's only the surface water that's missing."

"It's going somewhere else," Hector clarified.

They all stood there for a moment while Eleanor processed it. "Have you looked?" she asked finally. "I mean, water goes downhill, so the source must be uphill, right? In the mountains." She made a brief, vague gesture to the series of hills in the distance. "Have you checked?"

They looked at her like she was an idiot. "Of course

we've checked," Dolores said. "As well as we could. They've got sentries and drones and all sorts of guards around the mountains. There's a no-fly zone, too, so you can't just rent an airplane or copter and take a look."

"You could ride a broom."

She shook her head. "I've been riding it less and less. I'm worried I'll be discovered, as a spy and a witch. I do it now and then, but I'm careful where and when I go. I can't take any chances."

That sounded odd to Eleanor – why couldn't she take a chance? Witches had spells, after all.

"I see," she said. She would try to find out more later. "Sounds like they're hiding something?"

"Of course they're hiding something," Hector said. "There's a lake up there. Is the lake gone? Where does the water go? It has to go somewhere."

She understood that everything she said was something they had discussed over and over again, but she still wanted to hear their conclusions. "They're selling it to us? I mean, we have to pay for it. That's the bottled water, isn't it?"

Hector shook his head. "That's not enough. Remember, it was a whole river. That's tons of water flowing constantly, not just thousands of bottles."

"They've diverted it?" she said finally, and both Hector and Dolores seemed to relax. Their faces approved; their shoulders approved. It was obvious to them, and now she'd caught up. "But where?" she continued. "How?"

"Pipes?" Hector asked. "Can you run enough pipes to take all that water? Where do the pipes go?"

"What's on the other side of those mountains?" she asked, pointing.

"Arizona," Dolores said.

"An arid state. Probably would like some water," Hector said.

"Could they do that? Sell water to another state?"

"What's to stop them?"

"Who's to stop them?"

"But can people *own* water and sell it? Who's selling it?"

"We've been searching Wiggle," Dolores said. "Wiggle claims we get the bottled water from a government-sponsored workers' cooperative, and that the sales go to a nonprofit that builds schools. We went to look at the school, and yes, there's one there. Even some students. Not a lot of them."

"Okay, so it's got a face for the curious. But one school? For all that water?"

"The workers get paid, there's bottles to be made, bottling machinery, transportation. I admit, I can see it, there would be a lot of expenses. And the computers that handle distribution in the city – I mean, how else can they allocate it? – that costs money, too. It's hard to figure out all the possible charges. Most people by now are used to things this way. That's hard to change. Some people are angry, but not enough to make a difference or even some kind of effort to track it all down."

"The parades. The messengers. The heads. Distractions."

"Yes, well, they're pretty good distractions. Isn't anyone trying to figure it out?" Eleanor asked.

"That's what we're doing," Hector said. "Trying to figure it out."

Eleanor took a slice of cake and looked around at her companions and the mountains in the distance. She wondered if it was enough. All they were doing was complaining, after all. She frowned. And just what was *she* doing?

Exasperated, Eleanor decided to see what Stan knew. "Have you wondered about the water situation?" she asked.

He jumped a little. "I paid the bill! I'm sure I did."

"I'm talking about the drought and the water bills and all the bottled water, which is apparently local water even though there's no local water anywhere."

He relaxed and immediately looked bored. "Have you tried the internet?" he asked.

"That's also a problem," she said. "It's not the internet we know."

"It's not the Google we know," Stan agreed. "They use something called Wiggle for their search function and their universal browser. It's a very strange thing."

Eleanor studied him. Knowing him, and his addiction to social media, he should be going crazy. But his body language was calm. He wasn't bristling at all. In fact, he was on his phone, using his rubber-tipped pencil to tap out – what? What was he doing?

"You've found another site for Augment," she said, suddenly illuminated. Augment was his old social media site. "Wow. I'm impressed. How did you figure it out?"

Stan continued to tap, but she could see his eyes peering sideways, watching her reaction. "I'm pretty smart," he said in a soothing voice. "You hate to admit it, but I'm smarter than you are."

Her first reaction was to protest, but she kept her mouth shut. *She* hadn't figured out how to get what she wanted from the Liberty internet. But Stan had.

She nodded. "That's pretty good. I really am impressed, Stan."

A small purr escaped him.

"You've found something similar to Augment?"

He had a special cat grin for occasions when he felt he was a genius.

"You've *started* a site like Augment," she said, reading his expression.

He was delighted with her remark. "I found a kind of back door. A growing community of people who want to engage outside the limits of the social constraints."

"That sounds like an advertising hook."

"Good, isn't it?"

"How many people do you have? And do you have advertisers?"

"Not many. And yes."

"So you're getting some revenue?"

"Not much. And yes."

"I wonder. This back door. Can you use it to get information?" He paused thoughtfully, cleaning his left paw while he considered his answer. He put his paw down. "Practically speaking, not really. This internet uses Wiggle as both its browser and its search engine. I take it you already know how limited the search engine is? It's blocked the major outside domains, and created its own sets of domains and subdomains, which it allows. That's what the back door is using, actually. There's a small subdomain we're using as a sort of organized chat area."

"Why do they allow it?" she asked. "I mean, it's a very restrictive internet, isn't it? Why this area?"

"Just a programming flaw," he said airily. "Actually, a few people have said that they think a programmer did it deliberately and will become rich someday. He'll be the next internet billionaire."

"Or *she* will."

"Probably not." He smirked.

It occurred to her suddenly that the old Stan would have laughed – a short, abrasive, blaring laugh. "Huh," she said. "You can't laugh, can you?"

"Only on the inside," he said. "You can't hear it, but I'm sure you can feel it."

She nodded. "But about this 'back door.' I was looking for a good geological map where the rivers and lakes are marked. Everything I find online or at the library contradicts everything else and leaves out things or moves things."

"Part of the plan," he said wisely.

"What plan?" she snapped. He always pretended to know more than he did; she was sure he was doing it now as well.

He loved irritating her. "Don't you think there's a plan?" he asked, and got up and left.

He had nothing in mind, but the weather was good and he felt inclined to walk about and see the city, which was always interesting. That day, for instance, there was a parade of small children with musical instruments. They were terrible. Everyone laughed and clapped, and he was pleased to follow along with the parade out of sheer gloating superiority, until he heard a kind of hiss nearby.

"Psst!" A presidential head winked at him and said, "Psst!" again. Stan stopped and looked around, in case the head was talking to someone else. Nope.

"You want me?" Stan asked.

"I do. I wonder if you'd mind having lunch with the real president, not just a head. Fish tacos," it said. "Beer," it added.

Stan stood there in stunned silence for a moment. "Spicy fish tacos?"

"Not too spicy," the head said. "Come to the palace at one pm tomorrow. Side entrance, near the drawbridge."

Stan nodded in delight and took off on his way. He was finally being recognized.

He wished he could whistle.

CHAPTER 6

The president provided decent fish tacos and beer. They were presentable and passable. Still, Stan had expected tremendously high-end fish tacos, maybe from some exotic fish with a lingering tingle. Instead, it had merely been good.

"This is terrific," he said, however. He knew his place. His place was to lie and cajole and flatter. "I'm so delighted to meet you. I haven't been here long, but I've been so impressed with what I've seen."

"Have you?" the president said. He motioned to a woman who sat apart from them, a notebook in her hand. "You don't mind if my deputy sits in? All my meetings are historical, and require records."

Stan glanced quickly at the woman, and immediately forgot about her.

The president beamed. "I have to tell you, the reason you're here is because I've been reading some of what you've published on Whispers, and I was curious to see what kind of person managed to tap into the heartbeat of the public the way you have."

Stan's heart had fallen at the beginning of the sentence but raised to the heights by the end. "You've been reading it?" he asked hesitantly. "I don't know very much about the way you run things here, so I'm wondering if I offended you in any way?" He frowned, trying to remember the most incendiary of the items he'd posted.

"Not at all," the president assured him. "I'm all for an open society." He paused, raised his fish taco, took a considerate but tiny nip of the end, and continued to be silent. Stan could hear him crunching in a small, insignificant way. Wasn't he hungry? He lowered his head in thought. This president might have layers. Stan hated layers.

"The reason you're able to post, by the way, is because I am so interested in how the populace is handling my reign." The president stopped. "Regime." He stopped again. "Term." That seemed to satisfy him. "So, I'm allowing a sort of underground commentary to keep track of satisfactions and dissatisfactions." He took a fork and speared some of the fish out of the taco, which was the worst thing you could do to a fish taco. Ignored the point, in fact. "Some dissatisfactions are actually good for business," he said. "As long as they're mad about things you want them to be mad about, then the gears are grinding smoothly."

"I love a well-ground gear," Stan said.

"Have another beer," the president said, pushing one forward. "What I really wanted to talk to you about is your friend and housemate, Eleanor."

"Ah," Stan said. "I should have guessed. Does she annoy you as much as she annoys me?"

"Do you know what she's looking for?"

"Sure. There's a missing witch, Daria. I hope you're not offended by calling them witches? I have to tell you about my experience with them–"

"I'm sure it's interesting, and I'd love to hear about it later. So, they're looking for Daria." He considered this, his hands steepled. "Who is she in touch with?"

"Oh," Stan said. He was becoming a little uncomfortable. He certainly had no obligation towards Eleanor, and he didn't like her, but on the other hand he felt a kind of psychic connection.

The people you dislike, he thought philosophically, can feel closer than the people you like.

"Stan?" the president asked, intruding on his thoughts.

"I'm trying to think. She did mention someone, but to be honest, I don't pay much attention to her. The only reason I remembered the name Daria is because she said it endlessly for a few days. Daria, Daria, Daria." He shrugged. "And 'water.' Daria and 'water.'" He brightened. "Daria is a water-witch! That's what it is. Important because of the drought? And speaking of the drought," he added, "you know, the prices keep going up, day to day? It's a little hard to keep up with."

"Yes, well, those Easterners keep stealing the water."

"I don't know why," Stan said, in good humor as he began on his third fish taco. "We Easterners have plenty of water."

He heard the silence almost immediately and his chewing slowed. He drank half a beer before he had enough saliva to take another bite. He considered that he might have gotten too comfortable, and might indeed have crossed a line. Mentioning that he was from the East? Saying the prices were too high? "I mean, of course I don't know. It's beyond my intelligence. I'm sure you have a great deal of knowledge," he said, keeping himself from either stuttering or hissing, both of which seemed about to surge out of him. "It must be difficult, being president. A lot of decisions?" he asked querulously.

The president forked out another bit of fish and nibbled at it delicately. Why, Stan thought, he doesn't actually *like* fish tacos! The idea hit him all at once with the force of a wall of water. It had never occurred to him that there were those who actively disliked what he loved. It was a great betrayal of his faith in the world. And the beer! The president had barely sipped his beer! What was he, some kind of rich man with only rich man's tastes? The populace was wrong to think he had them in mind, if he couldn't even eat or drink what they did. He was just pretending to be normal, that's what it was!

"Stan," the president said softly. "I need you. I need your

help. Your expertise. Only you can do it, use your brains to tell me what's going on. I've had my eye on you right from the start." He sat back in his chair, put his hands on his thighs, and smiled benevolently. He rang a bell. "Dessert? I believe we have some cream buns."

Stan had begun a soft song in his throat at the start of this speech, and by the time he heard the mention of cream buns, he was ready to roll over and offer his belly. But he wouldn't do that, of course. He had done it once, just once, when Eleanor offered him olives. He didn't know what it was about olives, but they were as delightfully psychedelic as catnip.

"All I need," the president said, "is a clever brain and sharp eyes to find out what this Eleanor is really up to. Do you think you could do that for me? I wouldn't be able to offer you much more than a minor post – a very minor post – but it would pay more than these rants on Whispers would. Don't stop those, though, whatever you do. You're brilliant."

The cream buns arrived, and some nice cappuccino, and Stan was prepared to sell his soul – or rather, lease it, with pay.

"We should get in touch with Gloria," Eleanor said the next time she saw Dolores.

"What will Gloria do? She's in New York."

"She's good, she's really good at bad situations," Eleanor said. Where did this come from? Eleanor had never even known she believed that! But she realized it was true. Gloria was steady and clear-thinking and saw farther than she could – and she didn't just mean her witchly talent. She meant her human talent, too.

"I don't mean to be rude," Dolores said. "But she doesn't know this situation. She never met Daria, who is nothing like New York witches. It's a complicated world here. A complicated life. The other witches left because they didn't feel safe. Or just because they wanted to. I admit that. But what would Gloria

know about what any of us wants? I don't know what I want
at this point. Do you? Do you know what you want?"

The question had a sharp point to it. Eleanor wanted to be
rid of Stan; she wanted Gloria to be proud of her and to let her
learn more. That sounded like she wanted to be back in New
York... but did she?

"I don't know," she finally admitted. "I want to know what
I want, that's as close as I can get."

"And even that seems like too much trouble, sometimes,"
Dolores said, nodding. She waved goodbye and went inside. It
seemed a little abrupt.

Eleanor walked for a while, took the subway for one stop,
then got out along President's Avenue, moving with the joyous
people down the jubilant streets.

She turned down a side street, heading one block over to
Palace Boulevard. She passed one head who said, "Hello, there,
Eleanor! Good to see you!" Her heart froze, but she continued
on.

She hadn't gotten far when she heard the messenger's horn.
It was down near the palace, and she ignored it at first. But it
kept getting closer. She picked up her pace. She was no more
than ten minutes away from home. She passed another head,
and it said, "Always a treat, Eleanor!" and she drew in a breath.
The siren kept coming.

She was walking faster now, but as the noise got closer, she
turned to see where it was headed. It was coming towards her,
straight towards her, but surely it was going to turn and go
after someone else? She began to run, and people all around
her stopped and watched. Some of them pointed; all of them
were interested.

The van with the chicken logo cut in front of her, pulled
over, and stopped. She turned and ran a different way, but the
doors popped open, and four men jumped out and caught up
with her so easily that she was ashamed of herself. (Really?
She couldn't run any faster than that?)

Two on each side grabbed an arm and pulled her forward. The other two formed a wall behind her. People everywhere murmured and pointed, but this might be one of those messengers with prizes, so there was no need for alarm. It could be good! It was almost always good!

She was pushed inside, and the doors slammed shut, and the men guided her into a rather comfortable seat. There was light; the men nodded at her as if they wanted to reassure her.

"It'll be all right," one of them said. "The president's a decent man. He'll help you."

"I don't need help."

"That's right," another man said, scoffing. "You're doing just fine."

"Well, I *am*!" she said.

"That's why you're here," the third man said. Were they a skit? "Because everything you've done is perfect."

She clenched her jaw. "I demand to see my lawyer," she said.

The first man sighed. "All these New Yorkers," he said. "They all have lawyers."

At that, she realized that Liberty wasn't just a different state but a different nation. And she didn't know the rules here.

She was taken to a bland but locked room, very much like a hotel room. Large bed, large TV, small refrigerator, separate bath, drapes that could be drawn against a barred window. A chair and a small table. An ironing board in the closet.

"You'll get dinner at six," the guard said. "Any dietary restrictions?" He was very polite, and it was unsettling. She was a *guest*, not a prisoner. But she was trapped, just like a prisoner.

"I'm vegetarian," she said.

"Of course." He made a note on his phone. "Not vegan?"

"Not vegan."

"Good for you," he said, and disappeared.

She got up and paced, looked out the window at the edge of a parapet, and the moat surrounding the palace. There was a drawbridge just within view, no doubt accounting for the rough and rumbling part of the ride just before they arrived.

She'd always felt the moat was a good touch, though.

She tried the door and to her surprise, it wasn't locked, so she opened it. But when she stepped out a bell rang, and men emerged from rooms to her left and right. She hesitated. The men stood where they were. She took a step to her left, and the man to her left took a step towards her. She stepped to the right and the man to her right loomed towards her. She paused. They did not seem aggressive. They did not have guns. They were tall and thick, yes, but would they do anything? She took a breath and walked purposefully toward the man to her right, because the corridor seemed shorter in that direction, and she hoped for stairs or an elevator.

The man mirrored her in an unnerving way. As she walked towards him, he moved with her until they met, body to body. She tried to edge around him, and he stepped to block her. She turned and saw the other man had gotten closer, too.

The two men formed a silent vise. When she stepped in the approved direction, the man gave way. When she stepped in the wrong direction, the man approached.

She went back to her room.

She turned on the TV which had only one station: cartoons.

She thought about many things while she waited; how she had become a witch, how she came to be here, how everything was Stan's fault, and what, if anything, would happen next.

PART TWO

CHAPTER 7
New York, Election and Secession

Far too many people thought it was a joke. No states had seceded after the Civil War. New Yorkers had heard Staten Island threaten to secede – but it never did. Texas threatened it; California threatened it. It was a political stunt, and no one took it seriously. Until it happened.

This particular election had been even nastier than usual, Eleanor thought. Politicians! Usually, none of them did anything more than talk in sound bites and truisms and puff themselves up and scorn the opposition. But then it happened – a state seceded from the union and declared itself a separate nation. It was all being contested at the same time that it was all happening, legally or not. And then, with a referendum at the state level that supported the move, the state of Liberty ratified itself as separate and at least temporarily indivisible. Or so it said.

Although New York loved a good protest, there weren't that many marches and protests about the secession at the beginning, because most people found it both interesting and laughable. If it was laughable, then no one really had to worry. That's what lawyers and constitutions were all about, keeping the system going. And hoo boy! What if *everyone* seceded? What if the US became kind of like Europe, with separate countries instead of states? As far as language went, it was almost there already. *You* try to figure out what those Southerners are saying!

But the secession continued, from November into December into April, as legal challenges went through the courts, and regional courts refused to hear the conclusions of federal courts and vice versa. Suddenly, it was looking like a done deal. They were getting away with it!

And when anything new happens in America, you march.

It was a little confusing.

Some Easterners said, "Good Riddance!" But then there were others who said, "Save Our Nation!" And there were some on the other side who shouted, "Freedom to Choose!" And in this case, they meant choose which nation you belonged to.

Eleanor didn't go on marches at first – what good was a march, let someone else do it – but then polls began to overtake the news cycles. How many agreed, how many disagreed, who would be left without federal monies if they seceded and how that meant they'd have to admit their own poverty. How could a state that relied on federal money *leave* the federal government? And wasn't it good for the rest of us if they did? Our own taxes could be reduced if we didn't have to support them! Let them go!

Taxes, Electoral College, Supreme Courts, tariffs and interstate highways – suddenly everything needed to be discussed and viewed from all angles.

Marches were the perfect vehicle for showing angles.

Eleanor had gone to one of the laughing protests because she'd seen them on the news, and they looked like they were fun. They had started when those old-style secessionists from Staten Island marched through downtown Manhattan on a cold day in mid-February. There were counter-protests on all the streets around them and it was the same mix of shouting and slogans as the other protests had been. So a young New School student, Andrea Roxitt, got a few dozen of her friends and fellow students together, aligned on both sides of the avenue, and as the opposition marched past them, they laughed in an exaggerated, loud, long way. Other protestors tittered, unsure at first, but eventually joined in. And the laughter rippled through the crowd down the parade route, in step with the marchers.

The laughing protests caught on, even behind police barriers. The laughs ran on unbroken, as protestors took their own individual breaths whenever they needed. You could laugh for a long or a short time, you could just stop by and laugh and go on your way to work; the laughter was unstoppable. Once, the conservative marchers tried to laugh back, but they were applauded, as if they'd joined in.

Eleanor worked part-time at a museum gift shop during this period. She had almost gotten a degree in business years before, but she finally realized she had been trying to force herself into being something she wasn't. The truth was that she felt at odds with herself and her surroundings. She wasn't like everyone else.

She could think things into being – which was to say, she thought a thing and it often happened. She thought about a taxi, and there was a taxi. She thought about stopping the rain, and the rain would stop, sometimes only on her side of the street. She had injured other children slightly when she was a child, and injured an adult or two as well, but never seriously. A trip, a paper cut, a pinched thumb – these all frightened her when they happened to someone who annoyed her, or even when she idly thought to herself, what if that ball landed in his eye? There was no denying the connection. She tried to put up a mental door when she was annoyed, a red door with intricate carvings on it. She tricked herself into looking at the carving, with its animal heads and its trellises and trees and flowers. It didn't always work but she learned to be less impetuous with her magical thoughts. Even so, she was branded a sneak and a troublemaker at school for some of the accidents that happened around her. A bug jumped out of a girl's hair right after she said Eleanor was a freak. A boy's bicycle chain broke whenever he passed by her. A girl tripped and broke her collarbone after Eleanor heard her snickering while looking at her.

She didn't know how to prove even to herself that she could do what she thought she could. A whole month could pass without an incident and then suddenly, it would happen again. She reacted and someone got humiliated or hurt. She didn't trust this part of herself, but at the same time she suspected that it meant she was special. But what was she to do with this ability?

She chose to try to make herself as anonymous as possible. After a disastrous series of relationships, she gave up men. After some numbing jobs, she moved out of the finance sector and into smaller jobs in kinder surroundings.

The museum shop wasn't perfect, but it had a soothing atmosphere, and she took some comfort from the routine orderliness of the shelves. The customers always changed, and if anything weird happened, she could summon her boss – who, unfortunately, annoyed her a lot as well, but who kept to his office most of the day, watching porn. He had a small office, and his screen was always facing the door. He liked to keep the porn on screen until she noticed it, at which point he would click on the screensaver – a picture of a kitten with its mouth open wide. That was his sense of humor.

One day she overheard a group of women talking about some of the candles for sale. These had various ornamental engravings along the sides or the bottom, copied from one of the exhibits.

One woman said, "It's a triquetra. Look!" She held the candles out to her friends. Her face was fresh and open, freckled and surrounded by sandy curls.

"It's not as good as the ones we have at the house," her companion said. She was a thick-set woman, with a short lavender jacket and a loose, flowing skirt. She wore thin boots and leaned heavily on a cane.

"Still, it's nice," the third woman, who was thin and rather old, said. "Nice to have a change from our usual assortment." The second woman nodded. "Of course. Let's do it. Did you see anything else?" They agreed there was nothing else and brought the candles to the counter.

"What's a triquetra?" Eleanor asked. She held one of the candles in her hand, looking at the pattern shaped on it.

"It's a Wiccan symbol," the woman with the cane said. "It symbolizes the triple goddess."

"Goddess?" Eleanor repeated without thinking. "A goddess would be nice. And you said a *triple* goddess?"

They all smiled at her, together, as if suddenly seeing something wonderful. "Hello," the woman with the cane said. "My name is Gloria."

"Ruth," the thin one said.

"Becca," the young one said.

They continued to smile at her benevolently, and Eleanor felt a sort of glow spreading from them. She found herself smiling back. All four of them calmly smiling at each other in the middle of a museum shop.

"This is so lucky," Becca said. "We were getting the candles for a Wiccan meeting tonight."

"You might be interested," Ruth added. "It's all about goddesses and forming a circle with other women who have small or large powers."

Eleanor felt a surge of hope. Her body almost lifted up in delight. "I'd love that," she said. "I don't know what Wiccan is, but these candles are my favorites, and you all seem nice."

At that, they laughed, and Gloria handed her a card and said, "Come right before sunset. We'll wait for you."

The women left, with a rush of air and a lingering laugh, and Eleanor looked down at the card in her hand. It was pale blue, bigger than a business card, with silver along the edges. The script was mostly italic, with flourishes at the beginning of each capital letter. There was a picture of a pentagram, which she recognized as a witch's symbol, and some old-looking Gothic letters that might have made up words, but they were not words she knew. She smiled down at the card and slipped it inside her pocket. The day was much better than it had been. She bought the last candle with her employee discount, and went home to eat and check what time sunset was these days.

She noticed her own level of excitement and tried to quell it. Would these women like her? Would she like them? It was almost like preparing for a date; she noticed it and didn't care. Either she had misunderstood them – and she would find that out – or these women would understand what she had gone through all her life, when the things she was thinking actually happened.

They were very far over on the east side, in what had once been known as Alphabet City, but had been gentrified years before. There were still pockets – on 10th Street, on 11th Street – with unrenovated tenements housing people who had been there all their lives, watching to see when they would be gentrified out.

She didn't care if she saw a rat or heard a laugh cut off abruptly inside a building. The air was warm, and a ghostly moon sat sickle in the sky, waiting for darkness. She hastened, her chin up, her right hand carrying her candle like a knife, her left hand holding her purse and (because she was uncertain) a bottle of wine.

It was not a very imposing building. It had stone steps, worn and dipping in the middle, and large wood-framed doors and a single bell, which she rang before stepping back.

Gloria, the older woman with the cane, opened the door and regarded her with approval. She had warm dark skin and hair cut short. "I'm so glad you came. Eleanor, is it? It's such a lovely name. We like strong names. Strong women. Decisive women."

"Oh, Gloria, give it a break. You'll scare her off if you don't stop." It was the thin white woman, Ruth, who pushed Gloria gently aside and grinned at Eleanor. "Come on inside. Is that wine?" She held out her hand. "Gloria frowns on wine, but she's the only one. She prefers weed."

"Ruth," Gloria said patiently, "you're ruining the moment. I was trying to impress our new member with the exaltation of our cult."

"It's a cult?" Eleanor asked.

The two women laughed merrily. "It is a cult," Gloria said finally. "An old, old cult. Passed on from woman to woman. Held in secret and out in the open – both – and one that is essential for the earth to survive."

"The earth is in terrible shape," Eleanor said solemnly. She felt that there was no danger in stating the obvious.

Gloria nodded. "Our numbers got too thin. We wouldn't ordinarily talk to a stranger, as we did. But there were all the signs–"

"You have the mark on you," Ruth said in pure delight.

Eleanor's hand went to her face, though there was no mark there that she knew of. She had just become enormously self-conscious. "The mark?" she asked feebly.

"Oh, it's not on your face. It's in your eye."

"Oh," she said. "Oh!" There was a gold flake in her iris. Only in one eye. She looked curiously at Gloria.

"Yes," Gloria said. "There are three possible signs: a scar in the shape of a sickle. A sixth finger or toe. And a flake of gold in the eye. Do you know your power?"

She nodded shyly. This had all gotten straight to the point rather quickly. "I wish for a thing, and it often happens. But only as it relates to me. I can't end a war or create peace or cure cancer, but I can change the things that affect me directly. Like move the rain away, or make my coat heavier, or cause a hand to burn if it touches me."

"Tsk," Gloria said. "There's always an issue with hands touching us, isn't there? Are you entirely in control of it? Your power?"

They had been standing in the doorway all this time, when suddenly a voice from inside called, "Why don't you let her in so we can all meet her?"

Gloria rolled her eyes and winced. "I got carried away," she admitted. "I forgot my manners. But be warned, there is a whole roomful of witches waiting for you." She raised her voice on the last sentence, for the benefit of the witches behind her.

This was certainly better than an ordinary day, Eleanor thought. She could feel her own excitement creeping into her face, and she tried to organize her idiot grin. Gloria stepped aside and motioned with her cane for Eleanor to follow Ruth down the hallway, which was well-lit with electric sconces. It had a maple chair rail running down both sides, and faintly flowered wallpaper. The well-worn carpeting muffled their footsteps, but she could hear voices down the hallway, a little raucous and persistent.

At the end of the hallway, she entered a good-sized kitchen with large picture windows looking out into a private garden, with young beech trees leaning gracefully along fencing at the edges. In the middle was a small clearing surrounded by benches.

"This is Eleanor," Gloria said, her hand firmly guiding Eleanor forward to the middle of the kitchen.

"Welcome," came a chorus of voices around a large kitchen table. There were close to a dozen women, of all ages and shapes and colors. There was an aroma of spices, and she noticed a medium-sized black pot on the stove, bubbling. Apple cider and cinnamon and nutmeg and a few other things.

"You can add vodka or rum or just about anything, and we freely encourage you," a grinning witch told her. "Just about anyone could have read the look on your face, but I'm better than most in trickier situations."

"She is. That's Sheri. Her gift is guessing."

"Mind-reading!" Sheri cried. "It's mind-reading!"

The group jostled and laughed, introducing themselves and their talents. The talents didn't seem so remarkable to Eleanor. There were healers and clairvoyants and a finder. Sheri shook her head. "She thinks we're poor representatives of the power of witchcraft."

They all turned towards her then, their faces bright. "These are the powers we knew about," a woman named Jessica said gently. "Once you're initiated, you'll learn about the other powers you have, and how to control them."

"If you *want* to control them," a sort of goth-looking witch said, and another one rolled her eyes.

"Go easy on her," Gloria said. "I just gave her my card and told her to come over."

"That seems a bit unfair," Carmen said. She was one of the youngest ones, in her early twenties perhaps. She leaned forward and put her elbows on her knees. Her hair was wavy, and she tended to twitch it slightly. "But here's the short version: we're witches. We have a code of ethics and we have an educational system. We're also very secretive about our rituals and our requirements. If you join us, you have to abide by them. If you don't, you'll get thrown out and something important will be taken away from you. Like the power of speech."

"Not always the power of speech," Gloria pointed out. "But something that matters to you."

Eleanor stood there, her eyes slowly traveling around the room. The women looked back at her with interest. They seemed a very diverse group, yet completely and utterly comfortable with each other. She thought of the troubles she'd gotten into simply because she was who she was and what she was. She thought of the punishments she'd received as a small child who hadn't understood that what she'd done was awful. She had sometimes struck out, out of sheer frustration, and gotten into further trouble, lying her way out when she could, or being taunted and sometimes beaten when she couldn't.

This group had talents and they had community and it was hard to believe that she had finally arrived at the one place where she might fit in.

She could feel her face beaming out at them. "Can you fly?" she asked, and they cheered.

"So, when did you know you had a power?" Monica asked, indicating a seat for her. "A lot of us only found out by accident. Ginny, over there, for instance, fell off a wall and froze herself a foot off the ground."

"Or the ground froze a foot away from me," Ginny said smoothly. "Or I stopped time and got off the wall... or I stopped place." She looked interested. "Never thought of that. Maybe I stopped place!"

"That one's too difficult to think about," Becca said. "I wouldn't know how to begin."

"You begin by thinking of a place – let's say, this room. Then you think of making the room into cement, let's say. Or into smoke. I like smoke better. Maybe an instant freeze?"

Oh, Eleanor thought, they like conundrums. It's a game. "What does smoke do in an instant freeze?" she asked. "Does it fall down and break?"

Monica nodded happily. "Perhaps it can be sliced up. Slices of smoke."

"I don't know if slicing is a way of stopping," Ginny said. "In terms of place. Does smoke equal place?"

"I'm getting tired of this," Gloria said. "You keep changing the parameters. First it was place, and then it was smoke. One or the other."

Ginny shrugged. "It was just a thought. I think what I actually do is separate myself from place."

"You mean change place," Gloria persisted.

"I don't think that's what I mean at all."

"Because if you separate yourself from place then you're in no place at all and we don't know if that exists. Does it feel different?"

"No. It doesn't. It feels the same, only stopped."

"Here we are again," Alison said.

Through it all, they had gotten up one by one and gone into the dining room that the kitchen opened into, and came back again, picking up objects, pausing, and putting them down. Eleanor was puzzled at first, but she continued watching as the conversation went on and realized the various women followed the same route. "I can see what you're doing," she said. "You've gone in a circle."

"Well, yes, of course we have," Gloria said. "The circle is always drawn when we meet. It can be simple if it's just a casual meeting, or we can get very ornate. You know about the circle, I can see. What else do you know?"

"Not much at all," Eleanor said. "And really just some words. Covens, charms, curses, mating with the devil–" she looked around expectantly. "Do you mate with the devil?"

"That was really just a rumor the devil started," Ruth said. The group burst into laughter.

"It wasn't the devil," Monica said. "It was just some man with a goatee horning in on our territory. You know how men are. It was just one of their campfire stories, you know. Someone trying to impress someone else. Of course, there's always been mating, but it's really consensual."

"Sensual," Becca said. "At the very least."

For a moment, everyone drank their wine or hot cider or ate their cake, their eyes drifting uncomplicatedly here and there around the rooms. Eleanor got up and went about the circle as she had seen the others do, stopping at the objects they had stopped at, lifting any she had seen lifted. There were statuettes of stone or pieces of blown glass or little trinkets shaped like bells or cupids, nicely done but by no means seeming to have any threatening or supernatural importance. But what do I know? she asked herself after a while. From then on, she just looked at them, picked them up, felt their weight, and put them down again. She liked the smoothness and the feel of a small mahogany box, but it was plain, and she thought that meant it was unimportant. The one object that she thought might have consequence was a small chalice, with stones stuck in the stem. She spent a few extra seconds on that one, noting the intricate etching around the jewels.

When she put the last object down and turned back, she saw that, once again, everyone's eyes were on her.

"Well done," Gloria said, and Eleanor felt an unexpected pleasure in having done a particularly good job.

"It was the goblet," she said. "The goblet was important, and I recognized it?"

"The goblet? That's just a souvenir from Oaxaca. No, you completed the circle. We can begin."

Eleanor sat down and saw that Gloria had brought out a pack of cards, and began to deal. "Deuces wild," Gloria said pleasantly.

They played poker for a few rounds, and Sheri turned out to be a particularly astute player, but then the game changed into one that Gloria called Foxes. In this, the wild card actually became wild and could move surreptitiously from one player's hand to another. The trick of the game was to predict when it would stop and with whom, with rapid-fire bids exploding around the table. Eleanor had no idea how they figured anything out but just for fun she joined the bidding and accidentally won one round.

That's when she began to actually see the fox, who leapt from one hand of cards to the other in a blurring hop, or stuck its head out from one hand for a second and then scurried to another. Eleanor looked up quickly, but the others were calling hands and rounds with equanimity. Only I can see it? she wondered. I'm the only one? They're testing me, she concluded and sat back with an air of indifference.

The fox then made a big show of pointing out where it was going, and Eleanor saw it and won two hands in a row. It lied to her on the next round. She deliberately just watched the next hand (a hand ran only a minute or two as wagers flew about where the fox was), not bidding. She saw the fox leap to Alison's hand, and Becca called it. All the witches' heads were lowered over their cards, but their eyes roamed, and they could see perfectly well what was happening around them. She tried it herself and yes, peripheral vision was good enough to see around the table, to catch a movement. There! That was a movement! The fox had leapt to Gloria's hand. Eleanor waited for anyone to bid, or for the fox to move, and nothing happened. There were sounds of someone yelling in the yard next door. Something got knocked over. She felt poised in the moment.

She wanted the fox to come to her hand, because the tension was extraordinary. Her shoulders ached; her eyes were straining; she wanted to get up. She could get up as soon as the fox came to her.

And there it was, peeking out at her from Sheri's hand. Eleanor refused to look at it directly, but there was a sudden round of bids. She bid herself and then made a firm "Come here" in her head and then, all at once, the fox was in her hand.

"Very good start," Gloria said, relaxing and leaning back.

"Went on too long," Becca said, putting her cards down and stretching. "Took forever to figure it out."

Eleanor, surprised, asked, "Figure what out?"

Alison, who had been quiet up until then, sighed. "Gloria, are you sure you picked the right person?"

Gloria smiled stiffly at Eleanor. "Don't listen to that. Don't worry about it. This was a good first meeting. Please come back again this time next week."

The witches smiled politely at her as they relaxed around the table. She felt her face burn. Were they dismissing her? Had she failed their expectations?

"Don't worry," Sheri said. "We always start this way. You're invited back, aren't you?"

She would have to be content with that.

CHAPTER 8

Eleanor was on her best behavior for her second witch meeting, trying to find a way to please them and convince them of her value. They liked puzzles. They liked intelligence. "I keep thinking about how Ginny stopped herself from falling," she began.

Gloria nodded. "Or stopped the floor from accepting her. We are not the only stoppable objects."

"No one ever thought you were a stoppable object," Monica said, laughing. "It's one of your charms."

"It's too soon to tell her about charms." Sheri turned to her and asked, her head tilted slightly, "Or are your thoughts your charms? Have you ever directly addressed the rain and told it to stop, or do you merely want it?"

That was putting her on the spot. They were always asking her about things she hadn't even considered. Why hadn't she considered it? These women threw her inadequacies back at her. Would she drown in this wordplay if she didn't admit her ignorance? She didn't know. She was out of her depth. "I suppose both," she said cautiously. "I mean, I know I've said, 'Stop' once or twice. Or more than twice. It does seem that a lot of things need stopping out there. The joke about stoppability – is there a particular reason for it?"

"She's catching on, at least," Carmen said, nodding

vigorously. "Oh yes. Stopping and starting are important considerations for just about everything, aren't they?"

Eleanor kept her mouth shut, waiting for the next clue. Was Carmen always this arch? Was she supposed to respond to this question?

Ginny continued with her explanation. "I was so surprised the moment I realized it, that I fell the rest of the way. But it was only a foot, so it was just a great way to learn. Though of course I didn't *know*. My family was always telling me that I never paid attention, so I thought, I just wasn't paying attention. I wasn't as high up as I thought. I had tripped during a daydream. I had lots of ways of explaining things until I gave up and admitted it."

"A lot of us hid our powers. But not everyone." Becca looked merrily at Gloria.

"I'm a distance-viewer," Gloria said. She sat back with her arms crossed on her chest. "I learned when I was a baby that I could see things and people when they weren't near me. I was a very contented baby in that way. I never felt that I was 'left' by anybody. And then when I was a teenager–" here, she grinned, "–I used my powers for evil. I spied on boys I liked, on girls I didn't like. I never watched TV because I had my own TV. And spying gave me information. The TV never did that. It was full of people I didn't know or care about."

"You said you can cause things?" Ruth asked Eleanor. They were all direct, but Ruth seemed to be the least obscure in her questions.

Eleanor nodded. "But only the things around me. I can stop the rain or move a cloud, that kind of thing. Make something small fall. Kind of just like pushing it aside. Or making it disappear."

"Is it only when it's urgent?" Gloria asked. "Do you try to do it when it doesn't matter to you?"

"Why would I?" she asked, startled.

They looked at her intently.

"Those are all different powers," Rose said. "Adjusting nature. Telekinesis."

"Maybe they're all the same power, just being used differently," Gloria said. "You can move the rain away from you or towards you. You can push things away. I don't know about 'disappearing' though. Where you think they go?"

"I don't know," she answered. "It never bothered me when they went away. Is that a problem? Can I still become a witch?" Eleanor asked, looking a little embarrassed.

The women around her looked up and then continued in their separate conversations. "Of course," Ruth said. "That's why you're here."

They ate their pieces of cake and drank their wine, as if it were a book club, Eleanor thought. "But how do I become a witch?" she asked, a little rattled. This was a piece of information that was eluding her.

"Well," Gloria said, "I assume you already are a witch. We've all felt it."

"But I don't know how to do witch things though!" she protested. This was so frustrating.

"What things are those?" Gloria asked.

"Why – transformations, curses, spells, flying. You said I would fly! I'm sure you said it." Did her voice really have to be so petulant?

"And where will you go when you fly?" Monica asked.

"Why, why–" she stopped suddenly, realizing she wasn't sure. "Why, just up in the sky, just up in the air, just going from place to place."

"Flying has to have a purpose," Gloria said austerely. "It's not a kiddie ride."

"What do you want me to say? You invited me, and really, it seems like you've been challenging me the whole time."

"We've been studying you," Becca said sweetly. "To see what kind of witch you'd be."

"It doesn't seem too promising," Carmen said. But then she

laughed, and they all laughed. She was teasing her, Eleanor realized. They liked to tease each other. She was one of them, after all.

The gift shop didn't pay much but it didn't demand much either. Eleanor was expected to deal with customers, restock the shelves, dust and straighten up, and then reconcile the cash register at the end of the night. Since most people used credit cards, this was easy. She was required to work one weekend day (she often got Saturday) and four weekdays, and there were two other sales clerks – a part-timer, Marianne, and Stan, a youngish guy with a thinning man-bun. She hated man-buns, but she tried to be charitable. And, of course, there was her boss, Charles Peter. She hadn't been sure at her job interview if Peter was his last name or if he was one of those eccentrics with two first names.

He annoyed her. He sometimes stood right behind her while she sorted items on the shelves and when she turned, she would smack into him and he'd grab her "to steady her," as he said. "I wouldn't want you falling and suing me, now, would I? Or is that what you were planning?" He'd dust off her shoulders as if she had indeed fallen. And he'd place his hand gently on her waist to direct her out of his way as he scooted around her for no good reason.

He was always finding a reason to touch her. It had been "accidental" at first, then it had become obviously intentional, but also nowhere near what anyone would consider assault. He touched her shoulder, her chin, the small of her spine, never her breasts or her ass. He did it to tell her he was behind her and coming through; to get her attention when he saw a customer before she did; to point out an area that needed straightening; to praise her work by squeezing her arm. He grinned. He winked. And whenever she went to his office, he looked up and smiled, then slowly closed the porn on his computer screen.

She mentioned all these things to Stan, and he just shrugged. "You're too sensitive," Stan said. "Women are always on the lookout these days."

"On the lookout?" she repeated. She tried different responses to him when he said things like that – freezing him out, not replying to his stupidities or, in this case, repeating them back at him.

"I mean, what's the point if you take everything seriously? Will that change the world?" He looked at her brightly.

He obviously expected an answer. "No."

"And being serious will make you miserable. It always does. So loosen up a little. He's a jerk, but really, he isn't much of a *force*, is he? So he watches porn, so he gets too close. Use it against him. Take a photo of him watching porn in his office. It might be useful. Accidentally hit your elbow in his crotch when he's behind you. You can always *smell* when he's behind you."

"That awful cologne," she agreed. "Awful." What was Stan up to? She had yet to figure him out. He was nice and then he wasn't. He backed her and then he snickered at her. He sucked up to the boss but rolled his eyes when the boss wasn't looking. Not to be trusted – obviously. But he was the closest thing she had to an ally, despite the man-bun.

The inventory for the gift shop was pretty standard: painted boxes with flowers on them; stationery; letter openers; posters; candles and candleholders; mugs; salt and pepper sets; jigsaw puzzles; scarves; place mats, all with some artistic influence. Notebooks; calendars; some mobiles; ceramics; some famous portraits and the more approachable abstracts. Jewelry as well, including scarabs and amulets. Key rings. Books on art. DVDs on art. Pens with art on them.

The museum had started twenty years ago as a private collection, open only by appointment, but as the collection grew it had taken over the building, causing the elderly owner to move elsewhere and dedicate his former home to his possessions. Not all of them, of course; he kept the most beloved ones with him. He had different collections, too: old books, music boxes, little spring-loaded banks.

She'd had a normal day with the boss watching porn, Stan hovering around her or disappearing altogether. There weren't many customers, and the day was almost over.

"Look who's here." Stan nudged Eleanor to look at Charles Peter, standing in the doorway.

"I got a call about a Magritte poster," the boss said. "Do we have any?"

A customer came in and Stan, with a grin, moved towards him, leaving Eleanor to field the question.

"Of course we have Magritte," she said. "Let me make sure which ones." She went over to the lateral files, pulling out the drawer of artists whose last name was L-P. It was low and she squatted down and began to go through the posters. When she smelled the stink of his cologne, she slowed down, stretching her arm out to jiggle the edge of the drawer. She pictured him behind her and glanced up to see what was nearby as she continued to jiggle the drawer. There was a paperweight right at the front of the shelf above her and she thought, yes, that's it, and the paperweight toppled over and fell on his shoulder. He yelped.

"Oh!" she cried out, sitting back on her heels. "I didn't know you were right on top of me like that. Are you hurt? Did it hit your head?" She stood up and grabbed his elbow, hard. "Should I call someone? How did it happen – did I do something? You should have warned me where you were!"

Stan came rushing over, adding to the atmosphere of alarm, winking at her, patting the boss' shoulder, until the man left, wincing and muttering.

"We have two Magrittes," she called out after him. "But I can't tell if there's blood on one of them – are you bleeding?"

He waved her question away, and Stan leaned in to whisper. "You're fearless," he said. "How did you do it? Did you slam the drawer or something?"

She looked at the drawer and saw that it was still open. "I must have yanked it too hard," she said. "I must be very strong." She smiled. It was just a small bit of magic, the kind she'd always done without thinking. But now, with the coven challenging her sense of feeling, she thought of it more as a pull, not simply a wish for something to happen. Was everything she ever did a pull? She'd never thought about the varieties of magic, the variables, the specifics. Nor, to be honest, had she ever spent time thinking about what she was about to do. But the paperweight had been chosen. She had called out to it. She had pulled it down.

It was a week before Gloria came into the store again, walking slowly around the objects, picking things up off shelves and replacing them, leaning slightly on her cane to see what was in the lower cabinets. She nodded at Eleanor, not saying anything while a couple who were also in the shop debated over small gifts for their family. They settled on coasters and mugs.

"I wondered what was happening," Eleanor said, going over to Gloria. "I didn't know if I should call or if I'd been rejected."

"You weren't rejected. And I've left you a present. I won't tell you where it is, and it won't be visible for two hours. But you'll know when you find it, and I think you'll enjoy it." She laughed and limped out of the store.

That cheered Eleanor up immensely. The store was moderately busy for a while (tourists: they bought prints and scarves), but there was a lull during the late afternoon, and she settled into dusting, straightening, keeping an eye out. There were a few things out of place, and she paused, wondering if there was something about them that was Gloria's clue, but she continued until she got to the spot where the paperweight had fallen onto Charles Peter's shoulder. There, propped against the replacement paperweight, she found a small book. It was only a few inches square, and it was beautifully bound with a shiny blue-green cover that had a pattern on it of outlined cubes containing black and white eyes. It had the smallest zipper she'd ever seen securing the three open sides, but it slid easily. The tiny pages inside had minuscule writing on them; there was only one page she could really read and it said, *Eat me.*

She closed the book and slipped it into her pocket. Her heart raced; this was the beginning, the true beginning.

She waited until she got home to inspect it further. She climbed up to her fourth-floor tenement apartment, with its bathtub in the kitchen, and the 1888 regulation window between the kitchen and the living room. She loved the idiocy of that regulation – the law said each room had to have a window, but never specified that the window had to open to the outside. She made a quick dinner and a cup of tea and sat on the chair in the living room. She took out the little book and placed it on the small table next to the window and stared at it for a minute. Then she tore out the postage-stamped page that said *Eat Me* and put it on her tongue, where it melted in a soft taste of strawberry.

It was a quiet night with a bright moon. The stars poked through the sky, and down below, the street sounds were benevolent. Eleanor gazed out at the blue-blackness of the night. There was a magical age – was it seventeen? – when it was possible to feel oneself bleeding into the universe, experiencing the intensity of everything – mood, anticipation, belief, eroticism. The desire for life had been urgent and wonderful, and it felt like that again as she looked out the window. She told herself she still had the chance to achieve everything – honor, fame, art, love. All of it. She could feel her own strength spread through her arms. She had power. She knew she had power. She had simply not taken advantage of it before, not channeled it, not tested it.

The moon was full and gawked at her. She gazed back and

the moon's face seemed to glare. Or was it sticking out its lower lip, challenging her? Suddenly she thought, I could make it come closer, because the taste of strawberry on her tongue was still there, and that taste told her there was magic in her.

She stood up and raised her right arm and pointed her fingers straight at the mouth of the Man in the Moon, who grew even more astonished at her. "Come closer," she commanded, and the moon moved an inch or two, wavered, then moved a few more inches, twitching to the right and then over to the left, then going back to its start. She could see it was struggling to stay put, and failing. Its eyes widened as the force of her mind willed it closer to the earth, to her. She could feel the pull of the tide and the earth as the moon neared her, and she thought maybe that was enough; she couldn't hold it and the tides and the earth all in balance, so she released it, pushed it back, and then pushed it back a little bit more so that the moonlight grew farther and farther away. But that, too, she thought, might disturb the earth's waters and things she quite possibly wasn't even considering, so she let it go again, and felt the letting go as if it were a string she had ceased to pluck. The moon went back to its normal position, looking aggrieved.

She turned away from the window and looked at the room she was in. Without moving, she pulled a footstool from the corner of the room towards her, and pushed it back. She saw a pen near a lamp and pulled it towards her and then pushed it away. Her mind had fingers! She could grasp items from across the room, push them, pull them. She felt good. She felt that she had learned something about her own abilities, and she wanted to learn more. Why can't I move myself? she wondered, and she tried to push herself up in the air. The idea of flying still thrilled her; she had been thinking about it since she had met Gloria, and she wanted it desperately. Everything else was a periphery; flying was the center.

But she couldn't push and pull herself. She tried repeatedly, sometimes thinking she was getting closer to doing it, only to be dropped back into despair. Finally, she stopped, afraid that she had lost what little she had gained. The exhaustion was overpowering, weighted with the fear of failure, and so she went to sleep, having no disturbances or dreams.

In the morning she woke. This new part of her life was the only important thing and she felt flushed with determination. She would become a witch and not just that, but a powerful, generous, marvelous witch. She would do kind things – is that what the other witches were doing? If they had power, how were they using it?

CHAPTER 9

"There are three degrees of initiation," Gloria said. "We explain it, and then you agree to it, and so on two more times. It is, of course, always voluntary."

"We kill you if you don't agree though, of course," Jolene said and grinned.

"There are more ways of being dead than you can imagine," Chantel agreed.

"Oh, don't start about the zombies," Becca said, laughing. "I hate the stories about the zombies. You like to make them so gruesome."

"A good zombie story has to be," Chantel said. "It's called *genre*."

The women were drinking punch and wine, and once again, they got up one by one and touched an item as they circled the room. Ruth nodded at Eleanor, and she circled the room in turn, once again picking up the smooth box, touching it on all sides, and then replacing it.

"Why do we do this?" she finally asked. "Go around the room and pick out one particular item?"

"These are our icons," Gloria said. "There's one here for each of us. We touch each one, as a way of incorporating all of us into the spiritual circle."

"I see you've already chosen one," Ruth said. "The box."

"I like it, yes. I'm not sure why."

"Sometimes the items choose us. It can be intuitive. It can be spiritual. Psychological. All the words mean pretty much the same thing. You've selected it, or it's selected you."

"I do like it," she admitted. "Do I take it with me at some point? To bond?" She felt a warmth spread over her face. A stupid thing to say.

"To bond!" Carmen repeated, laughing. "I like that! If you two chose each other, you've already bonded. No special dates! No movie nights!"

"Very funny, Carmen," Ruth said. She inclined her head to Eleanor. "You take it as you need it. You'll know when that is. Every step invites you in. We are careful about who joins, because each witch increases the strength of the coven at least two-fold. We magnify each other's abilities. So, our first activities when we gather are always to reconnect spiritually and politically. That's from *polis*, the idea of an informed citizenry. It means people work together using all their different skills to create a knowledgeable and engaged society."

"And then what?"

"We discuss concerns, choose a topic, form a circle, and begin an action."

"Do you choose the topic ahead of time?"

"We've been stuck on the same topic for a while," Gloria said, getting up and going from item to item as the others sat around the room. For a moment, Eleanor wondered if she was supposed to get up and follow the movements, but all the women nodded when Gloria was finished and came back to sit down. She had been the final one.

"You won't be invited into the circle yet. But it won't be long," Ruth said. "And there's an initial public, social aspect that involves our learning about you first. We need to know each other. So right now, the invitation is to learn about each other, not proceed."

"Are you an only child?" Gloria asked.

"I am now," Eleanor said. "I used to have a family, but we split up. My father died, my mother went insane, and my sister took off and never got back in touch."

Gloria sighed. "I'm sorry. And yet they produced *you*."

Eleanor paused. They had indeed formed her life. There were some quite good memories in the mess that had been her family. Sounds of occasional laughter. A smiling face. Before the spitting and screaming. "I got used to making sure I didn't feel a thing about my family. I have a life that has a certain kind of meaning, but it doesn't… it doesn't reach out."

"Carmen?" Gloria asked, inclining her head to the red-haired woman.

"Of course." Carmen nodded. "I came from a bad marriage. I did a little of the bad part myself, when I realized what I'd gotten into. But I got myself out, after sorting restraining orders and finding out who was, and wasn't, my friend. Something that will always surprise you, by the way. You can be absolutely sure about loyalties and still be wrong. But anyway, I got away and moved to a small place by the beach and spent the next few years staring at waves and imagining a different life. And then one day I went to a small concert of Chopin Études, and my heart burst open. I had denied myself Chopin because everything that belonged to my past had to be abandoned. And when I heard it again, I realized that no, not *everything* had to be left behind. All I had to do was retrieve the things I loved and get rid of the things that were destroying me. I didn't have to taint everything. That's the mistake I made. I was destroying what I loved in order to be free of what I hated."

The room murmured as more stories were shared. Women spoke and women listened, and Eleanor found herself a part of the sound of their stories.

Eleanor was afraid the initiation would be somewhat boring, potentially farcical, and a bit on the woo-woo side. She had gone through various rituals in her childhood, due to her parents' religion, as well as a fair number of dances and such at school. Most things involved dressing up and committing to things she didn't believe in. But she liked the witches, and she wanted to be initiated. She wanted to move forward. She was done with all the things that held her back.

She had been told about the start of the ritual, so when Gloria met her at the door and invited her in, she knew that the invitation was the first real step. Ruth stood next to Gloria and admonished Eleanor about witchly principles and asked if she would abide by them. She said yes. She felt a lightness in her heart.

"Once you cross this threshold, you're bound to us," Gloria said.

Eleanor said yes again, and the two oldest witches led her inside, back to the kitchen table.

Gloria indicated that she should stand in the doorway. "You're bound by our rules. They're pretty simple: you cannot expose yourself or us to the world because it has harmed us in the past. People believe we are evil and it's not worth our time to argue with them.

"Nor can you use what you learn to further your own aims. That's pretty broad and it's probably best to make it simpler. You cannot hurt anyone in any way except to prevent a larger harm. But even then, you cannot expose us. If you were to use witchery in public, it must be in such a way that the most obvious explanation is not witchery. You can make it seem like a trick, if it's a *possible* trick."

Gloria had lately progressed from a cane to a walker, and she shifted her weight a few times. She must be in pain, Eleanor thought.

Gloria straightened herself and took a breath. "Another way to look at it is that you can no longer act on your own. As a witch you are part of our community, our organism. Again, you can protect yourself as a witch if you're in danger (though again, it must not be recognizably witchcraft) but for anything that is not life-threatening and immediate, we discuss and decide and obey the group decision. To go against the coven is to declare yourself above the coven, to declare your existence and your ego have more weight than the combined existence and egos of the community. We operate as checks on each other. And yes, we don't always agree, but we accept a decision as long as the majority agrees that it is the right decision."

There was still a part of Eleanor that wondered if she could subject herself to other people's edicts forever. Did they *mean* forever? She cleared her throat, raised her chin, and asked, "And what happens if someone doesn't follow these rules?"

Gloria looked at her and then stared past her. "It's a good question. There's no single answer. Each occasion merits its own decision about discipline. The punishment is meted out to make the offending witch see what the offense was. We don't water-board anyone or whip them or anything terrible. But a witch will have to see the results of her misstep, one way or the other. I don't mean to suggest that it's pleasant – it never is. But each time there's a punishment, it's decided after deliberation and it's always unique."

"And what if I wanted to leave? What if I found I didn't fit with this particular group?"

Gloria nodded. "It's happened. If it's mutual – if we all agree that it's the best decision – then we'll just say goodbye. That's if you don't represent any kind of threat and we don't think you'll be guilty of reprisals, it's safe to have you leave. If there's doubt about that, then again, it's decided by the rest of the coven. We've never killed anyone who left." Gloria smiled faintly. "But we've done spells and curses to limit their ability to harm us. Our goal is to protect ourselves and have the separated witch go back to her life as it was before she met us."

Eleanor nodded. "I understand that. I just don't want to be harassed or anything like that. If we part ways, no repercussions and no remorse."

Two women stood up and motioned for Gloria to sit down, which she did heavily.

"Witches are indebted to the earth," Ruth said. "Our power comes from nature, and it is our obligation to protect the earth and its processes and beings. Protecting animals and children. Getting women the power they deserve. That kind of thing. And since we never take an action without a consensus, it tends to make our positions very moderate. Sometimes more moderate than some of us would like."

Becca grimaced. "She means me. I'm the current hothead. We do seem to take turns on that score. I'd be happy to give you a shot at it."

Eleanor nodded. "I sometimes have a short fuse."

"You'll learn to lengthen it. I did. Now, Gloria, will you invite her in?"

Gloria turned to Eleanor. "Do you wish to join this coven?"

A very simple question, Eleanor realized, and she was grateful for the simplicity. It made it easy to say yes, and she did so. All the witches stood up and led her into the living room, which had the furniture pushed back to make a wide clear space in the middle of the hardwood floor.

"There are some rituals that go back so far we don't always know why they began," Gloria said, "but since we respect the centuries that have led to us, we continue with them." She turned to the other witches. "Draw the circle."

They drew a chalk circle with a hexagram inside it on the floor. They put candles at the corners of the room and lit them. The only light besides the candles was the fading sunlight filtering though the curtains. "We begin now," Gloria said.

There was some sandalwood burning, or a candle with that scent. She watched as the witches finished the preparations. Objects were placed carefully, more candles were lit. A small broom and a rope were laid out around the perimeter.

Gloria pointed to one particular spot outside the circle and Eleanor went to stand there. "We invite a new witch into our circle if the whole of our community agrees. Witches, do you agree?"

One by one, in order from west to east, the witches individually agreed.

"We invite our initiate into our circle if she agrees to abide by the principles of our coven. Do you agree?"

"I agree," Eleanor said. Her heart was skipping round a little. What was she agreeing to? How far could she trust these women? She swept her gaze around the circle, looking each in the eye. They were not strangers; she was beginning to know them. "I agree," she repeated.

"Then step into the center of the circle," Gloria said. "Your spirit must be encouraged to move from the world outside this circle to this new world, with us. No passage is without pain, even if it leads to wisdom. The ways you learn will require you to show perseverance and strength and resolve and charity. These are not done without cost. Once you agree to bear the pain of this you will no longer be a solitary witch. That means you can no longer do just what your impulses dictate."

Becca and Ruth stepped forward with lengths of rope and laid them in the center and Eleanor felt her heart pump faster. They placed a small rough straw broom in the center, too, and some of the statues and ornaments that came from the living room. She saw the mahogany box, her favorite, among them.

They were done placing things and turned to her. "Are you ready to join us?" Gloria asked.

"Yes."

"Have you studied the commitments, and will you abide by them, letting your will be subject to the combined will of the coven?"

"Yes, I will."

"Will you hold secret and separate from the rest of the world all those things that you learn here?"

"Yes, I will."

"As a token of your new life, please strip naked."

She hesitated. "I'm menstruating. There's a string."

Gloria shrugged. "We all menstruate. I take that back. Ruth and I don't anymore, and I believe at least one woman is pregnant, but I can assure you we won't fall down in a faint like a man."

She took her clothes off, piling them on the floor. The women took a pace away from her and stood shoulder to shoulder around her.

"You must select someone to be your guide," Gloria said.

"Not me. I'm a kind of general guide – this must be a personal guide."

Eleanor was ready for this. She was sure that the most relaxed, least pushy witch was Monica, and she wanted the least pushy guide she could have. She stepped up to her, and Monica inclined her head.

"The circle accepts you," Gloria said. "Now, please go to the center of the circle. Pick up the broom and go around inside the circle three times, west to east, tapping each person on the shoulder and saying, I am part of your circle."

She did so. They each looked her square in the eye and that impressed her.

"There's a cup in the center of the circle. It's nothing terrible, just a slight intoxicant. It will allow you to see something you can't see now. Drink all of it."

She did so.

"Now, we need to take your measure as a witch, which is to say we need you to know that all of you is now a witch and we will commit all of you to our society. You cannot retain any part, you cannot withhold your heart, you cannot withhold your mind or your spirit or your sense of right. We measure you and tally all of you, all that combines in all the realms, to make you a witch."

With that, Gloria took up one of the cords and another witch came to help her. They held the cord against her and then tied knots into the cord, always measuring it against her after each knot, so that the final cord matched her height with knots gathered at head and heart – that cord, she was told, was her spirit, her ghost witch.

"We keep your cord here, in the altar. It's not an altar like in a church, it's just a witchly consecrated space."

"What does it mean, if you have that cord? Is there some power you have over me?"

"I suppose, in theory. But it might be the power to heal, you know. It's the manifestation, the holding, of your witch soul. That sounds like it's too much. It's more like when folklorists bury the child's umbilical cord, the connection to the earth. This is your connection to us."

"Psychological, mostly." This was Ruth. "I've never heard that anyone did anything with it. But rituals are psychological, mostly. The cord knots us together."

"Okay," she said. She would not want an enemy to have it. She supposed she had at least one enemy – her boss. Maybe even Stan – if only because she couldn't figure out what he wanted. He seemed to be too aware of her, too alert to everything she did, as if he were keeping track of her. She thought, for a moment, that she might be too suspicious. Perhaps she was too harsh.

But no. The world was harsh. Women needed to be vigilant. She'd had a man hold a knife to her throat and she had a friend who was raped. And immigrant and native women were even more at the mercy of individuals and power structures. Maybe she was becoming more political. She had gone on one march and she had signed petitions. She worried, in a careful sort of way, about anyone who didn't fit in to the scheme. You didn't get to be a politician by being virtuous.

She should do more.

A lot of men had armed themselves.

Maybe the women should, too.

It was at this point that she began to feel a correction, a psychic shift. She opened her eyes, and all the witches were watching her, their arms linked, making a complete circle around her. They took a slow, graceful step towards her in the center. She could feel a power surrounding her, and she filled her lungs and breathed in.

It lifted her up. What a thing! What a thing, she thought.

She had never been determined to save the world. But now, this moment, there was a force reaching her, a force that had another vision, a different way to view the world. As if the world were flexible.

Well, she reminded herself: witches, spells, transformations. Change of one kind or another. Of course the world must be flexible. It would be wonderful to forget the headlines – no, in fact, to have the headlines change into something that didn't reflect the way people in power treated those who were not. She was not a political person.

What had they given her to drink? She noticed that they were moving now, moving around her, circling her in the middle of the circle. Oh yes, Gloria had told her to choose something, and that object would become her talisman.

A wonderful word.

How amazing it was that they connected to physical objects in the middle of – what? A metaphysical group? That was one of the things that had appealed to her. She had always felt as if she were struggling to keep herself in place. The Red Queen syndrome. Something had been missing, and that was the nonphysical world. But the two had a thread between them.

She already knew which object it would be.

The little wooden box had no hinges, just a fitted lid that slid down to its groove with a tiny little click. The top was smooth as could be, but the sides were rough, as if recently whittled. She sniffed the box, which had an herbal, outdoor scent to it, nature away from the city, out in the woods. She could store small things in the box, and they would be secure. She could keep keys inside it, for instance, and keys were wonderful, unlocking and releasing, safeguarding and securing.

She chose the box.

She crawled inside the box. The oils in the wood made her skin feel warm. She could feel the texture of the wood even when her hands were not touching it. It wasn't just the wood, she realized. It was everything wood could be. Paper came from wood, and she imagined or tried to imagine, how wood became paper. Once she started thinking about it, she found that her fingers were pale and fibrous, and her arms were folding around the flatness of her body. She fit inside the box, a piece of paper, thin and warm. Her mind flattened out as well. Her mind became quiet. A piece of paper was a perfect thing when it was folded and protected inside a box of wood. It held itself with utter purpose. It might contain words; it might be ready to contain words. It was knowledge preparing to happen.

Paper kept its own counsel. It studied itself, holding itself poised and prepared. Paper rested on the bottom of the box and felt the wood, the kinship, with the box. It was sure of its fibers. It was also expectant. It could remain what it was, or it could hold the notations from some other part of the world. It could hold a paw print, a shoe print. It could hold a drop of wine. It could retain words for those who forgot them. It was malleable, open to suggestions, nonjudgmental, tolerant. Paper consisted of strands, of threads, all woven or warped together to form a purposeful version of itself. It was both old and new, wood and fabric.

She existed then, folded and accepting, until she felt a touch of the broom on her shoulder, merely a brush of it, and she found she was sitting on the floor, knees bent, arms bent, head bent, pressed into herself. She slowly unfolded and stood up again.

Sheri and Ruth brought her a warm blanket. Becca said she would make some tea. The witches moved back to the kitchen, sitting around the table, murmuring to each other.

The teapot was large and decorated with stars in a dark sky. The cups were of all kinds, china or clay. She took a clay mug as cups were filled and distributed. It was light and sweet.

"What do you think?" Gloria asked her.

She rolled it all slowly through her mind. "I think I'm going to enjoy this," she said softly and took another sip.

The lift she'd gotten from the ceremony didn't last long – or at least there was no change in her essential being. She found her work boring and her boss as offensive as always. But she did look through the selection of little boxes at the gift shop to see if any more spoke to her or just the box she had been presented with at the ceremony.

That particular box now formed part of the collection that was placed around Gloria's living room and kitchen. When the witches walked around and handled items, they had been touching the spirit of the witch whose totem it was, connecting with her. Eleanor understood that and looked forward to the next meeting, when her own spirit would be touched, and she would touch others.

That sense of being part of a larger event retreated, and ordinary life resumed. Stan had been getting on her nerves for a while now, sidling over when she was talking to the boss or when it looked like she had annoying customers, just standing there listening with a slightly open mouth. What was the deal with him?

Finally, he cleared his throat one day and said, "You seem to have a lot on the ball. I've heard some of your comments and they're pretty eye-opening. I wonder if you'd like to make a little money on the side? This is just between you and me." His voice got lower as the sentences ran on, so by the end she was leaning forward, as if what he said was irresistible. She hated it when people did that. She should have just said that she couldn't hear him.

"That sounds pretty suspicious," she whispered back, forcing him to lean in to her.

"It's perfectly legal. And fun. Though you have to have the right attitude and be pretty flexible."

She frowned. "Flexible in what way exactly?"

"Socially. Politically." His eyes rose as he considered. "Maybe even a little bit morally."

"This is getting creepy, Stan. Why not come out and say what it is?"

He sighed. "You've heard of Augment?"

"Oh. Yes. It's a new social media thing, right?"

"It is. You can still get in at the beginning, pretty much. The thing is, you can use it to generate rumors and also stir up some controversy. And you get a cut of the ad revenue if your Augs go viral. That's not hard, by the way. Everyone's prejudiced about virtually everything. I started one last week, about the election. I said that the candidate had a particular phobia. I won't go into it because it started about one thing and morphed into another thing. But there were over fifty thousand hits. There was only twenty bucks on that one, but you don't just have one Aug going at a time, of course. I made over three hundred dollars last month. Anyway, if you Aug something and I pick it up and blast you about it – and vice versa, if I start and you blast – well, in theory we can reach wider audiences. I'm sure most of our Augs won't overlap. Women and men are different, right? *That* was a great thread, only I started out by claiming that women could never be in the army because they had lousy gun skills. Turns out I was wrong, unless that whole thing about women sharpshooters was a lie, and it doesn't matter if it was or wasn't as far as I'm concerned because it was all good money either way. You see what I'm saying?"

"I hate it when people say, 'You see what I'm saying?'" she answered. "It's a way of controlling my attention. It's a male move. Aggressive."

He stepped back and grinned. "See? That's something you can write, and you'll get a lot of responses. The angry ones are the best, so it's always good to make your first comment kind of pushy, like, 'Men always try to control the conversation and I'm sick of it. The next one who...' and then threaten something. There are lots of guys out there who love to get threatened by women. It's surprising."

"Gives them a little tingle in the balls," she said, and he beamed.

"That's the idea," he said encouragingly. "That kind of phrasing gets them all riled up, and that's more income for you. And, like I said, for me as well if we cross-fertilize."

She thought it over. It might be interesting, and could even be a way of handling her new-found political concerns. That was politics at its core, wasn't it? Confronting attitudes and sentiments that defended prejudice and hate? Stan wanted to upset people to get more revenue. Eleanor would love to have more money, since the shop paid very little. And provoking people into thinking seemed like a positive move to get it.

She looked at Stan's eager, shining face. "You get something from bringing in new people?"

"I get a bonus, double points for a week. If we work together, it could be an awesome week for me! I have a feeling you're a natural."

So she did it. There were all sorts of demographic forms she had to fill out and, because she thought most of it was none of their business, she answered a lot of it with what she thought they would like. Thus, she was a perky twenty-something with lots of followers on other sites, and she ate out a lot and went to parties and had seven best friends.

And she got in. As a starter, she had to do the first hundred Augs for free, but after that she would get the going rate. She started safely – when do boys and girls start to be different? – and built on it through various common complaints – how long did it take you to get to work with that service disruption? What does your dentist do that you hate? Did you hear one of the candidates is building a castle? If you keep out the

Mexicans, who will pick the crops? – and then it started getting really swayed by the numbers of people who couldn't shut up, who were itching for a fight, who kept her numbers thriving.

Her best Aug was: If you had to decide between killing a candidate and killing a stray dog, which would it be? After the flood of angry answers jumping in once anyone named *their* candidate as the one to be sacrificed, she hit her one-hundredth Aug. From then on, she was paid.

She learned that anything about candidates or pets would start a big conversation. Or she could raise the issue of gun control. The debate about it was getting increasingly heated. She would pose provocative questions: Your child hears guns down the hallway. What have you told her to do? You're in the post office with your kids and someone screams, *He's got a gun.* What do you do? For that particular one, a lot of people recalled something called "Going Postal," where deranged postal workers came in and shot up their workplace, often ending in one or two dead.

One or two dead. Such a thing was unimaginable. Dozens now. Many dozens.

So there was another Aug: In the Good Old Days, when a deranged person got a gun, it wasn't automatic. They didn't kill as many. Would you sell an automatic to a postal worker?

The debate raged on, and she wasn't going to stop it, but she hoped her Augs were getting someone to think. Probably not. People really were just defending positions they already held, and shifting questions onto their personal platforms.

Aug: An admitted rapist was given joint custody of the resulting child. Well, it is his child, right?

A teen posted a video of a girl dying of an overdose. Aug: Is there a law against letting someone die?

Aug: What's the silliest thing your kitten did lately?

It was changing the way she viewed life, a little. Now she went through the day weighing everything as a possible question. If you saw a parent hitting a child in punishment, would you step in? Elephants are about to become extinct. Do you care?

And, of course, there was politics. Does your candidate need to be defended against more things than the other candidate?

It was all very interesting, and it certainly gave her a sense of being in control, perhaps even of controlling others. It was exciting when she saw a lot of hits. It was easy to jump in when it was slowing down and say something maybe a little outrageous to get it moving again. Of course, Stan excelled at that because he was constantly outrageous.

"You want everyone to have a gun?" she asked after one of his Augs.

"That's why I love what's going on in Liberty. Everyone there is required to own a gun. I want a gun."

"I don't think that's true – I think everyone *can* own a gun, but I don't think you have to carry it."

"Not a paradise then," he said sadly. "Guns are an indicator of the strength of a society."

"They're a sign of weakness."

"How?"

"You can't win an argument without a gun? What does that say about you?"

"It says 'I'm a man of action'," he answered smugly. "No one like a man who talks too much anyway." He grinned. "Too girly-girl."

Despite their disagreements, Stan approved of the traffic her comments usually generated. "You're really good at this," he said with a smile. "I knew you would be. Look, I've commented on your Augs a few times this week, and you haven't commented back."

"Oh, I'm really sorry," she said. "I got so wrapped up in it I forgot."

He nodded. "Yeah, I know. It's pretty addictive when you're new to it. But remember who brought you on board."

"You're right," she said. "I'll get on it."

His latest Aug was about pizza. Yes, that had a lot of comments. "I love pizza with pineapple!" she commented. That would get them going.

"Someone already said that," he complained later. "You're not really trying."

Another one of his said, "If you had to live in one movie, which would it be?" That was an awful Aug, she thought. There were lots of one-sentence dead ends, and then nothing. It wasn't going anywhere. "Star Wars," she said. "So I could travel to the spinoffs." That got a bit of a burst into sequels and prequels.

"Not sure that's technically one movie," he said.

"I didn't think we cared about technically?"

She wrote notes to herself, lists of possible Augs. Her boss saw her writing things down and demanded to see what it was. "What's this? It doesn't make any sense. And it's not about work. If you have spare time, go clean a shelf. Straighten something."

"Your last one was a good one," Stan said. That had been about the legal age of marriage in the United States. A whole fight broke out when someone reported the states where girls could be married at twelve with parental consent. Half the post accused the other half of lying and then there were case references and mentions of state legal codes and horrible accusations of revenge. Some people threatened to get their guns and kill each other over it. "And that was a relief. Because, you know, if you don't maintain a certain level of traffic, you can get booted off Augment, and you might get me booted off as well."

"You didn't tell me that."

"I told you what you needed to know. It's by invitation only to get into it, and it has to maintain some traction, or the ads don't get bought. That's obvious. I mean, that's really obvious."

Totally typical of him, or people like him, to hold you accountable for things they never told you about. She answered stiffly, "Yes. You're right. It does make sense, even if you didn't tell me about it. Anything else you want to tell me about?"

He looked at her with irritation. "You can't tell anyone your real name. That's obvious, too. Or do I need to keep telling you about obvious things? Only a few people get paid for posting, and I'm one of the few people who can invite people to join."

That was interesting. "How come? I mean, I'm impressed, but why you? Why you?"

He grinned at her and walked away.

CHAPTER 10

Eleanor had trouble occasionally with some of the terminology of the Craft, as the belief system of historical witchcraft was called. The Craft was an old religion or way of life – they used both descriptions. Most called themselves witches, and a few called themselves Wiccan but either one was good. They believed in a pantheistic world, a world imbued with spirits in all varieties of life.

"I'm having trouble with this," she admitted. "I don't understand what the point of it is. Do you need to believe there's some sort of supernatural being out there? Making rules?"

"There are rules," Jolene said. "Things mate, grow babies, babies grow up to be like their parents. They start the cycle again."

"Well, I never thought of it as a rule."

"You don't have to. It's a cycle. And besides, you're arguing about words. Call it what you will."

"A cycle seems good."

Another witch smiled. "Do you see other cycles? Seasons? Agriculture? Day and night?"

"Okay. Okay. I get it. What I don't get is why so many people think it's... intentional."

"The intent may come from itself," Gloria said gently. "The

whole business of 'first cause' never worked because the way monotheism explains the complexity of life is by suggesting there's a being who created it without being able to explain where that being came from. But if you assume that there is vitality in the universe, unraveling and playing itself out in various patterns, then some of it becomes easier to digest. Where did the complexity come from? A god who wasn't created? Or from the spirit of the atom?"

"Same thing," Eleanor said. "Essentially. Who created the atom?"

"The force that through the green fuse drives the flower," Ruth said.

"The knights who say Ni!" Monica said, smiling.

"An explanation for the 'first' doesn't matter at all," said Eleanor. "Look at monotheism – the excuse for war, the excuse for class structure. Polytheistic societies aren't as bloodthirsty. I'm not saying they're virtuous, it's just that if you can see gods everywhere, you're less inclined to view another society as a threat. Because that society also has gods, and since there are gods everywhere it's best to respect those other gods, too, as well as your own. And by gods, perhaps we mean a different thing. None of these gods have created a hell to burn people up for eternity because they touched their genitals."

"On the contrary," Gloria said. "Please touch your genitals and get relaxed."

"Look at the expression on her face," Leslie said, laughing. "Check out that stubborn face!"

"Time for a road trip," Gloria said. "Time for a festival."

"The full moon is in six days. I don't know – don't witches like the full moon?" Eleanor was doing her best to pick up some witch lore, though it was haphazard at best, and sometimes they outright laughed at her.

"It has a toxic effect. Or a nontoxic effect. Depends on who's writing the article."

"We'll go to Fort Tryon," Monica said. "To our regular spot.

Eleanor will keep it from raining. Won't you, Eleanor?" Her smile was winning. Her eyes were delighted.

"Well, I can try," Eleanor said.

It was a clear night (Eleanor really had nothing to do with it) and the weather was warm enough so that they wore light clothing and no jackets. They took two cars and found a garage outside Fort Tryon Park and followed the winding roads up to a small rocky clearing.

A few of the women had baskets which, it turned out, held candles and little bells and herbs and oils and matches. They began to gather wood in a flat area marked by rocks and built a tent of sticks in a portable barbecue placed within the rocks and lit it as the night fell. The wood crackled. Ruth sprinkled oil and the flames licked up and then settled. They sat in a circle around the flames, some on chairs (like Gloria) and some on the ground. One by one they began chanting. It was hard to actually figure out what the words were because the oil was making Eleanor's thoughts drift.

"There's a full moon," she said when she noticed how bright the night was.

"You knew that," Carmen said. "That's when the life force perks up, so to speak. Life rises or it dies."

Two of the women took off their clothes, others took off their shoes or left themselves clothed. It was a warm night, and the smoke from the bright fire made Eleanor's head a little hazy. Oils and herbs were piled on, creating a great, aromatic cloud.

Gloria began to speak. "There used to be a unity in the world. Oh, I don't mean the Garden of Eden or some such. Life, for whatever reason, requires killing something else. But there was a compact between those who died and those who killed – that it wouldn't be for sport. That life was necessary and essential and interdependent. We seem to have stopped believing that. We now believe life is for us, that the more we grab the more we have." Gloria's voice was deep and soothing, and when she spoke it made an internal sense.

"Are those fireflies?" Eleanor asked.

"There was a network of wise women all over the world once," Gloria continued. "Women who knew herbs, of course, but who also knew how to address the world, how to read it. When diseases raged, these were the women who talked to the disease, discussed why it was there, and found the remedy. Life was harsh but it was also in harmony with the seasons and the animals and the plants. It was broken by the single gods."

"The single gods," Eleanor repeated. She felt the presence in the trees and on the ground, multiple movements of grains of earth and individual particles of wind. Gloria's voice was expanding.

"Monotheists declare their god is the only god and all other gods are deception and must be destroyed," Ruth said quietly. "I was a Christian for a long time," she added, "but there were always creatures calling out to me from within other orders of life. I never felt that I was the most essential animal on earth. I found myself at a festival once and met other people who believed as I did. I was eighteen; they were Wiccans. They accepted me and I met a world of people who deliberately set out to experience the whole of life, rather than constrain it. I joined the goddess then, but the goddess is not a monotheist; the goddess is life."

"Huh?" Eleanor said. "Goddess? You all say you're independent, but you talk about the goddess, and I'm just curious what your beliefs are."

"Following the goddess is a way of life, and as we've already mentioned, life has rules. So do we. The first rule is–"

Everyone chimed in. "Do no harm."

Gloria smiled happily. "We believe in freedom to act and to believe as long as it does no harm to another living being."

Ruth was obviously used to playing counterpoint to Gloria. She prompted, "Second–"

"The goddess. The goddess can be whatever you imagine. But the world, our world, is feminine and masculine, and there is a goddess and a god. We do not say above or below; that is a judgment about worth and value that does more harm than good. Our main focus is the goddess. The goddess is displayed throughout the earth, especially in birth and development. It is the force that through the green fuse drives the flower, as Ruth said the other day. It is the birth of life, it is the encouragement of life. The male god is the needed component to this, the empowerment of vigor, though the goddess is certainly vigorous enough."

"Third…" Ruth's voice was gentle.

"We believe in freedom. All religions believe they have the one true knowledge and that all other religions are false. We believe that we can all find a path to the goddess in individual ways, and as long as the path respects others, it's the right path.

"And we believe that we are stewards of the earth, protectors of life on earth. We profoundly disagree with all the plunder, all the destruction. The poisoning of our planet is the poisoning of all of us. It is murder."

The women nodded and murmured assent. "These are the things you must embrace with us," Ruth said. "If you truly wish to be one of us."

"I do," Eleanor said, "I absolutely do." She had a quiver, because a part of her knew perfectly well that she wasn't a very good steward, that she certainly resented people and was perhaps not as charitable as a witch should be. She thought she was very flawed. But hadn't they all explained to her that tolerance was good, and therefore tolerance would urge her forward?

"What we do here is just connect again with the universals," Gloria continued. "And we experience it as joy. Music is joy; movement is joy, so we dance. Chantel, you can begin the music anytime now." She smiled at Eleanor. "We make a circle, and we dance and we invite the goddess to join us. That's all it is." Chantel turned on a strain of flutey pipe music, joined by a violin or fiddle and then drums.

The music was very lively, and the women danced in a loose circle around the fire. One held out her hand to Eleanor, and she joined in. She never did things like this. It was a heady experience, letting restraints go, and the music and dance kept pushing her forward. Three women had their arms around each others' shoulders, their heads lowered, spinning around in their own small circle within the larger circle. Gloria, in a collapsible wheelchair, was pushed from one woman to another, her arms raised to the stars, her smile beatific.

"Praise to the mother," Gloria cried, and the women echoed her.

"Praise to the world," Ruth said, and the others bent down and swirled like birds.

"To the earth."

"To the sky."

"To the air and the water and the small, small things."

"To the sun and the moon."

"To music made by bird and bug and rushing streams, and the great thick sound of thunder."

"Let us praise this world and protect it."

"Praise to the goddess."

"Look to the sky, Eleanor," Gloria said, and when she looked up, she saw the moon again, seeming closer, and she saw the stars winking and shuffling in the sky.

"What is it like to be a star?" Gloria asked, her voice low and deep.

And Eleanor felt something lift out of her body, a long silver ghost of some kind, winging up to the sky, shooting up among the gang of stars. She felt a celestial cold spread through her, but it was pleasant and sharp as life. The stars moved out of the way to allow her to join them, and she hung there, looking down at the earth, blue in parts and burning in others – no, that might be clouds. She hoped it wasn't really burning. A flush began, pushing the cold away for a moment. What had she done to keep the earth clean? The blueness had gray at its edges.

It was remarkable that she could even see color in the darkness, but the stars put out their own light and the moon grew brighter and wider. She turned slightly and the depth of stars amazed her. They were beings, those stars, creatures of a different kind of life, but truly alive. She shifted and rode the gusts of space, slight winds that comets had left behind, and she passed star after star, drifting away and then back again, like seaweed.

She heard Gloria saying, "The sky is yours," and it felt both true and modest.

She turned back to see her own planet as if shrouds or curtains were parting. There seemed to be a massive shadow behind it; she moved in closer and discovered it was an enormous turtle. This was so startling that she bolted backwards and looked more closely at the planets. Yes, she could just make it out – behind or beneath every planet or moon there was a faint turtle. It took concentration to see it.

Her eyesight was getting sharper. She moved closer to the earth, intent on seeing the turtle better. The earth was turning, of course, and she went against its rotation so that she could get to the turtle faster. To her annoyance, the turtle always seemed to be beyond her, moving at the same distance, always out of reach. Her perspective or vision changed slowly as she traveled towards it; now she could see that the turtle stood on a much larger, less visible, turtle. As she strained her eyes, there was yet another turtle under that one, and she could squint and see another and another.

Around her she could see, far off but still palpable, turtle eyes and heads behind every object in space as the stars rotated and the cosmic winds shifted. She found their eyes to be calm and loving; their mouths smiled gently. She had never thought of turtles, or cared about turtles, but at that time and in that place, she loved them.

She could hear the women again, laughing and murmuring, and it drew her attention back to the earth. She was back with them. Women stopped dancing and went over to the blankets spread with wine and cheese and brought back plates and cups to share.

"That was something," Eleanor said tentatively. "Very... vigorous."

Becca looked at her and laughed. "Admit it. You were pulled in. You felt it."

Eleanor felt a small piece of shyness drop away. "I felt amazing. As if I were being lifted up, held, holding – all of it mixed together."

"The goddess spoke to you," Monica said.

"The buzz will last for a few days. You'll feel inspired to do things to support the goddess' mission."

"Which is?"

"The world is being destroyed," Monica said simply. "Without the earth, we're nothing."

"We don't have to wait for an alien invasion to see everything die out. Did you see that they're allowing chemicals that are known to cause cancer – spraying it on the crops?" Carmen shook her head in anger.

"It amazes me," Ruth said. "It's hard to know if this is the start of the end, or the end of the end."

"We have to fight harder," Gloria said fiercely.

Eleanor looked alert. "Fight?"

"We're to blame. There's nothing growing on the earth now, it's all commerce and plastic. Plastic is not a female principle. We have to combat it. This is a battle between good and evil."

Becca nodded. "We saw it in this past election, though not even this side is altogether good. But better, definitely better."

CHAPTER 11

Stan was always helpful when the boss made Eleanor do things like bend down and search for an object in the lower cabinets, or stretch high up and lift something from the overhead. The boss would just stand there with a smile on his face. If Stan was working that day, and if he was around, he would offer to get it first and the boss would say, "Oh, never mind, I think I have one in my office," and Eleanor would feel just a little bit grateful. That gratefulness was a thorn, though. She was being singled out by one man and being "rescued" by another. There was no way to win. She decided once to say that she couldn't bend down because she had cramps, just to see what would happen. The boss looked disgusted and left.

"Do you?" Stan whispered, coming up behind her. Really, he could be so creepy that way, almost like a cat or a snake, something predatory.

She looked at him, at his eagerness. Why did he want to know? "Yes," she finally said. "Bleeding like mad, too. I'm surprised it's not showing."

Then Stan, too, turned and left. Good.

Now that Stan had introduced her to Augment, he was always demanding that they get together and discuss a strategy. Or he texted her to like one of his Augs, or he told her that the Aug she had posted was *almost* good. Her strategy on how to deal with him changed from day to day. The witches emphasized responsible behavior, so she tried to be nonjudgmental and still independent, but he took her noncommittal smiles as a kind of passive dependence. "You really have to get a little nerve up, Eleanor," he said once. "You let the boss push you around and you lean on me for all your Augments."

"I do not," she snapped, dropping the noncommittal bullshit. "I'm trying to be patient with you. You can be very pushy. You never leave me alone."

She expected him to be annoyed but his reaction was the opposite. He had once said that the thing he liked most about himself was being unpredictable. He must remind himself every morning to meet every opportunity sideways, she thought. How come she couldn't do that? How come she just reacted and reacted and reacted? She held herself back when it came to the boss, since she needed a paycheck, but Stan? How much did she have to put up with from Stan?

She didn't bring it up with the witches, other than a comment she made once that the gift shop was a pleasant place to work, except for the men who worked there. Chantel had laughed. "You know what rattles them? Look at their crotch. Just let your eyes drop and look at their crotch."

She tried it. The boss looked uncomfortable after a moment, but Stan liked it. He liked watching her looking at him. She didn't want him to enjoy it, so she stopped. She would have to find a better path and follow it, which is what the whole witchcraft thing was about. As an initiate, she had to learn about her own relationship to her power – what prompted it in the past, how she used it and what it meant.

"Well, I don't know if I can actually say I 'use' it," she had replied to Ruth's question. She very often felt lazy or ineffective. She had seen Monica find objects others had hidden before she arrived. Sheri had read her mind, very casually, and mentioned things Eleanor had never spoken about. Chantel cured another witch's headache. What had *she* done? "I can keep the rain off me; I can repair small things, like a cracked cup. I can trip someone, sometimes, not all the time. Very small things."

A few women looked meaningfully at each other. "It's all about you," Gloria said. It wasn't said in a hostile manner, merely an assertion about facts. "You're stuck at the one level because your mind is stuck at that level, too. Your thoughts are only about you, aren't they? About the day-to-dayness of you, the irritations, the failures, the successes, the needs, the wants."

"Well, of course," she replied, looking quickly around the room at the faces watching her. Were they all saints? Did no one else think about themselves? She could feel her face flush. "Please explain what you mean. I'm lost."

"No surprise," Chantel said. "She's privileged."

"No, I'm not."

Chantel smirked. "You're pale. Your teeth are good. You might not be rich, but you've had benefits."

"Well, yes, I have," she admitted grudgingly. It was a surprise to be defensive about her own background. Chantel was mixed-race. Of course her life had been different. But even white people had troubles. Though of course they didn't get shot by police as much. She winced at her privilege.

"Outside yourself, name the things you care about. The things you love and want to keep."

"I'll get back to you," she said, disliking how personal this had all become. She was sure they all considered her to be a poor excuse for a witch, limited in both powers and perception.

She forced herself to remember their kindnesses, the experiences they had encouraged her to have that had surprised and delighted her. She would strive to be better. Instead of dwelling on how offended she felt, she did her best to pay attention to their conversations. There were discussions about the election and the secession, of course, and Jessica had warned them that there was trouble ahead. She was the most powerful witch at predicting the future; she had foretold the previous two hurricanes and the volcanoes and earthquakes.

If Jessica could see anything about the future, then Eleanor suspected she could also predict people's deaths. It was something that just struck her, just hit her in the forehead as they discussed the latest news about the secession, and she couldn't help it. She had to say it. "Can you predict when someone will die?"

Jessica smiled, and she wasn't the only one. "Everyone new asks me that. And the truth is, yes, I can. Sometimes. I don't have a perfect gift, or it has some qualification I don't understand, and Gloria has warned me about developing it too highly in that regard. It's a terrible burden, carrying that knowledge around with you. It can easily change how you behave, and more importantly, how you advise someone else to behave. We're all seeking to develop our gifts, not to be immortal. It's the wrong skill. So I stay away from it."

"But if you knew, for instance, that someone would die of cancer in five years' time, then you could send them for tests?"

"See? You think I can keep people from dying. That makes me powerful. And it could get me thinking I'm almost a god. It's a temptation. I don't have complete control – I might see the future that's possible if someone continues on a particular path. But people often change their direction. And I can't decide for them which is the right one. I can't affect their futures. That's what it comes down to. Do I advise people to start a totally new action that, in fact, might not lead to a better future for them?"

"Which is not to say that she never sees it anyway," Gloria added. "Despite her attempts not to. But she has promised not to act on anything without approaching us first for full discussion and advice."

"Are we all supposed to get permission before we use our gifts?" Eleanor should have found a better way to say it; she knew it was belligerent even as she said it; she didn't need to hear Ruth clear her throat warningly.

"Not small actions, no. But if it affects another being, yes. Quite a few members here could change a cockroach into a butterfly, but it would be an idle and judgmental use of power. A cockroach is not less beautiful than a butterfly."

"For some of us it is," Chantel said, laughing.

Gloria acknowledged the comment with a sideways tilt of her head. "That's what I mean about judgment. Who can say, ultimately? We do harm to the earth just by living here and the way we destroy everything for our own purposes. That's wrong. We are against that. It is fundamental to our beliefs. We do not destroy life or alter its values out of judgment. You cannot be here if you have any doubts on that matter." She glared at Eleanor.

Eleanor took a few moments to collect her thoughts. She had already spoken too quickly at least once. What were her own values, anyway? Did she have a system? Did she have laws? Not just the laws imposed on her by the state, but the laws she trusted as a guideline for her actions? She considered the implications of not changing or altering a living being. At the moment, she couldn't think of any reason why she would, except to save herself, and she was sure that would be permitted. Outside of that, what kind of change would be likely to present itself?

Finally, she said, "I am open to guidelines. I suspect they will make sense, and that you've thought about it all very thoroughly. It's all new to me, and therefore it doesn't seem right to give you a blanket statement about what I will and will not agree to. I'm an initiate; I am learning. I will promise to give a great deal of thought to anything that I see and hear within this group. I will not agree to anything without thinking about it, though. That's lip service, and I respect you all too much to do that."

Gloria nodded and smiled. "That's a very good attitude. Being open and considering implications and consequences. And, by the way, this is not a group, it's a coven. A small distinction, I know, but an important one."

Eleanor agreed politely. She wasn't that big on word-policing. If it got the point across, it worked, right? "Now about transformations," she said. "Changing a cockroach to a butterfly or however you want to paint it, how does that work?"

One day at work, Eleanor heard snickering from Charles Peter's office. She assumed that Stan was watching porn with his boss, but there was a difference in their tone of voice. They sounded admiring and congratulatory. She walked cautiously to the office doorway and saw that the two men were actually watching the news.

"He's named ambassadors!" Stan crowed as Eleanor came into the office. "To Europe, South America, Africa – to *continents.*" He grinned in admiration. "Why have separate ambassadors for each little country? He's right."

"And with the internet, his ambassadors don't actually have to go anywhere. Just pick up a phone. Genius!" Charles Peter agreed.

"Or send an email. Why do they physically have to go anywhere? A text or two and – bam! – everyone gets the idea. Saves taxpayers' money."

Eleanor's eyes darted back and forth between the news report, the ticker feed at the bottom of the screen summing up everything, and the happily astonished faces of the men. "But that's ridiculous. He's not a country, Texas is just a state."

"Liberty," Charles Peter corrected her. "You know he changed the name and declared it *is* a country. Separate and autonomous."

"He had to look at his notes for that word," Stand said, laughing. "You've got to love him. No pretensions."

"He's just declared a state a country," Eleanor pointed out. "I'd call that pretentious."

"It's genius. I wonder if I can declare myself a country? Or more likely, I'd have to declare my house a country." Charles Peter's eyes tracked off into the distance.

"I guess an apartment would be harder to do that with." Stan frowned.

"Guys, he's *saying* it, but that doesn't mean it's real. I don't understand what you love about him so much anyway. He's a buffoon."

Charles Peter narrowed his eyes. "He's a real man. He fights for the real man."

"That statement means nothing!" Eleanor protested. She could hear her voice get high-pitched.

"Look, everybody loves him," Charles Peter said. "He won the election—"

"Not with votes he didn't."

"—in his own state. The people of Texas voted for him, that's clear, so this is obviously the will of the people of Texas, now called Liberty. I like how he's shaking things up. Everyone else just toes the party line. Bunch of followers. He's a leader."

Both men turned away from her and went back to watching the news. She stood there, wanting to say something scathing but holding back. Being a witch meant being circumspect. She was as circumspect as she could be until the weather report came on, and then she left.

Stan was almost generous for a while after that. "I really liked your post yesterday about how the groups you belong to change your identity," he said. "Quite a few people disagreed with you, which is always a good sign. I don't belong to anything that can be traced to me, by the way. I don't like being tied down."

"You have a job," she said.

He shrugged. "Barely has anything to do with my personal life."

"What *is* your personal life?" she asked. It was true, come to think of it, that they really didn't discuss much about what happened outside work – maybe an occasional movie review (later to be shared on Aug) or, occasionally, food recommendations. He appeared to have very firm opinions on food.

He looked both surprised and shifty for a second, then he recovered himself. "Are you interested in me?" he asked.

She could feel the blood flowing into her face at the same time that she shifted backwards, repulsed. She could see him reading both those reactions. "Want to go out for a drink?" he asked. "My treat? So we can compare Augment strategies? I won't be making a pass at you."

If she said no, she would be outmaneuvered. He would think he had power over her. But if she said yes, would that mean he *did* have power over her? She stood up straight and looked him in the eye. "If you pay, I'll go. If you don't pay, then no."

"I like having it all clear," he said, and offered her his arm.

"I work until seven today," she said, and that luckily got rid of what to do about that offered arm.

"I know how late you work," he said. "I get off at six."

She met Stan at a local bar, where he nursed a beer. He got up and waved when he saw her. "Let's get a table," he said. "I'm hungry. They have good fish tacos here."

"I'm vegan," she said, to be mean.

"Of course you are," he sighed. "They have French fries."

She shrugged and followed him to a table. "So," he said, beaming with friendliness, "what do you think are your best Augs?"

"We've done this before. I got a good response on the election ones and the mansplaining one."

He almost shook with disdain. "Mansplaining," he said. "Women and their fashion statements."

"What?"

"One woman says it and then a second one copies it and suddenly it's all the rage."

"You can't help but be offensive, can you?" She was almost genuinely interested in that. When she was offensive, it was usually an accident. With him, however, it seemed to be a skill.

"What are *your* best ones?" she then asked, determined not to let him control the conversation. Or control her.

"Easy," he said. "All of them." He grinned. "Okay, okay, the best ones were actually: Describe boobs and–"

"What?" she snapped.

"Relax, relax, just a joke."

"Stan, you're being offensive. Why?"

"I do that when I'm nervous."

"You insult women when you're nervous?"

"Doesn't everyone?"

He was enjoying himself. She stared at him, as the witches had suggested. A waiter came over, but she didn't answer when he asked if they wanted any drinks. She waited until Stan shrugged finally and said, "I'll have another beer. She'll just stare."

"Enjoy your beer," Eleanor said, and left.

The streets were busy outside, but no one was carrying signs. Most of the political marches had stopped after the election, while the Texas secession went through the courts.

This march was slow and silent, and everyone was clothed in black. Of course, in New York, that wasn't odd, but usually there were people who broke the code – older people, foreigners, Midwesterners.

The crowd was going in her general direction, so she joined them and felt a strange solidarity with them, whoever they were, whatever they wanted. Walking with them through the dark streets felt kind of like being with the witches, she thought. I don't understand them yet, but it feels right, most of the time. I resent being dragged into politics constantly. I don't want to have to spend my time yelling about rights and things. Can't we take a break once in a while?

The only sound from the crowd was their footsteps. She had

never been with so many people in such profound silence. It wasn't disturbing; it blanketed them together, muffled them, swathed them. She looked surreptitiously at their faces, not wanting to stare, but their eyes were locked straight ahead, not just looking to the next block, but looking to the distance. At one point, an old man stumbled, and hands reached out to grab him. They waited for him to get his breath back and began to walk only a bit faster than before, to catch up with the marchers ahead of them. Eleanor had passed her own corner long ago, but she hadn't turned into it; instead, she was pulled along by the community of silence. The evening wore on, and the dark-clad figures marched quietly, around all of midtown, over to the mayor's office, over to the UN until gradually and with very little sound, the crowd began to decrease. She found herself finally walking up Fifth Avenue with only one other protestor, and then that one turned a corner and she was left alone. It was past midnight, she thought; the stars were too dimmed by the streetlights to be seen, but the moon hung up there, watching everything, commenting on nothing. The moon that night seemed vastly personal as if it could give advice if their languages ever matched.

She told the witches about that march, and learned that it was a march by relatives of those killed by guns. Murdered for love; murdered by accident; murdered by gangs, at robberies, at schools, churches, synagogues, mosques, on subways, on highways, by police. Because they were Black or Hispanic or women or even children sleeping in bed; because they argued or tried to escape or were just going home; because they were in the store when the criminals panicked; because they held a cellphone and police thought it was a gun; because in America on average twenty-three children were shot every day, and two of them died, and on this particular night those in big cities walked in mourning, remembering those they'd lost.

"Well," she said, "it was very moving. I didn't know what it was, but I didn't want to leave. I walked with them until it ended. I hope it was all right that I was there, even if I didn't know why."

"You don't know anyone who's been shot?"

She thought about it. Not directly, no. But a neighbor had killed himself – shot himself – did that count? And another one, too, now that she thought of it. And the kids who were killed at schools – she felt a connection there. The names of the schools were seared into her memory, from Columbine to Parkland. Certainly, she had felt it when the massacres occurred. Everyone should be walking, she suddenly thought, because there wasn't anyone in the United States who wasn't affected by gun murders. "I do," Eleanor answered. "Yes."

Jolene's daughter, it turned out, had been shot overseas, in the war, and then she had seen her friend killed when he tried to buy cigarettes – in the wrong place at the wrong time.

"The world is in trouble, so much trouble," Gloria said.

"Then why don't we fix it?" Eleanor said, and all the witches looked around the room, settling on Gloria, who nodded her head and said, "Welcome."

"You were pretty weird last night," Stan said at work the next day.

"I'm not going to put up with that shit," she answered. "It's disrespectful and, by the way, I had a great Aug last night. It said, If you could teach a man one thing, what would it be? It flew off like fireworks."

"Oh, pandering," he said. "Yeah, that works for me, too. But seriously, I was going to suggest that we try to get a few more people in our group so that we could support and share each other's Augs."

"You didn't know about my Aug last night, apparently. You didn't share it. And it looks like you didn't read it. I really haven't been keeping track. Aren't you sharing mine?"

"Only the good ones." He grinned, obviously thinking he was the wittiest man on earth.

"Stan," she said, fed up with his inability to stay on track. "I appreciate your help, I really do, but you've stopped being helpful and now you're just repulsive." His face fell and he looked, for a moment, stumped.

Then his face brightened. "You've got a crush on me. Oh, sorry, sorry, but really, you're not my type. This is so awkward," he said gaily, walking away in the general direction of the boss' office. "I might have to report it." He stopped and looked back at her with a smug grin. "Just to have it on the record, you know?"

And he went in and reported her. She could hear the two of them laughing.

CHAPTER 12

Eleanor spent months getting to know the witches and learning their rules. They were pretty predictable once you used "Do no harm" as your starting point. She could see that visualizing what you were about to do or say didn't stop her from action, but visualizing consequences did. For instance, visualizing throwing Gloria out of her wheelchair (which she was using more and more often), was just a step away from doing it, but the consequence would be to lose Gloria's forgiveness and possibly her acceptance. She had to see the whole picture, not just the immediate satisfaction. As she got to know the witches individually over time, their various quirks and overall humanity became apparent, and her own impatience lessened.

There was Monica, for instance, who had a horrible habit of laughing at everything past the point where it was funny. She was a person who punned. She couldn't help it. She couldn't stop it. And Eleanor hated puns. Monica was overeager about everything, though a great appreciator when you needed one.

Eventually, with a lot of work, Eleanor tried to see something endearing about her obviousness. She was like a comic fool. When Chantel said she was going to Maine, Monica would ask, Bangor? And grin. When Grace said she was from Boston, Monica asked if she was a Red Sox fan, and was delighted at her knowledge about Boston.

She always went for the obvious and thought it would make her look clever.

She would sing a snatch of a song if it matched the words. Once Ruth said, "This house needs a new roof," and of course Monica started singing, "Our house is a very, very fine house." The other witches politely waited for her to finish before moving on. She was never offended.

Monica was marvelous at finding and hiding all things great and small. Ruth's cat went missing and Monica said, "Check the basement." And, yes, the cat was there. When Felice's ex-husband, a nasty man, started waiting outside her house in his car, just waiting, day after day, staring at her, nodding once, curtly, it was Monica who made him hide. It was a question, actually, of whether she'd made him hide or made everything else in the world hide from him. There was a discussion about the morality of this, since Monica couldn't or wouldn't be clear about exactly what she'd done. "I just put him somewhere where he can't see Felice," she said. "See no evil, hear no evil."

"But, dear Monica, what does that mean? Is he alive and well and is he in the world he knows? Does he see the things he's familiar with and does he have a home and food and everything he used to have?"

"Oh, yes, of course," Monica said, surprised. "I wouldn't hurt him. Why would I hurt him? He just needed to have a few things disappear so he wouldn't hurt anyone else. So he can't see Felice, or Felice's house, or even Felice's street. I hid them."

"You said you hid *him*."

"It really comes to the same thing," she answered patiently. "Think of it as putting up a curtain between them. That's a good way of describing it."

"If he and I were standing in front of Felice's house, could I see him?" Gloria asked.

"Of course. I just imagine a curtain between him and Felice. The curtain is more like blinders, I suppose. It just blocks his view in certain directions. That direction is Felice."

"Ah," Gloria said, relaxing. "How nice."

Occasionally, Gloria would encourage one witch to explain her particular power as best she could. Not everyone had multiple skills, but some could get fairly good at talents they'd never thought about, and learning any new gift made their own gifts grow. Since Eleanor was new, and she seemed to have a talent for moving things and for weather, she was encouraged to show them what she could do.

They all gathered outside in the back of Gloria's house, and Eleanor stood, irresolute, trying to think what she could show them. She had never actually deliberately done anything before, it had always seemed coincidence. "Don't worry about what will happen," Gloria said, reassuring her. "We're all born with a special ability, but we have to train it to make it a skill. Now, start small. It would be nice to have a small breeze, don't you think? Look at that branch over there, bending down, the leaves so still. Can you imagine them moving? Start there."

And, of course, she was right. Eleanor stared at the leaves and the branch, feeling hopeless at first, but then gradually, she saw the branch as it was and stopped worrying about what she could or could not do. The branch seemed to look back at her, if she could phrase it that way. It became alert just as she became alert, and the leaves reached up and out, slowly at first, so gently that it was hard to see. But then they rustled, and they could be heard, and it was actually a happy moment, a release for the leaves, a kind of dance for them. They were glad of the movement.

As was Eleanor. She couldn't see but the others noticed how her face glowed and her mouth grinned and her eyes lit up with joy. She had connected! She had forgotten herself and connected with the wind by thinking about the leaves in the breeze. Once she caught it, felt it, she lifted her head and brought the wind on harder, pulled it out of the air, as if she had a long thread. She pulled and pulled, feeling her hair whip around her face, her body brace against the force of it, until Gloria shouted, "Enough! That's enough!"

Gloria's voice broke the spell and Eleanor stopped abruptly, dropping the wind, and she staggered forward a little, as a few of the other witches did as well.

"I've never done that," Eleanor said. "I mean, I've never deliberately and intentionally done it before."

Gloria laughed. "Well, I think you've got the hang of it now. How did it feel?"

Eleanor still felt the reaching out, the pulling in, the sense of connecting with the leaves and through the leaves with the wind. "Like I was part of something bigger and still natural. Like it was the same as waving my hand or blowing a bubble or anything really, just something that was a simple action. That's not the right term. But yes, as if there were a part of my hand that could reach, stretch, stir, move what's out there."

"Keep describing it," Gloria said, "so the others might be able to imagine it and experience it, too."

"I saw the leaves and I began to think of being a leaf and experiencing it. I thought about moving as a leaf moves, in the air, being moved around and how it must feel like being in a dance, always new, and how the movements would feel. And then, once I had that, I felt the wind. That's all I can say." She ended on an apologetic note. It was not an easy thing to explain. It was not concrete.

"What a beautiful, beautiful thing," Monica said, her curly head bouncing with appreciation. "What a thrill it must be!"

"Oh, but what you do is so beyond me, or anything I could think up," Eleanor said. "Really, you impress me so much."

Gloria laughed at them both. "I'm glad you admire each other. It's been a lovely demonstration. Eleanor, we'll move on to a few simple spells – how to transform simple objects; how to reshape objects; and then I think, perhaps next month – would you like to fly?"

An electric shock ran through Eleanor's arms and into her

face; she couldn't keep herself from grinning like an idiot.

This world of witches was different from anything she'd known. She had stumbled onto them, never having sought them out; they had found her. Little by little she began to yield to the longing for a community. She hadn't thought there was one for her; she had assumed there was something about her that frustrated any efforts made in her direction. She had found life difficult, and it had always been, she believed, better to be apart. Her father had died when Eleanor was sixteen. A little while later, her mother started showing signs of dementia. Eleanor's sister left it up to Eleanor to care for their mother, and then she had gone off to be married, not willing to look back. A few phone calls, one or two visits, and then she and her husband moved away, far away. Once someone had asked her if she was close to her family and she had said there was no family to be close to. That hadn't explained anything.

Her mother got steadily worse and more and more annoying in her inability to stay in touch with what was necessary to live. She wandered off. She didn't bathe. She took things and left them all over the neighborhood. She burned money once, and Eleanor had slapped her. Just like that. She had reached the end of her patience and without any thought whatsoever, she had slapped the crazy woman in front of her who had just burned all the money Eleanor had brought back from her job as a waitress.

She lost respect for herself when she slapped her mother, lost the ability to forgive herself. She had called her sister to ask for money to help take care of her mother, and her sister had sent exactly what they'd agreed on, and then changed her phone number. Her mother became increasingly erratic, and it had been a huge relief when she'd fallen in the street and been taken away, into the system, which dictated that she was incompetent. Eleanor had said she couldn't take care of her – which was true. If she worked, she would have to pay someone to watch her mother and she didn't make enough money for that. But if she watched her mother, she wouldn't be able to work.

It had felt sordid. The few friends she'd had were tired of her sad story and she herself couldn't bear to hear herself speak of it anymore. Life just ran on like that until her mother died, leaving her, at last, free, but empty.

With her mother's illness and all the strain of trying to figure things out, she had never finished her education or trained for anything that paid a decent wage. Her stint at the gift shop was lucky, really; she had called to ask about a job just when someone had given notice. She had gotten it and clung to it; while she had that job, she didn't really have to figure out what her next step was. She was afraid there wasn't a next step. There was no union; no security; she paid for her own health care out of a meager salary; her world was already closing in. She had a steel spine, however; she knew that. She had lasted when her family had failed, and she would last a long time still – though she was not able, exactly, to figure out why she bothered.

It wasn't until she met the witches that her freedom amounted to anything. The odd abilities she had always been criticized for became an asset. She looked forward to what she would learn and what she could accomplish. The witches opened up her world. They made her feel that it was right to be herself, to stand for herself, to fight for herself, and at the same time they reminded her that extreme actions and reactions always ended poorly. She should evaluate; she should calculate; she should plan, and then she would discover her next step.

Her mind began to fill with the idea that she was transforming into something she couldn't yet see. Working in the gift shop began to grate on her. It was too constricting there. It was demeaning. She wanted to learn more and more about the hidden, secret world she'd discovered. She searched for little books of spells in the cabinets, but of course she knew that Gloria would tell her if there was another one. Gloria did things the right way, practically and cleanly.

Two of the witches were healers, and as Gloria began to discard her canes for a walker, and her walker for an occasional wheelchair, Eleanor wondered why the healers couldn't heal Gloria.

Becca sighed. "She has been healed, a few times. She would be completely bedridden otherwise. But even witches' bodies fail, even witches die."

Eleanor was startled. "She's dying?"

Becca raised her eyebrows. "Well, yes, but not immediately. It's not a question of setting a bone or drawing out a fever – it's not a disorder. It's a genetic problem; it's in her cells. We can change the shape of an animal by reordering its being, but ultimately that's a mask. Behind the change, the true being exists. The same is true for Gloria. We heal her as much as we can, but behind that, Gloria herself is failing. She's breaking apart. We all die."

"You said that."

"Because you have to understand what you can and can't do; it's the only way to make good changes. You imagine that transformations change essence, but they only change perception."

She pondered that as she learned.

The first transformation spell was very modest. Gloria explained the theory behind it, how molecules or little spirits ("Don't get lost in semantics") organized themselves and were aware of their organization, and all a spell did was to guide them to a new organization. It seemed too easy, until Gloria gave her the words of the spell, which couldn't be written down because it would begin to change the nature of anything it was written on.

"I'm not giving you the last sentence in the spell," Gloria said, finally. "Not now. Because transformation spells are easy. Unfortunately, the undoing spell is difficult. The molecules can be persuaded to go forward into a change but not necessarily to come back, not without effort. So, you'll begin by learning how to undo your spells."

"My spells?" Eleanor asked, getting lost in semantics. "What about other people's spells – can I undo those?" She wanted to forge ahead, blindly ahead. She felt suddenly immensely competent; she wanted to learn everything and be better at everything than anyone else. She knew it was ego, but for the moment she didn't care. When had she ever had the chance to be boastful and filled with finesse? She wanted that; she wanted the moments to shine for her; she wanted envious eyes and clapping hands and a roaring crowd.

"Ultimately, yes. The undoing takes more power than the doing, and undoing your own is easier than undoing someone else's," Gloria said firmly. "The undoing takes more skill and a certain amount of knowledge about possibilities, since the spell might have diverged. There are lots of tales of people who have messed up with the transformation spell and couldn't fix it. You have to learn what the rules are about fixing it, because it has to be set up to be fixable. Do you see what I mean? If you turned a prince into a frog but you did it in such a way that the frog you created couldn't be turned back, because you didn't do the spell right, then you've caused irrevocable harm. What if you did it to save the prince from some potential danger, but because you did it incorrectly, he would always be a frog?"

"It would be a twist on the fairy tale!" Monica called out. "Kiss all the frogs you want – it won't change a thing, girls!"

"I knew a prince who smelled like a frog," a new initiate, Chandler, said, laughing. She was small with long tight dark curls, which she held back with butterfly clips. She had just joined the group and Eleanor was actually surprised to see her there. Wasn't she too new for this spell? "Like, he was probably nice, but he knew he smelled. If I still knew him, I would transform him into himself without the smell."

"What if the smell means something?" Gloria asked, exasperated. "What if it's a medical condition?"

Eleanor was surprised. "Wouldn't transforming the smell out of him get rid of the medical condition?"

"No. If you were a strong proponent of the Craft, you'd have to know what was medically wrong and correct it before the transformation, if it can be cured. Being able to cure everything would achieve immortality. And nature doesn't believe in immortality. Nature, the universe, wants renewal. If you could get around nature's vast laws, that would be a paradox and we'd have to discuss the consequences, at some point. There are limits."

She's talking about herself, Eleanor thought. About her condition. She's stuck in a different kind of transformation. There were an awful lot of things Eleanor hadn't thought about. She'd have to be patient. It was all ahead of her, and that was exciting, so she promised herself that she would be attentive and observant, which Gloria stressed every single week. Absent-mindedness was fatal to the Craft.

Gloria presented her and Chandler with paper, a stone, and a worm. "These have been changed," she said. "And you must perceive in them what they were changed from – only then can you change them back. For our purposes today, just go from animate to animate and inanimate to inanimate. Study them. I've put a recognizable key in each transformed item, so you should be able to figure it out. Listen to them and experience them. I'll give you five minutes for each item, and I expect you to discover what they were before this incarnation."

Chandler took the rock and Eleanor took the paper. Eleanor touched the paper gently, took it between her fingertips, rubbed it a little and felt with a strange, surprising certainty that she was actually holding water. Quiet water. Would that be ice? She was holding a sheet of ice? She looked quizzically at Gloria. That would mean that transformation changes properties – as an example, water at room temperature would itself change. So the transformation was, in some subtle way, a two-step process, because it would have to change again from ice to water at room temperature. She looked away from Gloria and down to the paper. It wasn't wet, so it didn't bring that property along with it. It might not need the brittleness of ice to maintain its shape.

"Switch," Gloria said.

Chandler took the paper, and Eleanor decided to try the worm. She picked it up and brought it up to her eyes. It certainly felt like a worm, in its softness, in the way it wheeled its head around, looking for something to latch on to. It was the attempt to find a perch – because that was how she felt it, felt the movements – that made her decide this was a transformed bird. That was a relatively quick insight, so she spent a moment trying to feel into the worm, to find its sense of itself, to find the core of its self-recognition. She thought to herself that if she could find the bird inside the worm, then so, too, must the worm possess some sense of itself as a bird. That had traveled with it. There was no fear, she was pleased to note. It was like being dressed up, almost; it was in costume, playing a role. It would prefer to be a bird, of course. But until then it would approach the world as a worm. She put it down and looked up at Gloria, who nodded.

She took the rock. It was warm and its shape fit into her palm smoothly, and the weight was reassuring, steadfast. She was puzzled because she had no sense of anything other than rock. There was nothing behind it. She strained her mind to it, flexing her thoughts around the possibilities – what else would feel so solid and smooth and... permanent? It had an assurance, an impression of itself that matched its outer appearance.

She was annoyed that she could not get closer to its former existence. Or was this a trick – had Gloria snuck in something that *hadn't* been transformed, as a test? She weighed the rock gently and thoughtfully, over and over again, but she got nothing more.

"All right," Gloria said. "Let's see how you did. What was the paper? Answer together."

"Water," they both said. Eleanor's face flushed; she had been sure that she would be better than Chandler, who seemed so cheerful and extroverted and therefore (she would have to examine this thought later), not as perceptive.

"And the worm? Answer together."

"Bird," they both said. The irritation began to prick at Eleanor's mouth. She could feel her jaw clench.

"And the rock?" Gloria looked at them both brightly. "Together."

Eleanor, sure of herself, answered, "Rock," just as Chandler answered, "Orange," and she instantly saw the orange in her mind. She could see it now, could feel the weight of the orange shift into the weight of the rock. "But you said inanimate," she objected, and then she felt foolish. It wasn't animate; she had confused that with "alive," and by what standards was an orange "alive"?

"Sorry," she said. "I missed it."

"Good. Can you feel it now?"

"I can." She hung her head. "It's obvious now."

"Then you'll never miss it again. That's a step forward. All right, now the undoing. As you can see, with a proper transformation spell, the object still retains the knowledge, if you will, of itself. Within that knowledge you have to implant a kind of corridor or signpost. So, we'll go over the spell now and see how you use that corridor." She took them through the undoing spell and indeed there was a point at which the spell paused, and the spellcaster had to search for the content or origin of the object – or animal, as the case may be. "But higher animals come later. I included a worm because it's a relatively simple animal."

And so they continued, undoing a series of objects that Gloria presented to them without comment or identification. They were warned that they must not try the undoing spell if they weren't sure what the origin of the object was. An improper identification could lead to a permanent trap inside a form not its own.

Eleanor and Chandler kept pace with each other, undoing

slowly at first but then gaining speed. Although Gloria had set up a screen between them, keeping their objects hidden from each other, Chandler actually whispered to herself when she figured out the original. Eleanor let her get just a notch ahead of her, and soon she came to a tulip on a stalk, and she couldn't see what it had been. She reached and reached and found nothing, but she had just heard Chandler whisper *pencil* so she put that in her spell and the tulip shriveled and died.

Eleanor gasped and froze.

Gloria let the moment stand there before she asked, "Were you certain about what it was? Could you feel it?"

"No."

The moment hung there again, and Eleanor felt the shame of it. She had cheated, and cheated badly. She looked at Gloria, trying to gauge how severe her punishment would be. Surely she wouldn't be dismissed, would she? This felt so vital to her now, so much a part of her belief in herself. What would she be if she couldn't go on to become a full-fledged Wiccan? How would she learn what she needed? "I failed," she said quietly. "I know it and feel it. I didn't want Chandler to be better than I was, so I tried to steal knowledge from her, when I didn't see it."

Gloria nodded, and to Eleanor's relief, she smiled. "That's progress, isn't it? You can't overcome your faults if you don't know what your faults are, can you? So you're willing to steal. And you're jealous. And proud. Anything else?"

"Impatient," Eleanor said. "Acting without thinking." She waited. "I think that's it."

"Can you imagine what the world would be like if everyone with those attributes had power?"

"Are you saying they don't, Gloria?" Monica asked. She had stepped in to see the testing.

"Magical power, not political power," Gloria said evenly. "So?" Her eyes seemed to intensify so much that Eleanor wondered if she were staring into her mind.

"I have weaknesses, and I have to learn to control them."

"Not control them. *Transform* them. That's what this lesson is about. The secret self may still be at the core, but you change it into something metaphysically related. Greed into protection, impatience into helpfulness, ego into care." She turned back to Chandler. "Thank you for your help," she said, "and say hello to Eric for me. And by the way, Chandler isn't a novice. She's a former member who moved away a while ago and was just visiting us. We always like to test our initiates, so don't think this was just for you. It's part of the process."

A flush crept over Eleanor's neck and up to her face. A routine test, one that she'd failed, and no one had been surprised. A bit of poison slid out of her heart and into her veins. She didn't like to lose. She didn't like to be known, either. She took a deep breath. Living in a society involved compromises; she would compromise.

They moved on from inanimate to animate transformations. As the tests continued, she understood that any object or creature had an essence and a form, and the witch had to be careful to manipulate both. She went for lessons three or four evenings a week, and then finally she was deemed ready. She would do a transformation.

"We will start small. A spider to a frog. Now, we've discussed finding the heart of a creature, the picture every cell carries of what it is. When you transform, you must carry two pictures in your mind – what it is and what it will be. It isn't as hard as it sounds, really. But let's start with visualizing. Imagine a frog, Eleanor." Eleanor relaxed as she'd been taught and assembled the memory of a frog. Gloria tapped her on the forehead, and she opened her eyes to see an image of a frog in front of her, just floating there. "Good," Gloria said. "Now mentally place the spider on the image, yes, just like that. Now the spell. These are the words." And she recited the spell with Eleanor, emphasizing the words that left a sort of key and lock thread between them.

And then there was a frog that scurried a little bit sideways, then stopped, then scurried again. "All good," Gloria said with encouragement. "Now undo it."

All that work, all that slow repetition with the undoing paid off. She did it.

Gloria picked up the spider and took it to the window and released it. "Good job," she said, and Eleanor wasn't sure whether it was said to the spider or to her.

She sat there, bemused. It had worked so well and so easily.

"It was simple because of all the preparation we did," Gloria said quietly. "I know how you feel – I was once in your place, remember – but the reason it went well was because we rehearsed every step leading up to this, over and over again. You understood exactly how to proceed. It's now a part of you, a natural way to harness your talents. I don't want anyone to make a mistake, to cause any suffering – and neither do you, of course. I'm confident of that or you wouldn't be here. I want you to stop now, to hold the feeling in you, to think about what this ability means not only in terms of power but in terms of responsibility. We will continue next week. You've done very well." And with that, she was dismissed.

It was good to have that week off. It gave her a new perspective. She looked at objects and people differently; she looked for the idea of them, the fundamental being of them. And she listened, too, because so much of the world had a voice of its own. Musical instruments spoke in their tones; buses groaned like old dogs; city trees rustled a longing to get more light, to be free. The birds kept looking for better vantages as well. She saw a woodpecker on a tree and didn't know if there had always been woodpeckers in the city or not. The world was opening. The world was revealing.

Of course, there had to be a downside to it as well. She didn't load Augments as often as Stan wanted her to. And she refused to repost his comments about Liberty. Despite his warning that Augment frowned on too many political posts, he kept sneaking in questions about states' rights and then about how popularity indicated the mandate of the people.

"I still don't get why you think the whole Liberty situation is so great," she said.

"Are you kidding?" He gaped at her in surprise. "That place is like school when the teacher's out. I mean, we've got rules rules rules all the time, but there, he says that everyone will have a say."

"I bet it's not everyone or it would be chaos."

He shrugged. "Okay, not everyone. The right people would have a say. Not like here, where the weak are rewarded."

She was shocked. "Rewarded? How?"

"Handouts. Everyone gets handouts. Not me, of course. I'm not weak."

She eyed him coldly. Here he was, a salesperson at a small, third-rate museum. Gloating over his accomplishments. No, not his accomplishments, she reminded herself. His worthiness.

"He's a man of action," Stan said. "It's what he *does* that matters, and so far, he makes me joyful."

"He'll never get away with it," she insisted.

"What are they gonna do?" he asked with a sneer. "Invade?"

He always delighted himself and assumed he delighted her. It was so tiring the way he was always sneaking up behind her, tapping her on the shoulder and telling her that her Augs were getting sappy and crunchy. "Who cares about birds?" he asked. "Nobody cares about birds. Talk about music. Talk about sex. Give up on this nature thing."

She stared at him, trying to control herself, and that unnerved him for a full day. "I get it," he finally hissed. "You've taken some feminist crapola training, right? Trying to come on all strong and defiant? I can see through you. I know what you're made of. You're a weak little wuss who won't talk back to her boss even though it costs you your self-respect. You're a little girl I have to rescue. Which I won't do, by the way. You're on your own."

She walked away and went into the storage area and kicked the wall. There had to be something she could do to relieve her feelings; she felt so angry. She looked around and saw a statuette out of its box, a David. It shouldn't lie around unwrapped, of course, it should have been shelved appropriately, but it was perfect. She reached deep into the statue, keeping it and another idea in mind, then recited the spell. And there it was, a vase shaped like a penis. She stepped back. That was better. She put it back in the box.

In the afternoon, a woman came in to pick up a special order, and Eleanor looked at the receipt with interest. She called Stan and turned to another customer. Stan oozed all over the first customer and went to get the order but came back a good five minutes later, all flustered. "Where is it?" he snapped at her. "Did you do something with it?"

"With what? Her order? Is that the box?" She pointed to the box he held in his hand.

His mouth was set hard. "It says 'David' but there's a penis inside."

She grinned. "David's penis?"

He glared at her.

"So, they messed up the order," she said. "I'm sure you can explain that to her."

He molded his face into a reluctant smile and went over to the customer, who was not happy, but then again, who is happy in this world? Eleanor thought. I'm happy with the witches, generally, but I hate this place and I hate Stan now – why did I think he was all right at one point, was I just being blind? – and my boss and this job. No, the job's fine, though it doesn't pay. But the objects are nice. It's good to be surrounded by these things.

She helped a few customers and began to tidy up, putting things back in their places, restocking where needed. She paused in front of the cabinet where Gloria had once left a special box for her. What if there was something new? The idea popped into her mind, and she couldn't get rid of it, though Gloria had specifically told her to look for something that first time. Maybe this time it was supposed to be sensed, however; maybe it was another witch test. She thought about it, examining her immediate surroundings. She felt something faint and witchy in the air.

Her heart was beating. She slid the doors back on the cabinet and there it was – the box she'd chosen, her emblem. She opened it and there was a many-folded piece of paper. She didn't want to read it here; she would see what it held when she got home, in private. She stood up and tucked it in her pocket.

"I saw that."

She swung around to see her boss and Stan both looking at her, Stan with a smug smile on his face. He looked extremely satisfied, like a cat with a snake in its mouth.

"That's stealing," her boss said.

"It's mine," she said. "I put it there to keep it safe. It's so small, I was afraid I'd lose it. Here, look," and she took it out and held it in her palm, outstretched to the two men, who stepped forward, peering at her hand.

"Stan?" her boss asked.

"I don't think it's ours," Stan said reluctantly. He took it from her, turned it all around, looking for a manufacturing sticker on the bottom, then lifted the lid. "It's got a paper in it," he said.

"That's private. That's none of your business." She reached for it, but her boss stepped in between her and Stan.

"What's it say?" the boss asked as Stan unfolded it.

Stan turned it over a few times, finally holding it up to the light. "It's blank."

"It's mine," she said. "The paper has sentimental value. The box was my mother's." She cringed. She hated people who did that – who went for the pity excuse, who went for the sob story. She was not that kind. "Actually, it doesn't matter why I have it. The real issue is that it's not yours and it is mine." She held her hand out to Stan.

He turned it over slowly, then gave it back. "Should we check her other pockets?" he asked. "Just in case we missed something?"

"Stan," the boss said. "If she didn't take anything, keep your hands off her."

"Keep your hands off me *no matter what*," she yelped, surprised.

They both smiled. "I don't think either of us wants to touch you," the boss said, and left.

Stan and Eleanor stood in place, looking at each other. How had she ever tolerated him? "Should I write this up on Aug?" she asked, finally, hoping it would annoy him.

His eyebrows jumped up into his forehead. "Oh, good idea! Let's both do it and see who gets the most hits!"

And with that he put his arm over her shoulder and led her back to the cash register, where a customer waited.

She didn't open the box and unfold the paper until she got home. At first, it did indeed look blank. But the more she looked, the more that faint letters began to appear, and finally she could read the whole thing. It was a recipe. That was startling. And disappointing.

She had glanced at it quickly, but now she read it slowly. There were oils and herbs and a bit of smoke and, yes, at the end, with the ingredients assembled, it clearly said, "Rub gently into the hands and face and the broom before attempting to fly. Start with a minimal amount, but gradually add more to your taste."

It was the flying recipe! Gloria had been promising that they would get to it soon, and here it was! She hadn't known that there was an... ointment? Salve? Potion? Oh yes, potion! But here it was.

She quickly wrote down all the ingredients on a notepad in case the recipe vanished, because it seemed that after the day she'd had, it was likely to thwart her and just disappear. Was there a disappearing potion, too? She checked the paper again, but there was nothing else.

She had to stop and close her eyes because her head was filled with the feel of wind in her face, with clouds zooming in closer, with birds keeping pace with her. It was more magic than she had ever hoped for, and it would soon be hers.

CHAPTER 13

One of Stan's Augs asked why women are always the last to know. He got hundreds of replies about female cluelessness. Her fingers were itching to answer this or throw the question back at him, but she was tired of him. She kept her eyes down at work, for the most part. When she looked up to see what he was doing, he was always looking at her, grinning.

A few days later, Eleanor realized that Stan was stalking her. He was also calling her cellphone. A lot. And there were those doorbell rings, too, which unnerved her. She only figured it out when she was going to put out the garbage just as he was about to ring the bell. He looked at her through the front door glass, gaped, and ran off.

She confronted him, but he claimed that he had been drunk and in need of help, so he'd decided to go ask her. She'd spooked him. He'd run. He looked very sheepish. "You know how it is when you're surprised. Just surprised about anything. Plus, I was drunk."

"I didn't even know you knew my address."

He shrugged. "Personnel file. The boss showed me your records."

She stepped back a little. "Why would he do that? Isn't it against the law?"

"Nah. He made me his assistant. So it's perfectly legal."

"Assistant boss?" she asked. Why would he promote Stan over her? It made her furious. She worked harder. She was less sarcastic with the customers, though it was true of course that she did occasionally get into little snits that she resolved by walking away. She should work on that, she really should. "What's your title?" she said, trying very hard to keep her voice level. "Assistant boss? Little boss? Not-quite-boss?"

He smirked. "Assistant manager of the gift shop."

She paused for a moment. "So. This gift shop now has two full-time managers and one full-time employee."

"That's right," he said brightly. "Solves the whole unionizing effort."

"No one's tried to unionize."

"It's very effective."

"Stan," she said and stopped. What did she really want to say? That he had tried to be sympathetic, on her side, talking about the boss behind his back – and now he'd flipped? Why had he flipped? Why had he been on her side to begin with? Or had he? He was exactly the kind of guy who got pleasure out of playing games, just manipulating people to see how he could make them jump. She hated men like that, and it usually *was* men.

He was grinning at her still, his eyes lit up. He was amused and preening. "Jealous?"

"Hard to say. It's not anything I ever wanted out of life, but then again, maybe it's exactly the kind of job you're good for. You know, opportunities to show your assistant-boss-like flair. But I think it suits you. You look like an assistant boss."

His eyes narrowed but he didn't answer her. He went away for a while and then came back. "I was just discussing how we haven't taken inventory in a while. I was discussing with Mr Chaps, the one you call boss. By the way, call him Mr Chaps and call me Mr Biggles."

"Huh," she said. "I didn't realize your last name was Biggles. How did that get past me? You must have been picked on as a kid."

"Nope. I wouldn't let anyone bully me."

"Which means of course that they did. Okay. Inventory."
She made herself sound bright and chirpy. "When do we start?"

"This afternoon, after the part-timer comes in. You and
me. You count and I'll write it down." His grin was ferocious.
How come she'd never noticed his mouth before? It was nasty.
Leering usually described eyes, she thought, but he leered with
his mouth, too. With his shoulders. With his body, which was
lithe and sometimes seemed to pour itself into different stances.

After they closed up shop and bid goodbye to the boss, they
went to the storage room. Stan took a seat on a box, crossed
his legs, put a legal pad on his knee and raised his pen high,
waiting for her. She began to move methodically, clearing one
end of a shelf and then moving things over as she went along
so that she wouldn't lose track. She did this with boxes as well.
She tore open a pallet of candles and grouped the candles in
stacks of ten.

"We used to be friends," she said suddenly, following a train
of thought.

"We're still friends," he said, and it sounded genuine.

"You've been a little creepy lately. I mean, following me
home and all."

"Just making sure you're safe."

"I was safe before I met you. Why should it be different
now?"

"A woman can't be safe alone, without a man." He was
smug. He licked his lower lip.

"What about two women together? Are they safe?"

"Two women together is an invitation for a threesome," he
answered blithely.

"My God, Stan, do you hear yourself? Do you hear what
you sound like?"

"Mr Biggles, Eleanor. I know it will be hard to change your
habits, but now that I have a superior position, I have to insist
on the appropriate respect."

"Respect," she said bitterly, hoping it was under her breath – or, really, did it matter whether he heard her or not?

"Would you read the product number of those items on the right, please?" he asked lightly, but she could tell that he was enjoying it; his voice was sweet and plummy.

He liked giving her orders; he liked watching her do as she was told. Once, she pricked her finger and he asked, "Do you want me to suck it for you?" and she stiffened in anger. She wouldn't look at him; she didn't want to see his triumphant face.

When it turned six o'clock, she said, "Oh, sorry, that's the end of my shift and I have to go."

"It's inventory night. You should have made arrangements to stay."

"You only told me a few hours ago."

"Well, you'll have to change whatever it is you planned on doing."

"Sorry, I can't. It's a doctor's appointment."

"At this hour?"

"It's the one day a week that there are late hours. It took me a few weeks to make an appointment, and well, this is the right time in my cycle."

He got a crafty look on his face. "No, it isn't. I keep track of you. This isn't the right time to see a gynecologist."

She froze, her thoughts slowing down as well, so what she said came out very slowly. "You're keeping track of my cycle? That's the most threatening thing I've ever heard. That's more than an invasion of privacy, that's something else. Stalking? Wait, is that *all* it is? I've never heard of this. Or are you just saying it to get a reaction? You would do that, wouldn't you? I don't believe you."

But then he said, "You've got your period. I know because you have tampons in your purse. You left your purse behind the cash register. If you wanted privacy, you shouldn't have left it out. So you lied about the doctor."

"It's a skin doctor. I had a precancerous lesion a few years ago and I go this time every year to get a checkup."

He shrugged, annoyed. "If you say so."

"Stan."

"Mr Biggles."

"Stan. You've been threatening. You're harassing me. I could go to the police and get a restraining order against you."

"No," he said, quite confident. "I haven't threatened you in any way and there's nothing the police would be interested in."

How hideous it was that for a moment she almost wished he'd done something more overt, something he could be punished for. "I think I'll report you anyway just to have it on the record. If they can't do anything yet, at least it will be written down."

His mouth turned down. "Look at all I've done for you, and the way you thank me is to threaten me?"

"I've helped get your Augs out. I've helped with every single one of them. You had me join for that reason, not out of charity. You just like to think that you're important and I'm not. Well, let me tell you: you're not important."

"And you?" he sneered. "Are you so important, then?"

She almost told him she was a witch and she could do spells. She could imagine the derision, the hooting, the relentless mockery. "I never think about whether I'm important," she said, which was true. "Important people don't have to announce it. Everyone just knows."

He shook his head. "You look so cute when you're annoyed," he said.

She willed herself not to look back behind her as she walked home (of course she had no doctor's appointment). She stopped off for a drink and to read a magazine. She stopped at a store to pick up some pasta. She looked back only three times and congratulated herself.

The next day was Sunday and her day off. She was grateful for that. She might stop by the store and talk to Dottie, an older woman who'd worked there for over ten years as a part-timer. She could ask her whether she had any issues with management. That seemed simple enough – so simple that she could put it off for a week. Perhaps she was reading into the situation. What she really should do was get in touch with Gloria and discuss what was happening. It would give her perspective.

That was settled! She would call Gloria the next day. She went to bed enormously relieved.

She lived in a second-floor apartment in the Lower East Side, with a fire escape outside the living room, and a tiny bedroom just off that. She kept the living room window locked, but figured that the four-foot or so gap from the fire escape to the bedroom window was pretty secure. She had the window half open, and her only security provision was a glass jar with pennies in it to sound the alarm.

When she heard the jar fall, she bolted upright and grabbed the lamp next to her bed.

Very faintly, she heard a me-ow. It sounded fake. But what did it mean? She heard a hiss, and it, too, was unconvincing. She crept to the window very slowly, lamp in hand, and was just standing there, all nerves alight, when a hand crept through the open window and very slowly felt around.

"There are no more pennies," she said out loud, and the hand snapped back so fast it hit the window frame and the "cat" hissed again.

"I know you're not a cat," she called out. "Is that you, Stan?"
Silence.

She plugged in the lamp near the window, turned it on and looked out. There was Stan, on the railing of the fire escape. They contemplated each other, not making any rash decisions. But Eleanor's mind was racing. The idea that he would think it acceptable to try to break in through her window; the idea that he was toying with her (she had no reason to believe he actually *wanted* her); the crazy compulsive need to manipulate her; the beginning of a fear that maybe she didn't understand what his long-term goal was – and there he was, crouched on the fire escape. His face was smug, his eyes were merry, he looked like he was about to launch himself at her. "You left the window open," he said triumphantly. "Why would you do that? It was for me, wasn't it?"

This infuriated her so much that she acted without thinking and changed him into a cat.

It happened so quickly that he actually snapped into his new shape, tensing on the railing to keep from falling. He blinked and looked around. He saw his paws and then his legs and twisted his head to see his body. "What have you done?" he asked in a weird, horrified voice. Had she thrown some kind of drug at him? Some fast-acting hallucinogen?

"I've cast a spell on you. As a warning. To let you know who you're dealing with."

But the instant she said it, she knew she had left out the key, the part of the spell that kept it open to being reversed. Her heart thudded, her mouth was dry; she could only think what Gloria would say. It didn't matter, at that point, how Stan felt. Gloria was the real issue. She would be furious.

"Change me back!" he yelled.

"I can't."

A window slammed open. "What's going on out there?" an angry neighbor yelled. Perhaps they *were* too loud, but it was a shocking development.

"Let me in!" Stan pleaded. "They're going to start throwing things at me."

"Yeah, well, I'd probably join them," she muttered, but she opened the window all the way and the cat jumped in neatly.

He jumped from the windowsill to the floor, his legs splayed out. He tested out his legs, his whiskers and tail. He licked his fur once, as if to make certain it was fur – or as a nervous, automatic, cat thing.

Oh, she wished she hadn't done it! She had been working on her impatience. She thought she had mastered it. It was really his fault as he was so annoying. Yet she would be blamed for it.

Finally, he asked, "How come I can talk?"

She could see no way out but to pretend it had been deliberate. "You can talk because I only changed your form. You'll still think and act human. And talk, of course. Seems only right, doesn't it? Pretending to be a cat so you could get into my apartment? What were you planning on doing?"

"I just wanted to surprise you. To persuade you of my ardor. I brought flowers." And indeed, he gestured to the fire escape and there were daisies, her favorite. How did he know they were her favorite?

"Breaking and entering is a felony, with or without flowers."

"Oh, come on, you know you love attention. Women can't get enough."

She turned away from him and went for her phone. She called Gloria twice, giving her time to get up and reach for her phone.

"Yes?" Gloria said.

"I'm afraid I've done a terrible thing," Eleanor said. She sounded truly repentant to her own ears. This was not going to be easy, and she'd better convince Gloria that there was a reason for all she did. "I've been stalked," she said, and she explained everything to her. She had mentioned Stan before, so there was history she could draw on. She explained about the promotion, about how overbearing he was, how he followed her, and finally how he had tried to break into her apartment.

"I can see justification for some action, yes. But there's something else, isn't there?"

"Yes." She paused and considered a lot of different ways to phrase it, but finally decided on the straightforward route. "I didn't put the key in to change him back. I don't know any way of undoing it. Is there a way of undoing it?"

Gloria's silence ticked on. It was obvious that she was considering a great many things, none of which she would mention until she had decided on one. "Is he still there?"

"Yes."

"I'll head on over. I need time to think."

"Yes," Eleanor said miserably. She hung up the phone and wondered what Gloria would do. Would she unwitch her?

Stan sat there glaring at her. "You weren't exactly honest," he said. "You should have mentioned that you were teasing me from the start. Your Augs almost always had something to do with me."

"Sometimes, yes. You're generically annoying. Women recognize that and have something to say about it."

"You went out with me."

"That wasn't a date. We were supposed to discuss how to get more responses to Augments."

This went on and on, with Stan pulling out one "proof" after another of how she had lured him, tricked him, and now essentially emasculated him. She did her best to defend herself, but she knew what she had done was wrong, and she knew she would pay for it.

When Gloria came, she sat down heavily on the sofa, her walker next to her. "We'll start from the beginning," she said. "We will recognize individual blame. No overdoing it, no excusing it. Begin."

They led her through the work atmosphere, through every aspect, each pleading their own case as being the wronged one. Stan said, "She has no sense of humor, that's the problem. Everything is so serious!" and Eleanor replied, "He does one creepy thing after another and then pretends it isn't creepy at all. What does this have to do with a sense of humor?"

At the end, Gloria sat there patiently, thinking it over.

"You're both wrong," she said finally. "*You* are a stalker," she said to the cat, "and God knows what you would have done if you'd gotten into this apartment in your true form. Flowers are not an alibi.

"And you," she said, turning to Eleanor. "Learning the Craft means learning the ethics of the Craft. You had a few choices here. You could have used a lesser spell. You could have called the police, even. Breaking and entering is a crime. Why did you change him? You know you're not allowed to. It's too early in your education. That's obvious, since you forgot an integral part of the spell. You did it because you were angry."

Of course she was angry, Eleanor thought. Her mouth dropped open. Didn't she have the right to defend herself by any means necessary? How was it that the women who she thought formed her community would hold her to this strict standard? This painful, humiliating standard?

Gloria's face softened. "You reacted, as we all do, and did what you thought was the most effective thing. But magic wasn't necessary here. You could have hit him with the lamp, for one thing. But by using magic you did two things. You forced a change you couldn't undo and that's a violation of our ethical rules. And you exposed us, the Craft, to criminal investigation. We now have someone who is not part of our society, who knows about our powers. That's never good." She sighed. "It's an unnecessary danger. And the person you've chosen to expose us to – do you consider him to be respectful, courteous, altogether willing to hold our secrets behind his closed lips? Is he the right person to know all this?"

Misery settled in Eleanor's veins as Gloria spoke; Eleanor was past her first sense of outrage, and she knew Gloria was right. Stan was absolutely the wrong person to have this knowledge; he would parlay everything he knew into either media attention or some kind of personal gain. "It's not a good thing, I admit," she said finally.

"Unfortunately, we can't kill him," Gloria said, raising her eyes.

Stan arched his back and then fell over in shock. "What the hell was that?" he cried. "What happened to my back?"

"You did a cat thing," Gloria said. "You had a visceral response to what I said. I was merely trying to lighten the mood. We won't kill you. On the other hand, we can't exactly let you go. It seems," she said thoughtfully and slowly, "that the only resolution is to force the two of you into exile together. In his current form, he can't harm you, Eleanor. And he'll be a constant reminder of how you disobeyed essential rules."

"Hey!" the cat hissed. "You're leaving me *like this* to teach *her* a lesson?"

"You don't see the lesson for you in all this?"

"I get the point, and it won't get to be more of a point in the future."

"We can hope it will," she said evenly. "But there's always the danger that I'll undo you wrong. The most perfect undoing is from the one who originates it. There's always a chance it will go wrong if someone else does it. We'll have to wait for the time when Eleanor has proven herself worthy and then I can help her correct the spell."

Eleanor and the cat were quietly sober, thinking it all over. "You want him to stay here with me?"

"No. No, I think the best thing would be to put you both in a new environment. Get you out of your known patterns and see what happens. And coincidentally, I have some interest in a coven in the south that's in trouble. A woman called Dolores is in charge of them, and she's a kind lady, Eleanor. Perhaps she can give you more guidance than I have. At least she'll give you a different perspective. We witches used to have stronger connections. I regret that we don't, and now that we have such political divisions, I think it will be harder. Yes," she said quietly, "yes, I think that's the best thing to do. It doesn't seem like these times will get better on their own, not with this kind of insanity, and I want to know what's happening. As the nation gets divided up, perhaps we need to find a way to save it."

She paused and Stan yelled, "Witches unite!" raising his paw in a fist.

"But yes," she said, pulling herself away from that particular train of thought and ignoring the cat. "It would be good to have you there, and you can keep me up to date on what's happening. You two have to prove yourselves, and that means that *you* have to stay a cat, and *you* are forbidden to change anyone. If you feel the need to do it, get in touch with me first." She muttered some words under her breath. "If you change anyone without my permission, you will be changed as well. I've just put that curse on you. Do you understand? You must always consult me."

"Yes," Eleanor said faintly. What were her options? She was halfway a witch and she wanted to be a full witch. She wanted to be a deadbolt witch, an awesome witch. She wanted Gloria to admire her, to have the other witches embrace her not because she was new but because she was noble. Oh, dear lord, she thought, when did I want to become noble?

Stan, on the other hand, acknowledged that he had no way to change anything at all. He was stuck with this life and considered what it would be like and dared himself to find a way to enjoy it. "Room and board?" he asked cautiously. "I won't be able to work."

"Room and board."

"And an allowance, maybe? Enough to have a few little catlike pleasures. Maybe a concert, a performance, a beer?"

"We don't have a lot," Gloria said severely, "but considering everything, I think that a small stipend would be reasonable."

"For me, too?" Eleanor asked.

Gloria sighed. She felt she was losing impact. This was a punishment, after all. "We'll work something out. I'm leaving now. I'll find you a place to stay and send you off tomorrow. You'll stay together until you've proved yourselves worthy. I can see that neither one of you is really thinking about how to repair your mistakes, but you'll have to face them before you can move on." She got up and moved her walker to the door. She turned around one last time and said, "It's a different world coming. I hope you'll start thinking about what life is going to be like now – not just for you but for everyone. And I hope that will help you with your learning curve. That is, if you can learn. Because sometimes, I doubt it." She shook her head and left.

PART THREE

CHAPTER 14
Liberty

Eleanor passed an uneventful night in her room in the palace. Her TV even had cable; it was hard to consider her kidnapping anything more than a theoretical hardship. When the palace guard brought her breakfast, there was a small envelope with a hand-written note inside. "Please join me for lunch," it said, and it was signed *The President.*

In an hour, there was a knock on the door and a maid brought in a box with fresh clothes. There was a loose shift, a sweater, and a pair of shoes. The shoes were a little tight, the shift a little loose.

She showered and made sure her hair was brushed and then sat on the edge of the bed and waited for someone to come and claim her, which happened a little after noon.

The two hallway men – she couldn't help but think of them as monitors – escorted her out of the building and across the yard to the back of the palace. They went inside, nodding at various people on the way, and then opened a deep wooden door, stepped back, and waved her inside.

"Oh, good!" a hearty voice said. "Come in, come in."

The heads on the streets were a very good likeness of the president's actual head, and it was a little startling to see, as if he were an imitation of the animatronics on the street. It put her off balance. She wanted her stubbornness, her suspiciousness, all her bad characteristics to be in evidence, but instead there was a sense that she might be out of her depth and therefore couldn't tell what her strategy should be.

"Oh, please sit down," the president said, ushering her to a seat at the very nicely set table. "I ordered some Chinese food. Lots of veg and tofu, that kind of thing. I have excellent chefs," he added, grinning. "Of all nationalities. Equal opportunities. My pleasure." He pulled a cord by the table. She had seen British dramas; that cord was to summon the help. She imagined people below stairs or upstairs or down the hall, standing by the bells and watching to see which one would move.

"Why not a wired bell?" she asked.

"Oh, but this was here; why would I replace something that works perfectly well without electricity? Saving the planet, you know. I thought that was almost a religion for you?" he ended very delicately with a rising inflection.

"But you built this place." She was honestly puzzled.

"Not at all. It was a museum. But very few people went to it. I forget what it was a museum *of*," he said thoughtfully. "I'm sure the children hated it. Which is why I'm making part of the moat into a water slide." He beamed at her. "I do love the children, don't you?"

"Waterslide?" she repeated, stumped at where to begin with the questions that rose up. "But what about security? And where will you get the water to keep it full?"

"A government that is well-loved doesn't need much security," he said soothingly. He got up and walked over to the large window looking out over the moat to the city. "Join me?" His voice was soothing and confident, and she stood next to him.

"Do you see how well it's all working? Look over there." He pointed. "That's a children's chorus marching down the street. They're singing a bunch of songs about their city and their homeland. They're off from school, so they're very happy. And their parents have the day off from work and get to see their children performing, so the parents are happy. That's a well-ordered society. They usually celebrate by getting ice cream or eating out, so the economy is happy." He gestured for her to sit down. The door opened, and two women came in bearing trays, which they placed on the table. "Help yourself," the president said. "I hate having people hover around me, don't you?" He reached for the bowl of rice and took a big spoonful, then added the veg and tofu. A trio of small bowls held various sauces and additional vegetables.

Eleanor followed suit. "Is everybody happy though?"

The president put down his fork and sat back. "That's the goal: Of course it takes a while to get there, but substantially – yes. It doesn't take that much. A good economy, low taxes, fairly good healthcare (we don't want anyone to live too long, to be honest), and a circus. That's all it takes." He beamed. He glowed.

His smugness was irritating, and his description ran counter to everything she'd ever experienced. "How can they all be happy? In any group, at least thirty percent – I don't know the real number – are dealing with heartbreak, death, pain, a sense of injustice, impatience, jealousy, all the human things."

"Not here. I doubt it's more than two percent."

She cast a long glance at the window. There was a faint sound of children's voices. "How?" she said.

"We give them what they want even before they know they want it."

She studied his face, which was friendly and open. He was smug, yes, but also convinced that he had the answer. Like a salesman, with confidence in his own product.

"Surprise equals delight," he added.

"And no one is unhappy?"

He laughed. "Are you expecting revolutionaries? You're thinking there's some hidden fault and you're determined to find it. Tell me, what is the hidden fault? Where is the worm in the apple?"

"Water," she said immediately. It was, she assumed, why she had been brought here. The suspicions people had about the water theft were true, whether or not they had the details right. "Where did the water go?"

"Conspiracy theories," he said, sighing. "It's really so predictable. There must be something wrong, so let's search for it. Isn't that what you were doing? Looking for the 'missing water,' as you folks say?"

"I'm not connected to anyone," she said hastily. "I'm new here, so maybe I just see what's obvious. A whole river has vanished and it's not the drought, because you don't actually have a drought. You don't get much rain, and everyone is now highly aware of how infrequent it is, but it's not unusual. Even in the worst droughts, the river didn't disappear."

He chewed thoughtfully. "It's the Easterners who have done something." He threw his arms out a little dramatically, his fork still in hand. "You should ask them how they've managed it. Retaliation. As soon as we seceded, the water started to disappear. You can look that up. It's historically accurate."

They ate companionably. The food was good if a little bland. She found a small bowl of chilies and added some. Much better. The cat would like that. She wondered for a moment if the cat was involved somehow with her being taken… but that was silly. Of course he was. He never took his eyes off her and he was still determined to get revenge for being transformed. What was he up to? And what had he gotten her into?

"What do you want?" she said finally, putting down her fork.

The president broke into a grin. "I love that," he said. "You'd be surprised how many people wait to find out what I know before asking what I want. It's tedious."

She put her hands together in her lap and waited.

"Here's the situation," he said, leaning forward confidentially. "There are a small number of unhappy people who are mostly unhappy about the water, even though I keep everyone informed. When I know something, everyone knows something. Our water has been stolen, pure and simple. By Easterners. They've diverted a river up north that used to come all the way down to us. Despite that, we've done a great job of setting up an infrastructure that works." He looked at her sharply. "It works. No one is dying from lack of water. If people can't afford it, they can apply to the Emergency Water System and get help."

"Never heard of it."

"Because you don't actually need it," he said smoothly. "People who need help with water need help with all sorts of things, too. Once they're in the system, they get guidance all the way through."

"That's very generous," she said, suddenly determined to be as bland as possible. "What do you want from me? As you pointed out, I don't know very much."

"Yet you seem to be involved in an attempt to overthrow my presidency." He glared at her.

"What?" This made no sense.

"By trying to prove that there's a conspiracy about the water."

"You're wrong. I'm trying to find a friend of a friend, who's gone missing and who's known to…" she hesitated. "Known to be good at finding water. A dowser."

"So you're looking for missing water in order to find the missing water-witch?"

She was surprised that he was comfortable calling Daria a witch, with no insults or prejudices. Was this a trap of some kind? "A dowser," she murmured. How did he feel about witches?

He shrugged. "Semantics. So you imagine you'll find, what, a hidden waterfall and a giant plug and that's where your missing person will be? Reading a book, perhaps?"

"Well," she said, "she would be drawn to a body of water. And if there was any kind of significant change, I'm sure she'd be involved."

"Ah, yes," he said, nodding. "She *is* a bit of a control freak."

The remark sent a shock through her spine; she was alert, her shoulders pulled back and her spine straight. "You have her," she breathed.

He held his hands out, palms up. "Or she has us. Hard to tell, sometimes. But yes, she's here and she's perfectly fine. Now see, isn't that delightful news?"

"Can I talk to her?" The immediate sense of relief had fled and been replaced by suspicion. He could tell her anything he wanted, of course. She had given him enough to allow him to present her with a well-packaged, plausible lie. "And that still doesn't answer what you want from me."

"Oh, it does," he said genially. He pulled the cord to summon the help. "Because I need a spy. Tit for tat."

Stan got home late and went to bed; he appreciated not running into Eleanor. In the morning, however, she was still nowhere to be seen. He checked her room; he looked out back. His heart lifted a little.

He went to get the newspapers and have a cappuccino and a scone at a café. There was nothing about the treasure hunt in the papers, which was at once reassuring (no one had found it) and puzzling (was it still going on?). And nothing about a crash or accident involving an annoying tourist from the East. His heart pattered a little bit more than usual at that. Was that what concern felt like? Where was she? Out with her witchy cronies? She actually didn't seem to be getting along with them very much recently. He'd only heard one or two names, and that stuff about the missing water.

He passed by a president's head on his way back, and it winked at him. The second head nodded, and the third one waved him over. Of course it had no hands, so it wasn't really a wave, more like a jerk of the head and a meaningful look.

"Yes?" he asked it.

"Everything good with you?" the head asked. "Is life better than it was?"

"Indeed," the cat said, pulling himself up. "Life is peaceful today so far. How about with you? Any news?"

"Why, yes," the head replied. "We have your friend in custody. She's fine and we're in discussions. She may be out soon."

"No hurry," the cat said, despite feeling the slight nip of betrayal. "No hurry at all, if she's fine where she is."

"She's fine enough," the head said, which wasn't all that reassuring. "We thank you for your help. It's people like you who keep our nation strong."

"You said you would give me another clue," Stan said roughly.

"Of course. Here it is: the treasure you seek is where you find it."

"Hey," Stan said, giving a long-drawn-out growl. "That's not a clue at all."

The president's head laughed. "Are you kidding? That's the clue to the way to live. It's the whole shebang. And I give it to you free!"

Stan launched himself at the head with outstretched claws, but it did no good at all. The head was mostly metal.

CHAPTER 15

The shocking thing was that the president wanted her to spy on Stan, not on the witches. Why was it always about Stan? How did that cat manage to get everyone's attention? She cringed at her own thoughts immediately. Did she want to be the one who got attention under these circumstances? Was she crazy?

She had asked, stupidly, "Are you sure? You know he's a jerk, don't you?"

The woman sitting off to the side snorted – she had forgotten that woman was there.

The president had laughed, his eyebrows way up on his face. "That's a good one," he said. "I thought you two were friends? Aren't you living together?"

"Frenemies," she said stiffly. "We're kind of stuck with each other."

"Well, then, this will be easy for you. No moral quandaries. Not that there should be anyway. We like him, we just want to know what he's doing, what his life is like. We value all citizens here," he said ponderously. "We select a few occasionally and try to see how life affects them. Each one is different."

She was astonished at the platitudes. His tone was so reassuring and comforting, but what he was saying was basically, "don't you worry your little head about it."

"It's not a betrayal of trust?" she asked, just to see what he would come up with.

He shrugged. "Trust is always questionable, isn't it? Many people are killed by people they trusted, aren't they? Or betrayed by someone they loved who went on to love someone else more? Trust is an ephemeral thing. You trust someone for the moment because it feels right, but what do you know of it? This person, Stan, do you really think he's trustworthy?"

She sighed. "I know he isn't."

"And yet you're thinking about protecting him from me. Because you trust him more than you trust me? And yet I've done nothing to upset you, have I?"

She rallied. "I know him well enough by now to know what to expect from him. I don't know you at all, so I don't know what to expect from you. That is as close as I can come to trust under the circumstances."

"He's the one who gave us your name."

"What?" she said, startled.

"Does that change things a little? Maybe you don't believe me. Do you think he would give us your name in return for something – say, a clue to the treasure hunt?" The president laughed.

She shuddered. Stan absolutely would. She would get revenge! "I'll do it," she said.

The heads were very polite as Eleanor walked away from the palace, took the subway the obligatory two stops, and then walked over to a store to pick up some groceries. She couldn't remember if there was anything at home, so she bought eggs, milk and bread. She threw in a can of beans. She added a bar of chocolate. And a bottle of wine. Then another bottle of wine. And a can of soup. She circled the aisles twice, because she kept losing track of what she was looking for and kept thinking about her moral dilemma.

She hated that damn cat, but of course she had a sense of responsibility towards him. Was the president looking to harm him in some way or was he looking to... to... to *elevate* him? The president hadn't seemed angry; he had seemed benevolent and interested. Which in itself was an issue.

This was a very strange place with all its surveillance, its nougats, those messengers picking people up so often that it no longer meant anything. And the drought. And the heads everywhere, and the constant parades. It was all meant to keep people unbalanced, distracted. From what? That bothered her, that she couldn't see what all this masquerade was about. It was terrible to think that it was all about nothing, that there was no agenda, that it was merely chaotic. It could be that, she admitted. So far, it was a fun chaos, but that could change.

The only real, known problem was the drought. She frowned. She had assumed that the messengers picked up people and then they disappeared, but they had picked her up and she hadn't disappeared, so it might be necessary to question her assumptions about the drought.

And where was the cat now? He wasn't at home, though that didn't give her much to go on. Was he worried about her and searching the city? She nearly laughed out loud. She looked around and couldn't see any clues of what he had been doing while she was gone. Her useless maps were where she'd left them; there seemed the same amount of food in the refrigerator; he might have helped himself to some money in the junk drawer but in fact she couldn't remember how much there should be. She had to remind herself that under no circumstances was she allowed to worry about Stan.

The president had said that she had to make a report on anything Stan said or did. If she never saw the cat again, her conscience would be clear. If she never saw the cat again...

She had to examine her reaction to that sentence.

Did she feel a little guilty because she also felt relief? She did. Was it because if he was gone, she could stop regretting that she had transformed him? Yes. She had caused him to be something he wasn't, and he was a constant reminder. If he was gone, she could forget about it and move on. That was wrong. It was true that she didn't like him, but she didn't like other people even more. Her boss at the gift shop, for instance. She really hated him! But she wouldn't knowingly transform him into a worm.

She had to face the fact that she had been fighting her responsibility, and she had been wrong. She *should* feel responsible. It was no good insisting that the cat had actually caused his own punishment; that if he hadn't behaved that way there would be no problem. He had been wrong, but she had been worse.

First, though, she had to do something about Daria. She called Dolores and the phone wasn't answered. She tried a number of times, then decided that Dolores was not going to answer. She went out to the back, stood before a certain bush, and said, "Gloria?" and waited.

After a moment, Gloria answered. "Hello, Eleanor. Everything all right?"

"Well," Eleanor said carefully. "There have been a few changes. Stan has gone off somewhere and I don't know where, and I was kidnapped by the president. He has Daria. I wanted to tell Dolores, but she won't answer the phone. I was hoping you could talk to her."

There was a silence of some minutes, which Eleanor expected. Gloria was like that. She weighed everything before speaking. Finally, she said, "Did you see Daria?"

"Not yet. They said I could see her next time. And at that point I have to sign a contract."

"That's interesting. A contract. What are the terms?"

"That I can have Daria if I spy on Stan."

"Why?"

"I don't know. I have no idea. He's gone more and more, and at this point I haven't seen him in over a day. He said he was looking for a buried treasure. There was an item about it in the paper. The president also mentioned the treasure fondly. I don't know why it would matter."

"It might not matter," Gloria said. "It might be merely a distraction."

Eleanor sighed. "They're certainly good at that."

Feeling overstimulated and awash with contradictions, Eleanor decided to visit Dolores instead of calling her. She walked to the bus then rode her broom the rest of the way.

She found Dolores sitting outside her house, staring at the mountains with half-closed eyes. The witch was looking more and more diminished; grayer, wispier.

"You don't look well," Eleanor said. "Are you all right?"

She shrugged. "Low thyroid. Common at my age, the doctor said. I take a pill."

Eleanor leaned forward earnestly. "I've been trying to call you to tell you what's happened, but you haven't answered."

Dolores shrugged slightly, making a helpless movement with her hands.

"The messenger van took me a few days ago," Eleanor continued. "The president kept me in a room for a day before he would talk to me, and then it was about Daria."

Dolores was shocked. "I'm so sorry," she whispered. "What did they want with you? How horrible." She shook her head sadly. "Are you all right?"

"I am."

"Is Daria all right?"

"I think so."

Dolores tried to sit up straighter. "Daria," she murmured. "I can't stop thinking about how I feel responsible, I really do. I failed her. She was a difficult person to deal with sometimes. She was always a proud witch, and she didn't think she got enough respect. After all, water is life." Dolores sighed. "She said that over and over. It got boring." She flashed a tight grin. "She's one of those people who won't let go of a thing. If she believes she deserves more – and she always believes she deserves more – then she won't let up until she gets it."

"I imagine a lot of people are like that – hoping to be respected for what they think is important about themselves. She thought she was more important than you did?"

"Yes."

"But you were the leader of the coven?"

"Yes. I don't think I was a good one. A water-witch is no greater than any other witch, I thought. But back then, we used to have a big river next to us, so finding water never seemed that crucial. Of course, it was more important out in the desert, but even here, we have resources. Sometimes a neighbor needed a new well, or off-the-grid people decided to come out here. They came to her to find water, and she always did. She had a powerful talent. She said she could sniff it, hear it, see the moisture rising from the sands. Out in the desert, they respected her and nodded to her and stepped back in admiration when she came, but among us, well, all the luster went away. She was just a witch among witches. Not enough for her.

"At first I just thought she'd ditched us. I went to her place a few times, and her things were still there, as much as I could see. She had a whole room of potted plants, and a beautiful garden outside. The garden was fine. She'd planted it on top of water, of course, though I couldn't see any. The potted plants were also doing well. I wondered if she was coming in every so often to look after things. I couldn't tell. I left notes. I left a small spell that would tell me when she was there, but she manipulated the spell and I think it ended up telling her when I was there instead. She was incredibly good at spells. It put me in my place. Always a small group, only four altogether with Annie and Maureen, but we did get together regularly. Once Daria left, though, we fell apart. We would get together but have nothing to say. We would do small spells, and they wouldn't go right, or we'd stop in the middle and lose all interest in the spell. Annie finally said she was giving up witching and moving to a commune – I didn't even know there were any communes left. Maureen went back to school to study art and began to design stained-glass windows. I know that witching doesn't interfere with either of those choices, so I don't know why they had to leave.

"But to be honest, I'm not much of a witch anymore either. Before you came, I hadn't flown in months. I remember the ride with you because it was perfect. I had a reason for it – to see if I could find Daria – and there was a breeze and a bright moon, and the desert smelled of rain. That's the creosote. There's no other smell like it, and it makes me yearn vaguely for my life. If that makes sense?"

"It does," Eleanor said. She knew that feeling. It was creeping up on her more and more. What did she want from life? How would she get it? The desert air pulled the questions out of her, and she ended up wondering if she'd sidestepped having a meaning to her life. But Dolores felt the same; was that a coincidence?

"It sounds like she left a spell behind on all of you," Eleanor said. "You all lost the will to be a witch. If it were just one of you – well, that could happen. But it's all of you. I don't know this spell," she admitted. "I'm not a complete witch, myself. But Gloria can help me through it, I'm sure. Is it all right if I talk to Gloria? Or you could, of course."

Dolores got a tight look on her face. "Gloria. She's bossy and controlling. I don't really want her interfering."

Gloria did control things, but it wasn't a problem for anyone; she was the head. "Dolores, have you always felt that way about her? Or is this new, too? Like your not wanting to be a practicing witch?"

Dolores looked off into the distance, her mouth working silently. She sighed, finally, and said, "I don't know. I just don't know anymore. It's so very odd, almost as if half of me is locked in, blocked off. I can look and see that these are things I once loved, but now I don't care. I can see that Gloria was once important to me, and I enjoyed speaking with her, but it seems so far away. That's certainly true, anyway: everything inside seems far away now. Yes, you must be right," she said finally. Her voice was sad and reluctant. "I can see what you're saying. Yes, talk to Gloria. I need to be restored. At least, I think I do."

"You do," Eleanor assured her. "You do."

Eleanor went out to her yard and spoke to Gloria once she got back home. "I just saw Dolores, and I'm really worried," she said. "I think this place is under some kind of spell. I'm sure Dolores is ensorcelled; she has no interest in being a witch anymore, and I really do suspect it's because of Daria. Can you come here? Quickly? Monica, too, if that's possible. Dolores really doesn't have any power anymore, and I'm just a beginner. With limited powers," she added. "Not complaining. I'm just not equal to what's needed right now."

"We're a step ahead of you," Gloria said. "Flying by broom would take too long. Monica and I applied for a visa into Liberty and we just got it. We'll take the first plane in. I met Daria once, and I know she had ambitions. I'm not against ambitions," she added easily. "I've had some myself. But she didn't want to learn the Craft for the sake of the Craft. She wanted to use it." She took a deep breath. "I'm just trying to say that it wouldn't surprise me if she'd become corrupted. And I'm sorry to hear about Dolores. Sometimes it seems there are people put on this earth simply to be taken advantage of. Oh well. That's not a helpful viewpoint, I know. We'll be there soon. I'll get back to you once it's all confirmed."

CHAPTER 16

Jem was very excited; he had had a dream. Stan had to listen to it as Jem drove away from the city. "It was right there, man!" Jem cried. "In the mountains. A big door! And behind it, a treasure chest, just like in the movies."

"Or in cartoons," Stan said. "I've seen that in cartoons."

Jem laughed and slapped Stan lightly on the back. "You've always got a joke," he said. "I like that. But we were going to go that way, weren't we?"

"I thought we were going to avoid the mountains. Because there's a lake there, and we're avoiding water."

"There *was* a lake. Lake Fortune. It's not there anymore."

"I think that's nonsense. Lakes don't just disappear."

"Lakes are *always* disappearing. There's that lake in Siberia that disappeared. The Great Salt Lake, which turned to salt–"

"It did not!" Stan said. "You're getting all mixed up."

"Well, *our* lake disappeared. I showed you the river, and it's gone. You can't deny that."

"I never saw the river, so of course I can deny it."

They had to pause for a moment. "The lake didn't cover all the mountain," Jem said finally. "The last clue said it was between two deserts, and we have deserts. We'll cross one to get to the mountain, and if we go around the mountain or to the left of the mountain, we hit the Sonoran desert. I looked it up, like I said. So, the mountain is between two deserts!"

"Well," Stan said, puzzling over it. "Hmm, it does sort of fit together. I hate agreeing with you. But I agree with you. I know you're wrong, but I can't prove it. Once you see you're wrong, we'll do something else." He rummaged in his fanny pack. "Fine. I have a bottle of water and a donut. I'm good."

Jem raised his eyebrows. "I brought *two* donuts," he said meaningfully. "One for you."

"That's good. I think I'll be hungry after a walk like that."

Jem sighed pointedly, but Stan wasn't paying attention. He was looking at the scenery, which he was very glad he didn't have to hike through in person. The mountains were getting closer and closer. It was odd that he hadn't really thought much about them. Of course, every so often, he had noticed them in the distance, but it was like wallpaper. There was bound to be a pattern in wallpaper, but he really wasn't interested in looking closer. Mountains had never been useful before.

They certainly got bigger and bigger. He didn't much care for that, because he assumed that sooner or later, he would be climbing on them. Still, they did look full of possibilities. Lots of shady parts. Lots of glaring parts. Some crooked trees in various places. Birds, too. He looked closely. Yes, birds, not drones. He couldn't stop looking at the birds. He really, *really* wanted to catch one. He made a deep chittering noise in his throat.

"Something wrong?" Jem asked, slowing down. "Did you see something?"

"Birds," Stan said stiffly.

"Okay," Jem sighed. "Look, I think we should go straight to the mountain. The clue said in between deserts and that would make sense because the biggest desert is over where New Mexico used to be."

"'Used to be?' Where did it go?"

"Seceded from them and joined us. Now it's part of Liberty. Actually, I don't know if all of New Mexico seceded. Parts. And parts of Oregon."

"Oregon? I mean, how can they join Liberty? Must be thousands of miles away."

"Think of it as an island that belongs to a land nation. The distance wouldn't really matter if it was water, so it doesn't matter if it's land, does it?"

"It does to me," Stan said stiffly. "It doesn't make sense."

"I like it," Jem said with satisfaction. "Little by little, we'll be a whole nation again. All of us in Liberty."

He sounded like it would all be easy, Stan noted. Like you could cut up a map and just move states around. Which was an interesting idea, actually. But also stupid. Otherwise Jem seemed like a decent guy. With a second donut just for him. Which was nice. Though of course, philosophically speaking, the donut would end, and the Oregon secession would not, so maybe one did not balance out the other.

Jem drove and drove, pulling over at official scenic stops and also sometimes just pulling over and getting out to walk around. Stan did not find this interesting, but Jem always said something like, "We have to keep our minds sharp. Maybe there's another clue. I thought that bush looked fake. But it's normal. Not a clue."

They got to the mountains and Jem moved some barricades and they drove up even higher. The road suddenly ended, and there were paths that were overgrown or filled with rocks. Jem scouted out a few, going ahead and then coming back with descriptions of what he'd seen. Stan actually went a few feet down a path that Jem had pointed to, but it looked very tricky, so he took his donut out and ate it. Why save it? Jem had two.

And then Jem shouted and came running around the side of the mountain, waving his arms like mad. Stan stared blankly. Was that wave the kind that meant danger or the kind that meant happy excitement?

Jem finally arrived and said, "You've got to see this. It's incredible."

Stan followed him around the mountain and saw the mouth of a cave. It was a good size, no crawling on your belly with spiders and bats racing over your neck. Jem kept waving for him to follow but what was the hurry? The cave wasn't going anywhere, unless Jem thought it was going to disappear like the lake – in which case, Stan wasn't interested in going in at all.

But he did go in, carefully, sometimes down on all fours when the footing seemed risky. Jem got ahead of him again – was he some kind of goat? – and kept calling back to hurry, see this, hurry.

"I am hurrying," Stan hissed. He was a little out of breath. Perhaps he should cut down on cream cakes. Or cut down on hiking, which made more sense.

And then he finally broke through into a cavern, with enormously high ceilings, and a light source.

"There's an opening above," Jem said, pointing, and Stan could see it, too, a hole at the top that let in the sun. The noise, which had been growing as he hiked through the cave, now made sense. There was a waterfall coming from the opening in the ceiling all the way down to a large lake before them. Or maybe not that large, Stan realized, because the lake was actually at least three feet below them, and it looked like that wasn't the normal height. It was still beautiful, however, and it made him thirsty, just looking at it. He leaned over to drink.

And Jem pushed him in.

This made him frantic. "What are you doing?" he screamed in a voice that was embarrassingly high-pitched, like a cat yowl.

"Do you feel a current?" Jem asked.

"Get me out of here!" Stan was scrambling, but it was against rock and he couldn't quite get his claws into anything. He was going to *kill* Jem when he got out! *If* he got out.

"I was thinking there was a current," Jem continued conversationally. "'Cause I think it's going somewhere. It can't just sit here. Don't you wonder where it's going?"

Stan finally managed to scramble up a few feet on some kind of root. He sank his claws into Jem's pants leg and gave a yank, falling back as he did so. Good, he thought, now we're both in. Let's see how much he likes it.

"What'd you do that for?" Jem yelled, bobbing up and down and spitting water.

"Why'd you push me in?"

"Poor impulse control," Jem said. "It's an affliction. A handicap. You basically grabbed a disabled man."

"I'm more disabled than you are, you idiot!"

"You look fine."

They were drifting together, pulled by a fairly strong current, and Stan began to hear another roar, just like the one he'd heard on the way into the cave. He paused in his argument to look back toward the waterfall in the cavern, but they had actually already drifted fairly far away from it. "Jem," he said, suddenly nervous. "Shut up. I hear another waterfall."

Jem heard it, too. He floated and looked around and Stan could see a sudden concern showing on his face, and then a strong concern, and all at once he was splashing, open-handed, at the water.

"That's not how you swim," Stan yelled, and realized with horror that he had to yell because the sound was so much louder than it had been. "You use your hands like a knife, not like a paddle. Like a knife!"

Jem grabbed hold of Stan and they began to spin slowly, round and round, and then they were moving faster, round and round, and then they turned a corner in the cave, and the noise was enormous. It was another arched cave, but there was a drop; they could see that the water stopped continuing ahead of them, and then suddenly, holding on to each other, they were over and falling down, down, down, screaming together.

And landing in more water.

It wasn't all that steep a drop, really. But it was fast and they landed separately. In between gasping and insanely slapping his paws to get leverage, Stan looked around and saw Jem up ahead of him, treading water in a slipshod fashion, gasping and desperately trying to gain some control.

Stan didn't think Jem looked like a man who would get control. But he accidentally gulped some water himself and was forced to wonder whether *he* would gain control either.

They moved along swiftly. The light was dim but at least it was something. He looked up once to see if there were cracks in the rocks above, but he tipped backwards and swallowed more water, so he gave that up. Instead, he tried to dog-paddle over to Jem. It took minutes and minutes and eventually Jem noticed what he was doing and dog-paddled towards him as well. When they met, they each grabbed hold of each other. In fact, Stan thought that the easiest thing to do would be to basically clasp Jem around his neck, his arms reaching over his shoulders. Kissing distance.

"Excuse me," he said. "This just seems to work best, given our body types."

Jem nodded, spitting out more water. "I was thinking..." he said.

That was surprising. Who had time to think?

"...this is going somewhere," Jem continued.

Again, Stan was dumbfounded. How was he thinking *ahead*? It was taking all Stan's resources to stay afloat and breathe at the same time. But perhaps Jem was thinking about being rescued? And knew how to make it happen?

"Yes?" Stan said with encouragement.

"It was really fast for a while, but it seems steady now. It doesn't seem to be getting faster or slower."

"Yes? Does that mean something?"

"Probably. If it was going faster, then I think it would be getting narrower and maybe heading towards another waterfall. If it were going slower, then I think it would be getting wider. All in all, I'd like it to be going slower."

They continued, locked together, as they tried to estimate

speed and distance. Stan also listened for the sounds of another waterfall, but he didn't hear anything. Gradually, the current seemed to slow down, or they adjusted to their situation, because they began to note what was around them.

"It's a natural underground river," Jem noted. "So that's where all the water's been going."

"How do you know it hasn't been here all along?"

"Oh, the cave's not new, that's for sure."

"I meant, maybe it's been flowing here all along." This guy was an idiot.

"Nah. I mean, why would that be? The water disappeared, and look, here, look, there's an underground river."

"But maybe there's always *been* an underground river! Didn't you hear me?"

Jem had been looking at the rockface as they were drawn along. With Stan's last comment, he turned his head to look at him (not an easy thing to do, the way they clutched each other). "I heard you," he said. "I'm thinking it through. This has been here a long time, but look, I don't see water marks along the sides, so the river has never been higher than this. And it's summer, which doesn't get much rain and it's past snowmelt season, so it's strange that it wouldn't have high-water marks, because the water level always drops in summer. Doesn't it?" He waited.

Stan was both annoyed and impressed. He hadn't been thinking about what it meant, at all. So it was pretty neat that Jem could look around and take educated guesses on what he saw. But it was also very annoying because that made it seem like Jem was smarter than he was, which was never going to be true.

"I'm new here," he said, in explanation.

"It works pretty much the same way everywhere," Jem said, trying to look noncommittal as he spat water out.

"Not in New York," Stan said firmly. "How far do you think we've come?"

Jem blinked. "How the hell would I know that?" he snapped, then he took in a deep breath. "Sorry. Didn't mean to shout. But let me think. I've gone rafting, and let's see, I once went a mile in half an hour, and the water was, I think, a little slower than this. How long do you think we've been here?"

Stan was silent.

"Let's say half an hour. So maybe we went more than a mile."

"How wide is the mountain? And which direction are we headed?"

"God," Jem breathed. "You're like a bratty kid with these questions. Why don't you let me ask questions and you answer them?"

Stan scowled.

They drifted along steadily, neither one of them speaking. Their eyes rested idly on pieces of debris – plastic bottles, plastic bags – along the cave sides. "We might be going faster than I thought," Jem finally conceded. "Or has it picked up?" He watched a piece of Styrofoam twirl close to the wall.

"It has picked up," Stan said stiffly. "There, I've answered a question. And it must be more than half an hour by now. I'd say it's more than an hour. So I'd also say, based on your statement, that we've gone a couple of miles by now."

"Could be."

They floated along for another burst of time. Their eyes had adjusted to the dim light, and Stan saw a pool noodle brush against a rock. "Did you notice that piece of rope back a way?" he asked.

"Yes. And I saw something that looked like a bumper to keep a boat from knocking against the dock."

"Could some of the things we're seeing come from that lake that disappeared?" Stan was becoming hopeful. He was, indeed, a buoyant personality anyway, and seeing things that were recognizably from civilization cheered him up immensely. He *liked* seeing familiar objects; the cave wasn't at all familiar and he distrusted it. Also, and he was proud of himself for this, if there were lost objects down here, there might be something entirely useful!

"Let's look for a raft," he said.

Jem rolled his eyes. "You think there's a raft?"

"Look, over there – a plastic box."

"Tackle box."

"So there will be other things. We should try to get closer to the side. Everything I've seen so far has been over to the side."

Jem nodded, and they both used their hands to paddle closer to the side of the cave. Stan had seen movies of people in rivers who grabbed onto tree trunks or branches to save themselves, but there was nothing like that here. The side of the cave wasn't completely smooth – there were ledges and cracks – but none of it was enough to grab onto.

"Look!" Jem said in disbelief. "Look!" and Stan turned to where he was pointing up ahead. It looked like the tree trunk he had been reminiscing about, or a branch or a series of branches. He could feel Jem kick fiercely with his legs to go towards it, and he joined in, kicking and splashing.

It was actually part of a dock, rotted and thick with broken splinters, but it was three boards wide and about two feet long. Jem pushed Stan off and hoisted himself up onto it. It sank a foot or so, making it more unstable, but Jem held on and twisted his body until he found a balance. "It's not much," he said, holding a hand out to Stan. "But it's a start. Maybe we'll find something else to lash to it. So we're looking for boards and for rope."

"There was some rope on that bumper we passed."

"Too late. That's the past. There must have been something that happened to make things wash down. Whatever it is, I'm thinking there may be more pieces."

Stan agreed to hold on to the boards with his claws until they found more to build with. It was a relief to stop holding himself up so high, so he relaxed and kept his eyes looking forward. They were on the right-hand side and they each saw a few useful things on the left-hand side, but they decided it was unlikely they could cross the river to get it before they were too far downstream. There wasn't a lot of junk, but it tended to be fairly large. The small stuff had nothing to snag on, Jem said. The larger stuff found bumps in the rock wall, ledges and fissures.

"I see an inflatable," Stan said, squinting. "Up ahead, see?"

Jem jostled his boards. "A doll," he said, squinting.

"I think it's a sex doll," Stan said with surprise. "Not that I've ever used one." It sounded a little prissy, even to his own ears, but he wasn't going to confess anything. "It's not moving along. I don't know why."

"Well, it's floating so it's not ripped," Jem admitted grudgingly. "Let's take a look."

They paddled over again and steadied themselves against the rock wall. "Fishing line," Jem said, lifting up a mess of it, knotted and tangled. "That's what's keeping it here. Line's stuck on some outcropping." He found the spot and tugged the line free. The sex doll spun around a little. "Well, it'll make a good float, I guess. You want it?" He generously offered it to Stan, who looked at him in amazement. He had never figured out exactly what it was that people saw when they looked at him, but surely – surely – however Jem managed to explain it to himself, surely he saw the claws?

"I'd rather have the boards," Stan said diplomatically. "I mean, I'm a little lighter than you are, so they wouldn't sink so low. And the doll's fully inflated."

"I promise I won't do anything lewd," Jem said, and grabbed the doll by the shoulders and climbed aboard. She rocked back and forth, and Jem splashed an awful lot and made various grunts, and for a moment Stan thought he *was* doing something lewd, but eventually Jem got his bearings and settled himself face down on the doll. He could now paddle more easily. "This is great," he agreed.

They paddled out to the middle of the river, and took turns grabbing one another so they could float together like two otters. "I think we're going faster," Jem said after a while. "And I think we're going downhill."

It was true. By their calculation, they had been in the water for close to two hours, and their speed probably averaged two miles per hour (could it be three?) so they were at least four miles from where they started.

"How wide is a mountain?" Stan mused. This was not a city problem.

"Really wide," Jem said. "Though we didn't start at the beginning of the other side. Let's see," he said, scrunching up his face. "I'd say we were actually pretty close to the western side of the range. And the range is pretty much north-south. So it's possible we're getting close to the end of it, the edge of it. That would be good."

"You don't happen to have any of those donuts, do you?" Stan felt a little peckish. What a good decision it had been to eat his donut before they'd gone into the water. His donut would have dissolved by now, but maybe Jem put his in a Ziplock pouch? That would be a sensible thing to do, actually. "Mine dissolved," he said serenely. "Or I'd share it with you."

Jem nodded, shifted around crazily, then pulled out a Ziplock pouch. He struggled to open it, so Stan took it from him. He had more leeway on his perch, so he opened it, passed one donut to Jem, and then took the other one. "I am grateful," he said seriously. "I was beginning to feel faint."

"This isn't so bad," Jem said after he finished his donut. "We're going somewhere, it'll be new and interesting, and I think this must be the way to the treasure, really. It's exactly the kind of adventure you'd have on a quest." His voice was plucky and satisfied, and Stan realized that this man was actually picturing himself as Harrison Ford or Chris Pratt or someone fighting his way through the galaxy, when of course it was Stan, and always would be Stan, who led the way in all things. Usually.

"Look up ahead," Jem said, and Stan followed his gaze. There was light, down at the end. Bright light. Stan wasn't sure what it meant. It could be a good thing, he admitted to himself. It could be a very good thing. He didn't really like being in the middle of a mountain. It wasn't his idea of an adventure. Both men stared straight ahead as the light expanded, or the opening got bigger, or they just got closer. When they were very close to the mouth of it, Stan saw the tops of trees and he had only the briefest moment to wonder if he really wanted to be at the top of trees, and then there was a relatively short waterfall leading to a kind of chute of rapids all the way down the slope, ending in a swirling wide pool which spun them around (Jem screaming "woo-hoo!") and then they were once again on a river moving somewhere.

Like a water slide ride, Stan thought, though he'd never been on a water slide ride. He didn't see the appeal.

"I think we should see where this goes for a while," Jem said. "It might lead us right to the treasure, or the next clue." And so they continued on. It was a strange thing to say but it was beginning to seem to Stan that this was in fact a metaphysical trip. Maybe Jem with all his theatrical belief in journeys had a point. Definitely a journey, had to hand him that.

"So," he said finally, following his thoughts as far as he could. "If this is a clue to the treasure hunt, which part was the clue? I mean, did the clue just lead us to the cave and so we have to find another clue? Or is this whole thing a clue?"

"Of course it's a clue," Jem said firmly. "And it's taking us somewhere, isn't it? I mean, we got the clue that led to the cave, and then the cave is leading us somewhere."

Stan sighed. "The cave is right back there."

"You do that deliberately," Jem said with a sigh. "You refuse to follow the logic. This is a step-by-step process, and the cave was just another step."

"Where is the treasure, Jem?"

They were still going hand in hand down the river. Stan

could see the same old desert around them, sandy brownish ground, dark green sticks and bushes. Rocks. Where were they and how would they get back? Were there buses? His hand crept to his bowtie and found that he still had his phone, but it was wet and he had no bowl of dry rice to stick it in.

Jem watched as he opened his phone and shook it a little. "Is there a signal?" he asked, and Stan snorted.

"Really, Jem? It's soaking wet. It's dead."

Jem was annoyed and said something, and then Stan said something, and they spun around and drifted with the current, which was steady but not all that slow, and their attention was on each other so much that it took a while before Jem noticed a soldier standing on the shoreline past Stan's shoulder. Stan saw two past Jem's shoulder, and they shut up and looked around and drifted some more. "Do you think they're friendly?" Stan asked.

"How would I know?" Jem whispered.

"I thought you would know if they were one of yours or not."

"One of mine? One of mine? What does that mean?"

"Are you guys currently at war with anyone?"

"Are all New Yorkers as dumb as you?"

Having gotten through a few rounds of insults, they settled down for a few moments, wondering whether to continue the insults or give up. Finally, they both looked ahead, and Jem said, "Do you see that?"

And of course Stan did.

"It's a lake," Stan said, staring ahead of them as the river they were on opened up and opened wide. He could see factories on either side, and trucks entering and leaving.

"It's *my* lake," Jem said jubilantly.

This irritated Stan enormously. "How can it be your lake? Do you think you can just peel up a lake and move it? It might be the water that would be in your lake if your lake was where it should be, but it's not your lake." He crossed his eyes in irritation. "Really, Jem."

Jem snorted. He was also irritated. "If it's the water that would be in my lake, then obviously since a lake is a collection of water – obviously then it is my lake. Ipso facto."

"Ipso facto," Stan muttered. "Ipso facto. Do you even know what that means?"

"Libtard," Jem muttered.

Stan stiffened. "Who says I'm liberal, you backwoods piece of crap?"

"I know who you are!" Jem sputtered. "You think I don't read Whispers and can't put two and two together? You call yourself Stan the Cat! And you know what, if I looked like a cat I'd be smart enough not to point it out to everyone!" He tried to land a punch on Stan's head, but the logistics were all wrong, and instead, he tipped over back into the water and began splashing frantically, trying to catch up to Stan, who couldn't puff up his fur as much as he wanted because he, too, was in the water and scrambling to get at Jem.

"Hey!"

They both stopped and looked over to the shore where two men with rifles grinned at them. They were both annoyed by those grins, though it was better than being shot at.

"You'd better get out of the water," the closest guard said. "That water's really not for swimming, you know. It's drinking water."

Both Stan and Jem quit thrashing, and splashed their way toward shore. Stan stopped in a shallow area, cleared his throat, and said, "Um, I peed in that water. I think you should know."

CHAPTER 17

The cat was still gone, and despite herself Eleanor was beginning to worry. He didn't answer his phone.

She met the witches at the airport and brought them home. No broomsticks, because it was daylight, and she managed to hire a private car service to get them back to her place. After lunch she took them to that day's parade. Dressed-up floats with flowered arches and animatronic presidents waved to the crowd.

The weather was good; the sidewalks were lively. At the end of the parade were three pickup trucks with children in them throwing out nougats. The crowd cheered and at once the nougats, still in the air, turned into butterflies. More nougats were thrown and there were yet more butterflies. The crowd cheered and clapped, and the butterflies circled around everyone, and then each butterfly turned into a drop of rain, a very nice drizzle, and the crowd roared with pleasure and delight.

"The drought is over!" a man in a hat cried, and a cheer went up. The trucks continued down the street, and the next street cheered, and the next.

Eleanor followed Gloria's glance at the pavement, at the mix of discarded nougat wrappers and butterfly wings. She saw Gloria freeze, and then Monica noticed it and looked closely at the ground, too.

"What is it?" Eleanor asked. Dolores was looking at them all with concern.

"Inanimate to animate and back to inanimate," Monica said. "It's a change spell, and it violates life. Which was it – alive first and then a wrapping and then back to alive and then on to rain? However it was done, it's cruel."

"And the butterflies that were destroyed," Gloria said. "Look at them. They're endangered. And they were destroyed heedlessly. For fun?" She shook her head. "How can this be fun?"

They walked along slowly, butterflies dying all around them, people laughing and eating the nougats, which Eleanor found hard to think about – were they, in essence, eating the butterflies? All changes were superficial, she had understood that; there was still the intrinsic self. She could certainly see that with Stan, who had not changed away from being Stan.

"This city has such a strange feeling," Monica said when they returned to Eleanor's house. They discussed what they should do, testing a number of possibilities. Finally, Monica started going through Eleanor's cupboards for cake ingredients.

"You're making a cake from scratch?" Eleanor asked, surprised.

"She's been taking cooking classes," Gloria explained.

"You'd be surprised how much cooking reminds me of witchcraft."

"You said that about weaving," Gloria pointed out.

"Oh, what a tangled web we weave, when first we practice to deceive! *That's* what I feel, you know. Deception."

"Thick as can be," Gloria agreed. "Dolores, you don't feel it?"

Dolores looked a little stricken. "No. I feel… weighed down. But that feels like me, like it's inside me, not like it's outside me."

"Good description," Gloria said gently. "Do you have any hyssop in the garden?" she asked Eleanor. "Any type of weed? Something sweet?" She took whatever Eleanor could gather and began to stew it all together, using bottled water and humming under her breath. Maybe not hums, Eleanor realized. Words. A spell.

Gloria let it cool, and then gave Dolores a cup of it to drink, and then another cup to wash her face with. "The eyes especially," she said. "Cup it in your hands and close your eyes and just let your face fall into it. Four minutes."

They waited quietly as Dolores did so, and then Gloria said, "Four minutes, Dolores. That's enough. You can just let whatever liquid is left go down the drain."

"Thank you, Gloria," Dolores said, drying her face and hands on a towel. "I feel refreshed."

Gloria nodded. "It will take some time. A few different kinds of potions, I think. It's a deep spell. She obviously didn't want you to find her, and she put in a lot of thwarts. One by one," she said briskly. "One by one we'll breach them. Did you bring something of hers?"

"I did. She left her cup behind. I can't imagine why she did. A talisman is so important." She handed it to Monica, who cradled it in her hands, her head down.

"It ties her to her coven," Gloria said. "I doubt it would slow her down in any way, but psychologically or morally, it would get in the way. Good for us, though. Monica?" She nodded briskly at the witch.

Eleanor went over to the sink to see if the water was on, so she could make tea. The water spat for a moment and then dribbled, and then poured. Monica stepped over to her swiftly and put her hand under the water and said, "Stop!" She didn't turn the water off, but she said, "Stop," again.

"Gloria?" Eleanor said in a low voice.

"Leave her alone. She's getting something."

After a moment, Monica roused herself and turned the water off and stood there, thinking. "She's nearby. Not sure how close. But the water has her signature all over it." She shook her hands dry. "She's using her power through the water, too. I'm sure." She stood there, thinking. "I can almost feel a web of water, a way of binding that goes through water. I wouldn't drink it without a cleansing spell."

"We did that before," Eleanor said. "I mean, earlier today."

"But you ran the water after that. We have to cleanse it. And we have to cleanse all parts of it, even the parts we've had to drink."

Monica consulted Gloria and they decided to create an amulet made of certain leaves wrapped around stone. They could carry it or put it in a pouch and wear it.

So the four witches carried out the instructions, thinking out loud as they did so.

"Did you get a good sense of where she is physically?" Gloria asked.

"She's in a very large building. With water around it? An island? I keep getting the impression of a castle."

"The president's palace," Dolores and Eleanor said together.

"He has a palace?"

"Yes. With a moat. That explains your feeling that it has water around it. So she's with the president. I wonder... There was a woman with the president when they took me in."

"Took you in?"

"The messenger came for me. He held me overnight in a very nice room with room service. I had guards. Nothing strange happened other than he asked me to spy on Stan, and he told me that he had Daria, and that she was fine. I think that woman was there when he said it, too. How strange. I didn't really pay much attention to her."

"By her choice, probably," Gloria said. "I heard some of this story but tell us everything you remember."

When Eleanor had brought them up to date, Gloria looked thoughtfully around the room. "Daria is in charge," she said. "We can see she's in charge. Dolores has told us enough to identify her as an arrogant, grasping woman who unfortunately has the power to deceive."

Monica made a little clucking sound. "Is it possible she's under some spell herself? Maybe she doesn't mean to be like this."

"No," Dolores said regretfully. "It's one reason the coven became so small. She was controlling and abrupt. Things had to be done her way. None of the rest of us wanted to fight her. It was easier to just leave. I should have done something. But it was easier for me not to do anything." She lowered her head. "I regret that."

They expected Gloria to say something, to admonish Dolores for not at least getting in touch with her, but she said nothing for a moment. Then, finally, Gloria sighed and said, "I don't know how much she has changed or influenced or destroyed, but it's easy to see, just from a quick walk around, that there's too much magic going on. Talking heads, those nougats turning into butterflies and then into rain – that was a demonstration for us, I believe. She knows we're here and she was showing off. That's why she wanted to see you, Eleanor, to get a sense of you and to see along with you. Did she touch you at all?"

"Touch me?" Eleanor murmured. And then, all at once, she remembered a moment when the woman had indeed reached out and touched her. She had held a tray with tea and biscuits on it. She had put the tray on the table and then, as she passed the teacup to her, tapped her on the arm to get her attention, and then tapped her again to see if she wanted sugar or milk. And then she had stepped back and remained on the other side of the room, silent and watchful.

Had there been a small smile on her lips?

"Yes," she said. "Was that Daria?"

"What did she look like?" Dolores asked. "Small face with a sharp little chin, big eyes, hair cut in waves all around her face?"

"I don't know." It was true, she couldn't quite remember her.

"She could have presented herself in any form," Gloria said.

"The question is: what do we do? Are there enough of us to confront her and win?"

"I don't feel very strong," Dolores said sadly. "I don't know if I'd be any good."

"Not today," Monica said firmly. "It will take a little while for the potions to make you yourself again. Tomorrow will be better. We should look at a map and see where we are and where she is, and think about what to do." Eleanor was surprised at how decisive Monica sounded until she looked over and saw that Gloria was huddled forward, her head slumped.

"It's been a long day," Eleanor said finally. "Gloria, let me show you to your room. Dolores, there are two beds in another room, if you want to stay here tonight."

"I think we should all stay together," Monica said in agreement. "Four heads are better than one."

"I just need a nap," Gloria said. "You start planning and I'll come back full force."

Jem and Stan crawled out of the water and onto the shoreline, where three men stood, pistols on their hips, watching them with interest. One had his hand on a gun. Stan automatically checked his bowtie for his own gun, but it was just as wet as his cellphone and of no use at all.

"What were you doing in the water?"

"We fell in," Stan said. "We were watching our reflections. Have you heard that story about Narcissus? We were talking about Narcissus and then boom!" He was good at this kind of mindless stuff, he thought. Distract them and let them tell you more than you tell them. "It's how we got the word narcissism. What have you been talking about?"

"About shooting trespassers," the man in the middle said. He was sandy-haired and a little beefy. Either he was in charge, or he just felt like he was.

"Oh, is this private property?" Stan looked around. There

was a wide river and around it were rocks and shrubs, same as ever. Ahead was a big lake and to the sides were factories and trucks. He waved towards it. "I bet that's private property! What is it? It looks like a bottling plant."

"I think you should shut up," Jem sighed. "You just can't seem to shut up."

"Is that you, Jem?" the tallest man said, and Stan was suddenly alert. "What are you doing here?"

"Looking for the treasure," Jem said with a sigh. "This is all an accident."

"Treasure?" the man on the left said with a snort. "That was a joke. Didn't you know that was a joke? We were all just high one time and came up with it."

Stan's fur rose unimpressively because it was so wet. That made him even more annoyed. He spun to Jem, his claws out, his teeth showing. "Joke? There's a joke here?"

"Take it easy," Jem said. "I can explain." He lifted his hands up in a calming gesture, which was lost on Stan, who now spun back around to face the man who'd called the treasure a joke. "I recognize you!" Stan cried, pointing his paw at the man, who smiled. "You're the man who gave me the clue." He stood there, staring at him. What was this man doing here? What was going on? And why was his heart sinking in despair?

The man laughed and slapped his neighbor lightly in delight. "That's right! I thought he looked familiar."

"You mean you saw him once and didn't recognize him the second time?" Jem asked, incredulous. He was wringing out various parts of his clothing. "He looks quite distinctive to me. Like a cat, is what I think. He says it's a skin disorder."

"Could be. I have a cousin with a skin disorder. Only his is all red and scabby." The man nodded at Stan. "And yes, I scribbled a few words on a newspaper and shoved them at you. It was fun. I watched from one of the neighborhood cameras. You were so excited! You kept trying to be discreet, but you couldn't help yourself!" He nudged his fellow guard. "I must be pretty good with words," he said.

"What words?" the other guard asked, interested.

"I don't even remember. I was just told to make up some words."

Stan staggered backwards slightly, his heart beating too fast. "Excuse me," he said, trying to gather his dignity together. "You mean, you *made up* the clues?"

"I made up most of it," the guard agreed. "Even the stuff that went to the papers."

Stan was still reeling. He felt the world slipping away from him. "You made up a treasure hunt just for fun? And put it in the paper? And got the president to play along? Why would the president play along?"

"Oh, he gets bored," the man said. "And he's a cousin on my sister's side."

"He's not a cousin on your side as well?"

"Could be. But I don't get along with my sister all that well, so I don't ask."

"But who are you then?" Stan asked, turning to Jem. "And why did you bring me here? You *did* bring me here, didn't you? It wasn't a mistake?"

"Oh, well, it went farther than I thought it would. I was just planning to show you the cave and then maybe send out a clue about the waterfall later. Or something else. I hadn't decided yet. It was fun figuring it out. You were so eager to find something that it didn't even have to be logical. I had to go to a lot of meetings just to be there if you showed up." He looked at the other guards. "None of the others wanted to do that, you know. But even though there's no treasure, it turned out to be a great way to recruit people."

Stan growled a little. "Recruit people for what?"

Jem raised his eyebrows at the guards, who stepped back. "We have to talk privately for this." The guards waved and headed back towards the plant. Jem took off his jacket and put it on the grass. "Good thing it's sunny. This will dry fast. Don't you want to take off your suit?"

"My skin condition," Stan murmured. "I'll just sit in the sun. Go ahead."

"I work *with* the president. I'm in politics." Jem cleared his throat. "I'm a political scout, actually. I keep tabs on interesting people, watching what they do and how they do it. If they get people's attention, for instance. Or if they're too boring to be of any use. I mean, sometimes we want boring. Local boards should be boring, or people would go to the meetings more. And we don't want that. We just want to have some meetings open to the community and let them come and see that they never want to come again. They can go to some court cases, too, so we want judges who are hard to understand. But the public likes lively debates and entertainment, so we have lots of parades and giveaways. We run it like a game show mixed with reality TV. It works like a charm. Plus, I know those nougats have something in them. I never eat them, anyway. Maybe you shouldn't either. Just saying." He shrugged. "We want to recruit you."

The cat's eyes half-closed in pleasure. "Who are 'we'? Recruit me for what?"

"I'm with the Press Corps," Jem said. "No one really pays attention to us in the palace, or at least mostly they don't. We do a great job of screening and whenever anything like bad press comes through, we send out some exciting news. The treasure hunt was a reaction to an incident with a faulty president's head. We immediately told the people about the treasure hunt. And gave out more nougats. There's such a mild serotonin uptake in those that I personally don't trust that it does anything. Still won't eat it, however."

"Wait!" Stan cried. He was on his feet and pacing, his tail held high and then low and flicking. He wasn't sure how he felt about this. It was interesting, but was it accurate? Which part wasn't accurate? "You make things up?" he asked finally.

The question was too narrow; the question wasn't really the question he wanted to ask, which was broad and infinite and had to do with inflating the world and changing it.

Jem laughed. He went to slap Stan on the shoulder, but drew back. There wasn't much of a shoulder to aim for. "It's really neat. We have meetings a few times a week where we sit around, drink beer, and think about things to do that would keep everyone from thinking about the water and the taxes. People love to be distracted! And they get bored quickly. So it's fun to toss things back and forth." He laughed. "We *do* toss things back and forth. Yeah, potato chip bags, pencils, sometimes we try juggling. Hey," he said, eyes lighting up, "we have juggling lessons coming up next week. And if there's something else you'd like to try, just say the word."

"Hang gliding," Stan said automatically.

"Hard to do at a meeting," Jem said. "But maybe we can figure that out. Anyway, it's terrifically fun and you get to use your brain full-time. It's just that," and here he didn't so much hesitate as wait for imaginary music, "you have to be okay with lying and deceit and stuff."

"Like what?" Stan had no problem with lying and deceit, but he was curious to see what "stuff" covered.

"Well," Jem said, and pointed to the factories and the lake. "This was diverted so we could produce bottled water and sell it back to the populace. And to a few other places as well. Mostly our allies, but we occasionally change the label and sell to our enemies as well. We have an army to do a lot of the logistics on processing and transporting, but if we need some more labor, we just send out the messenger and bring some back." He thought he saw a twitch on Stan's part. "This is all hush-hush. But they can't return, of course. We let them choose two people to join them. We have compassion. And we pay them." He looked virtuous.

Stan shrugged. "That makes it okay," he said. "Taking people is bad, but not if you give them a better life. Everyone wants a better life. All in all, I like your style. But I have to know – why have you been giving clues and stuff to me? Why tell me about the Press Corps?"

"We've been keeping tabs on you. Have you ever wondered why it was so easy for you to set up Whispers?"

"No," he said.

Jem frowned. "Well, you should have. I guess it's 'cause you were new here. Anyway, we knew about Augment – a few of us were followers – and we were curious what you would do. Every place on earth needs somewhere for people to let off steam without mounting a resistance, so we thought, here's our chance. And you were great!" He grinned. "You kept bringing up more and more things, good and bad, political and not, and it kept people from really thinking about any one thing too long. You have a knack, a skill. You're an artist at making people stop and look at themselves!"

Stan glowed. His heart thrummed. He could hear his song rising in his throat and he was afraid that it would be too catlike for the occasion, so he looked at a bird in a bush to center himself. "I appreciate that," he said finally, in control of himself again. "Not many people realize how much attention it requires. There are people who have no regard whatsoever." He scowled. He was thinking of Eleanor. "Who think it's easy. Who can't get at the sharp center–"

"Eleanor," Jem said. "Yes, we know. She's being watched, too, but not for a good reason. She gets in the way, doesn't she?"

"She does," he growled.

"Well, someone's interviewing her now, I think. Talking to her. Seeing what's what and whether *steps have to be taken*."

Stan's head snapped up. What did that mean? He was all for putting her in her place and telling her how insignificant she was and how important he was, but was there something ominous in that particular phrase. "Huh?" he said without thinking. "You're not going to hurt her?"

Jem looked at him steadily. It was a minute before he smiled. "That's nice. I mean, that you care what happens to her. I wish I could say she cares what happens to you, but nah. The president asked her to spy on you, and she said yes."

Stan ignored the fact that he had also said yes to spying on *her*. Instead, he leapt up to his full height, practically straining at the sky. "That bitch!" he cried. "That witch! Always messing with me! I don't care what happens to her, I really don't! And I like this whole Press Corps thing you've been talking about. It's exactly what I was meant for. I have a spectacular brain and I can't stop thinking marvelous, wonderful things."

"And the water plant?" Jem waved vaguely at the huge manufacturing plant.

"Who the hell cares?" Stan cried. "I only drink beer!"

CHAPTER 18

Gloria needed to rest, and various potions were given to Dolores to get her back in some sort of shape, so the witches were just preparing to leave the next day and set their plans in motion when Stan walked through the doorway.

Everyone stopped and looked. "What's this?" Stan said rudely. "More witches?"

"Is that the cat I've heard so much about?" Dolores asked. She looked him up and down. "Has he had all his shots?"

"I never thought about shots," Gloria admitted. "So, no. And he hasn't been neutered yet either."

Stan's claws were out but he forced himself to retract them and put on what he hoped was a grin. "Well, well, well," he said. "I heard you had a little visit with the president, Eleanor. Anything happen?"

Everyone became quiet and watchful. Eleanor sighed. "He wanted me to spy on you. I said yes because he said he would release Daria, or that he had Daria – now that I think about it, I realize I'm not quite sure what he meant. So yes, I know you can take care of yourself. I don't know if Daria can."

"Seems like she can," Gloria said neutrally.

Eleanor nodded. "Of course I didn't know that at the time."

"We wondered where you were," Monica added. "Catting around?" She laughed.

"I was on important business," the cat said, swelling up. "I also had a meeting with the president. He likes me a lot." He glowered at Eleanor. "But not you. I think that's a fair assessment."

"So you're his spy, too, then?" Gloria asked sharply. Eleanor really admired how she saw things quickly and spoke directly to them. "Fine. I suppose you'll be watching us and calling in your information?"

"Well," Stan said, suddenly remembering. "Actually, do you have a phone I could borrow? I dropped mine in the water. Or maybe rice? I hear rice works."

The witches glanced at each other and smiled. "I wonder if you hear yourself at all. You want us to give you a phone so you can report on us?"

"That depends on what you'll be doing."

"We're going to get our witch," Dolores said. "A friend of mine. She's had some trouble with her spells."

"Where is she?"

"She's a water-witch. She'll be near water."

"You're going to the mountains?"

"That's interesting," Dolores said. "There's water in the mountains? I thought the lake dried up."

"Oh, is that supposed to be a trick question? Because I'll give you a trick answer. There's water in the mountains and no lake in the mountains. How about that?" He was feeling tremendously important and tuned in at that moment. He loved knowing more than anyone else, and he especially loved knowing more than Eleanor. He looked smug.

The witches all grew quiet, thinking. Finally, Gloria said, "She moved the lake somehow. I don't know what spell could do that, so she must have caused something to happen. How do you move a lake?"

"Break a dam?"

"Then the water would have come here," Dolores said. "But our river dried up."

"It doesn't have to be the dam," Monica said. "You could punch a hole in the side of the lake anywhere at all and it would drain in that direction."

They all grew quiet again.

"They redirected it."

"*She* redirected it," Dolores said sadly. "Always arrogant. I didn't know she was this powerful, though. Or maybe I just didn't realize how aggressive she was. I'm ashamed at how little I knew her."

"Who said it was the witch?" Stan cried out. He was annoyed that these people thought they knew so much, and could figure out so much, and didn't even bother to ask him any questions about what *he* knew. "Dynamite would blow a way to the cave and then the water would just follow all the way down to the factory. And that's how men would do it!" He was triumphant. He didn't even care that Jem had said to keep his mouth shut, because he was going to have a lot to tell Jem, as soon as he got a phone. He was sure he'd be rewarded. And Jem had told him about a library where he could use a safe computer, and he'd given Stan the password for a special account in his name.

The best thing would be to go with the witches, see what they were doing, then go to the library and report what they were doing on Whispers, then get in touch with Jem, who would see how much in the know Stan was.

That was a lovely thought. To the witches' surprise he began to hum.

"Oh, who knows what's in his head?" Eleanor muttered. "It doesn't matter what he does now. Let's get going. Do we need anything special?"

Because there was no public transportation to the palace, and because Gloria was already disabled, they decided to fly. Gloria chose her walker-with-a-seat and the others chose variously a broom, a rake, and a mop.

They stood outside while Stan demanded to be taken with them. "I've never flown!" he complained. "And I've put up with a lot. You don't have to agree with me, but you have to admit that I've put up with a lot! Letting me fly once won't hurt you and it will give me some kind of compensation for being changed without my approval."

Gloria looked at Eleanor and raised her eyebrows. "No," Eleanor said.

"Then we're off!" and with that Gloria rose and the others followed. They rode at tree level, ignoring the pointing and the murmurs below them. It would just be another spectacle to the inhabitants of this place and, indeed, instead of shock there was sometimes applause and laughter. Another treat from the president! Another glorious treat!

They circled the castle when they arrived, going slowly around the moat, rising a little to inspect doors and windows, making themselves seen. Eleanor could feel it, the moment when the castle noticed; alertness leached from inside. Faces began to appear at the castle windows; whether they were guards or staff or the various faces of Daria, it was impossible to tell. But it was obvious that they had been seen and – more to the point – identified.

The witches landed in the public area outside the moat, in front of the drawbridge, which was down. Gloria landed first, stood up, collapsed the seat, and took firm hold of the walker. Eleanor and Monica stood to her left, Dolores to her right. The enormous carved castle doors were closed; there was a small human-sized door on the right side, which was open with a guard stood in it. He was uniformed in a vaguely familiar guard uniform, tight black pants and a red swallowtail jacket and tricorn hat. Revolutionary in some way? Eleanor made a note to herself to look it up. He stepped outside, onto the drawbridge itself, came to attention, and crossed his rifle on his chest.

"Give Daria's cup to Monica," Gloria told Dolores, and the witch scrabbled in her pocket and brought out the cup. Monica took it and pressed it between her hands, feeling her way into it, letting her mind wander and rest and observe. She had never met Daria, but her mind reached out and through the castle, searching for the witch's signature. She could feel the surprise, the sharp displeasure when Daria was found, and the swift and mounting psychic wall the water-witch was building.

Gloria had been watching Monica's face and she understood. "Are you ready, Eleanor?" she asked quietly. Eleanor glanced quickly at her and frowned. They hadn't thoroughly discussed each step of the process. She knew Monica would find her and then they would summon her as a group, but she also had doubts about her own powers. She took a deep breath and nodded.

"We are with you, Eleanor," Monica said.

Then Dolores chimed, "We are all together with you."

Eleanor felt a surge in her heart and lungs, a swelling outward. She lifted her head and felt everything in her reach out to the castle, and then rush inside. She heard the heartbeat that Monica magnified, the bit of lust and yearning that marked Daria as a human being, and the arrogance and insolence that marked her as a witch.

Monica touched Eleanor's arm and then held on as Gloria reached over, balancing herself on her walker, and took hold of Eleanor's other wrist. She was lit up between the two strongest witches, with Dolores on Gloria's other side, balancing them. They were all linked, a shield and a wall, and the power to find moved from Monica to Eleanor and was reinforced by Gloria's imperturbable strength. And then, in a brief insight, she realized that Monica would replace Gloria someday soon, that the foolishness that had always seemed a barrier to her was a last attempt at privacy, at guardedness, and that it was also her personality, and she realized this and used it, the power that would be and the power that was. The mix of all the powers swelled through her summons to Daria, racing through corridors and up the stairs until it reached a particular door, where Eleanor's summons rested for a moment. She wasn't the one who summoned; they all did.

"Daria," she whispered, and the whisper slammed into the door like a fist, and then it banged again, and the door flew open. Inside, a woman stood facing them, her arms outstretched. Her fingers were upturned, as if to catch a ball, and then the rain began.

It started as a drizzle and sped into a storm. Eleanor began to pull, using her imagined arms and her indrawn breath to drag Daria forward until the witch lost her balance. Daria increased the rain until it bore her through the corridors on a wave, and she used it to dash down a side corridor, or up a stair, but always Eleanor pulled harder, the strength of the other witches pulling with her. They stood physically outside, straining together, as Daria was drawn reluctantly, continuously forward.

Daria expanded, spreading herself out so that the rainstorm pushed through the walls and out to the moat and then on to the street. People stopped and hooted with delight. Rain! Maybe the drought was over! They smiled and laughed and pointed to the skies and then realized that the skies beyond the rain were bright and blue and had no clouds, and it began to disturb them. People turned to go home, and they walked faster as the rain hit them hard, and then they began to run.

"Daria!" Eleanor cried, feeling the strain of the pulling, the summoning. But there were four of them and only one of Daria. How much longer could she resist?

The water was rushing out of the castle now, into the moat, which began to overflow, washing up over the sides and into the streets. The last of the pedestrians were swept forward, down the streets. They scrambled to regain their footing and then ran.

Gloria braced herself against her walker, using just a little of her energy to transform it into a seaside railing raised above the waves.

"Daria!" Eleanor summoned her again, and the witches took a breath together, their heartbeats synchronized, their wills straining and stretched forward. All of them could feel

Daria braced against them, and all of them could feel the first slippage, Daria's first wearying, the effort she made and the resolution behind it. The rain began to drop off a little, just a little, as if the bulk of it was done or debating if it was done. But she was merely readying herself.

The moat leapt up.

It was in itself an incredible, terrible sight. It rose like a creature awakening at an alarm, surging forward and aiming at the witches. They braced themselves against the railing, and Gloria began a deflection spell, which Monica and Dolores joined while Eleanor kept drawing Daria forward. As the wave reared up towards them, she could see Daria's face within it, and then her arms spread out along the length of the wave. That was too much; she was spreading herself out too thin; there was no way she could maintain two spells requiring so much effort. The wave began to lower and recede, and Daria's face showed the strain, stretching a little at the mouth, collapsing a little in the forehead and eyes.

"I summon thee!" Eleanor cried, and out of the corner of her eyes she thought she saw the cat scampering towards them. She realized that the rain had subsided to a drizzle, and that the wave was collapsing with a long, moaning sound. Within a minute, a figure stood before them on the drawbridge – Daria, her shoulders slumped and water dripping off. But upright and proud.

Eleanor could see the cat now, off to the side, stopping and snapping photos. So he had used his time to get a phone on the way here. That was fine. But now he ran past Daria and up the drawbridge. Where was he going?

"Daria, come forward," Gloria said. But the water-witch stood there, raising her chin. "You can't continue with this, Daria. We are strong enough together to put a restraint on you, and make it stay. How deep that restraint needs to be is your decision."

The witches began easing the summoning, and Eleanor

sighed with relief. She had never done anything like this, didn't even know she *could* do anything like this. And a restraint spell was new to her; her education had stopped when she'd been sent to Liberty. She allowed herself to look around. She was surprised to see that there was very little destruction, though of course water would do little damage to a moat. The drawbridge looked unharmed.

And as she looked at the drawbridge, she saw Stan come trotting out again, on all fours, with the president, who was actually sitting on him. His legs dangled, and Stan looked anything but heroic, yet the cat stopped on the drawbridge and took a selfie. He took a few more, and turned to make sure to get Daria in the shot, behind him. Eleanor could picture it – the cat rescuing the president, with the witch in the background. Why, it would be all about him, of course. She gritted her teeth. He was taking more pictures, and the president was even waving at the camera now.

"What is your decision?" Gloria asked the bedraggled form on the drawbridge. Eleanor could feel it as Gloria began to wrap Daria in psychic restraints and she felt Monica join in. She could see the sunlight glancing off the sheer strands that began to wrap around Daria's arms and legs.

Stan saw it, too, and he and the president moved past the witch and along the drawbridge until they reached the streets. Daria watched them without reacting. It was obvious that she was too weak to fight the spell, but she wasn't giving in.

"I want you to admit that the only reason you were able to stop me was because there were four of you and only one of me," Daria said, her voice steady and implacable. "Will you admit that? I am that powerful."

"Yes, you are," Gloria said easily. "Which is why witches gather. Well, it's why any group gathers, I suppose. Armies do it. Villagers fighting wolves do it. Combined strengths are real, and I fully admit that it would be hard for a single witch to defeat you. You're very strong."

Daria swelled up a little.

"But we're stronger, of course," Gloria continued. "I'm grateful to my friends for joining together; I will always be grateful. I don't know why you took the path you did." She stopped, waiting for an answer.

Daria stood there, unyielding. Her eyes were slits in her face. She adjusted her stance, feet apart, straight spine, chin high.

"She never did like to explain herself," Dolores whispered.

"Daria," Gloria said. "If you respect your own gifts, you'll answer."

Nothing.

The witches watched as the restraints grew over Daria like sheer entwining strands. They covered her inch by inch, threading and weaving, until finally she stood immobilized.

"Let us discuss this," Gloria turned and said to the other witches. "What do we think is appropriate? It's obvious that she doesn't care about her effects on others, and that rules out any kind of re-education. She doesn't have the soul for it."

Eleanor looked around at the city that Daria had held hostage for water and power. She saw Stan wave to someone and when she followed that direction, she saw a bunch of vans coming towards him. Some people jumped out with cameras and one person at least with a microphone. They ignored Daria. The president had his arm around Stan's shoulder (he was now standing up) and was gesturing widely. The cat bowed.

The witches watched this for a few minutes and then Gloria turned to Eleanor. "You've been very helpful, Eleanor. This would never have been cleared up without you. As far as I'm concerned, you've redeemed yourself. Monica, do you agree?"

Monica laughed and said she did.

Gloria nodded and looked sharply at Eleanor. "And you? Do you believe you've done enough? Should you continue your education? I can help you to restore the cat to a human, although we should decide whether he merits that." She frowned and looked over to the crowd that was beginning to grow around the news van. "What's Stan doing?"

He was pointing at Daria, and all the cameras followed the direction of his paw and began to film the water-witch. The reporter was gesturing madly. "I believe he's giving an interview on the news about his part in destroying the witch that held the city's water imprisoned," Eleanor said, sighing. "And the president is agreeing. I think he already has something going on, something up his sleeve, and since the president is standing up for him, I think it might be a political position." She sighed again in exasperation. "And he managed this while looking like a cat."

"Which is why transformation as punishment sometimes is ineffective," Gloria said. "But we need to decide about Daria first. How do we contain her? What does she want?"

"Indeed," Monica said. "What can she possibly want?"

They looked over to where Daria stood, still immobile. But her lips were moving.

"She's answering us, I think," Monica said, "but the constraints make it hard for her to speak."

They moved closer, and Gloria relaxed the cords around Daria's mouth.

Daria took a deep breath and looked at them levelly. "I wish to be turned to water," she said.

There was a silence as everyone digested this. "To water?" Monica said in a worried voice. "But you can't be changed to water; that's against the principles of transformation. And I'm sure you could find a way to change back and create trouble again."

"I wish to be locked into the change." Her voice was steady and certain.

"Locked in? You will no longer be human," Gloria said. "Or at least, I hope you won't still be human. I don't think your human part could bear that. It's not what our nature was made for."

"I will spend every hour of every day of my life getting even with you," Daria said calmly. "I will dedicate my life to that.

The only way you can stop me from doing that is to imprison me for the rest of my life, or you can allow me to transform into water. If you do that, I will never be able to take my vengeance on you, and you can soothe your conscience by never having to think of me in prison – any kind of prison you would end up deciding on, something 'humane' yet adequate, would be intolerable to me. Water would not."

"A human being into water – we don't allow that kind of change. We don't know what the existential experience is – we don't know what would happen to your consciousness. You changed paper into butterflies or butterflies into paper without thinking of what the consequence was for the butterflies. How you affected their existence–"

"Because I didn't care," she interrupted. "Butterflies! What a very tender conscience you have! But don't let that stop you. I hope I have consciousness; I hope I can feel the water around me, the waves I am part of, the vast expanse of it. You think you're so powerful because you can enforce your rules, but the real power is in nature, not in human laws. Imprison me in one of your curses – or two or three – and I will spend years figuring out how to break them, and how to find you, and how to destroy you." She took in a great breath. "That is my promise."

As a kind of proof of her determination, a single crack of thunder split over their heads.

"Don't pay attention," Gloria told them. "That's just sound; that's all she can do. We'll discuss your request and determine it," Gloria then said, raising her voice so Daria could hear. "In the meantime, we will all four jointly lock you and thwart you. Monica, reduce her size so you can carry her on your broom. We'll discuss this when we get home."

Monica approached Daria slowly, speaking the spell distinctly, and raising her hand at the end, moving it down to push the size smaller. When she stopped, that was Daria's new size.

"You are also bound," Monica said, and lifted Daria up and

placed her in a small box inside the bag she always carried. Did she have an assortment of boxes? Eleanor wondered. She looked across to where the news vans were still surrounding Stan and the president. None of them had even glanced their way, and she assumed that one of the witches had thrown up a spell. Gloria caught her looking at Stan. "I suppose it's time to let him return to his regular form. Do you agree?"

"Let me find out what's going on first," Eleanor said. "I'll meet you back at the house. You can discuss what you should do and tell me about it. I'm sure I'll agree. I won't be long."

She walked over to the group surrounding Stan. He was standing between the president and a large sandy-haired man. The president was speaking into a microphone. "So, when I figured out that we were all held under a spell and the water had been stolen, I enlisted the help of two incredible resources in our beloved state of Liberty. This is Jem, he's my right-hand man, he's the one who told me about the conspiracy to defraud our great nation, which I'll look into, you can bet, just as soon as we blow up some obstruction to our river and make sure it all comes right again. Imagine that! The river will flow again! We'll have a celebration like no other. Right, Jem? Jem is brilliant at these things, as is," he turned to Stan, "this great liberator here, Stan, is it? He and Jem rode down a waterfall to find where the water was going to, and they discovered the whole secret, all of it. Nowhere else in the world could this have happened!" the president blared. "What have we done for you? Why, we fought witches and water thieves and people who blow up the natural environment – all of them from outside the country, from the East, I'll bet we'll find out, not one of ours. Though, yes, I hear a witch or two was involved, and that's godless! We will defeat the godless army!" he cried at the last and paused, expecting an outcry from the crowd, but there was no crowd, only the news van and Eleanor.

"I think they were expecting a parade," Eleanor said. "So they left."

"Ah, we've met," the president said and took a closer look at her and a closer look at Stan. "That's right, both of you working for my government. And it's much appreciated." He waved at Jem, who came forward, grabbed his elbow, and led him away. The news vans began to load up.

"So you're a hero," Eleanor said.

Stan beamed. "Should have been recognized long ago. This is just one in a series of–"

"What's your next step? I assume there's a next step?"

"I've been invited to be part of the government. I'll get an office and a two-bedroom suite in the castle in case I want my chums to stay over – and no, Eleanor, not you, ever – staff of my own, a terrifically fast computer with both Google and Wiggle on it. I'll be a kind of mastermind." He beamed. "As is only proper."

"I see," she said. "Well, I can't say I'm surprised. I'll be heading back now. Good luck. Oh – Gloria asked me about your rehabilitation. She's thinking of changing you back into a man. I don't know how serious she is, but of course she's the only one who can undo it. Is that what you want? I just thought I'd check."

Stan's cat eyebrows raised. "Huh," he said. He took a moment to think about it. "You know what, I don't think so. It's kind of interesting being a cat. I mean, I have the best of both worlds. People see me as a cat or they see me as a person, and that means I can practically be invisible when I'm a cat. I can hear all sorts of things, and that will be so useful in my new position. I haven't really found any problems, except with finger skills. Do you think Gloria could give me human hands but leave me a cat?" He thought it through. "Maybe not. That definitely would draw attention. But opposable thumbs? Can there be opposable cat thumbs?"

"I'll check, Stan. It sounds reasonable to me. I'll ask her and let you know tomorrow."

"Well, I may be busy tomorrow," Stan said, puffing up.

"Interviews. Staff meetings. That sort of thing. I'm a quick learner but I'm sure I'll have to meet everyone in the whole administration, and then some. I may have no time for you." He puffed up even more. "Just tell Gloria to give me opposable thumbs. I don't have to see you or hear from any of you, and I'm pretty sure that there's going to be a new law out in a couple of days that won't treat witches very kindly." He paused again and raised his eyes to the sky before dropping them to her level. "Yes, I can see that happening. If I were a witch – especially a witch that people knew about – I'd want to leave right about now." That last word came out as more of a yowl.

She heard the threat and nodded. "But you may find you need a little help with the parades and such," she pointed out. "They love strange things around here. Like talking heads. Like cats with opposable thumbs. But most of all, parades."

He nodded thoughtfully. "Parades," he murmured, and looked at her. "I always did think you were clever. We'll discuss how to handle the parades sometime soon." He nodded officially and walked away.

Back home, the witches were deep into their discussion about the morality of turning Daria into water. Monica informed her that they had gone round and round and the real problem was that they were all convinced that Daria would discover she had made a mistake, and that there would be no real way they could find that out. Water didn't communicate.

But Daria was adamant. She stood in her reduced size on the table as the argument swirled around her. Eleanor sighed. "I feel for her," she said. "She's simply not at home in her natural element; she wants to change it. I understand that. Who of us hasn't felt out of place? But none of us would ever consider permanently changing into another element, would we? I think the reason is that when we make errors, we make them because of who we are, not what we are. And then we adjust. I think Daria can no longer adjust to what we accept and take for granted. She wants another chance at life, on her own terms. She could be wrong. But enfolding her in punishment for the rest of her life is also wrong. I think that we have to allow her to be mistaken because I believe she's right. She is not meant to be what she now is, and so we should let her go towards what illuminates her. Change her to water. Release her into the ocean. Let her mix with the widest possible body of water and let her travel in what she believes is her true skin."

They sat together for a while, just thinking, and then when Monica called for a vote, they each voted yes.

They took Daria to the Gulf Coast and released her into the ocean, and at the last moment changed her to water, and watched the ripple dissolve into the vast moving shape of the sea.

"I don't know how this can be completely good," Dolores said. "Is she alive? Conscious? Alone?"

"All of that. And it's what she wanted. I hope it brings her some kind of peace. I don't understand it either," Gloria said, forestalling other comments.

Gloria's eyes were sagging; she huddled over her walker as if it was all she could do. Monica came up to her and put her arm around her shoulders. "Come home," she said. "I can help you." And she draped Gloria's arm over her shoulder and did a gentle lifting up. Eleanor understood and used her own ability to push as a kind of brace. They each took a piece of Gloria's exhaustion and rose on their brooms and such, and flew home, where they gave her wine and biscuits and helped her to bed.

Eleanor was having a glass of wine in the backyard when Stan appeared.

"I'm just picking up a few of my things," he said, and sat nearby, looking around. "It feels different here now. I mean, everywhere."

"I feel it, too. I think Daria had some sort of general spell going on. Kind of a mix between being stoned and being drunk. Slightly uninhibited. It's gone now."

"I think it kept people from being upset about the water," Stan said thoughtfully. "I have a feeling they'll be upset now." She looked at him carefully. His eyes were bright, and he had that slightly hungry look about him that she remembered from their Augment discussions. That hunting look. "I think you're right. What are your plans now?"

He tried to look bored which to him meant stretching his long cat body luxuriously out and then flopping over, as if he wanted his belly rubbed. "You know, without Daria, the president really isn't that smart. He's kind of a puppet. But I'm smart. I can be a hero. I suggested we divert half of the river back to its normal route, and let the remainder go to the bottling plant. People trust bottled water. I don't know why, because it comes from the same place as the unbottled water. But I'm fine with that. We can have a good economy if we do things right. And I'd like to see more competition. Newspaper wars. Maybe gladiator contests? Everyone likes gladiator contests. I do like the whole idea of a Roman theme. Togas. We could all wear togas..." His eyes gazed into the distance.

"Gloria said I can give you opposable thumbs," Eleanor said. "As a thank you. A kind of thank you, anyway. Because you..." and here she stopped for a moment. "Because you were instrumental in discovering the water situation. That's not a small thing. I've got my powers back," she added confidently, "and I've been shown how to undo the spell. I could even turn you back into yourself again."

"The thumbs," Stan said quickly. "Just the thumbs."

"Have you thought it through? It's the only time I'm going to offer."

"My picture has been in all the papers, on the TV, people recognize me on the street," he said. "I'm a celebrity. If I change the way I look I'll be nobody. The only real problem I have is with holding things and writing things down and, well, anything that requires a grasp. If you wanted to fly me on your broomstick someday," he said, leering a little. "I would need to grasp it, wouldn't I?"

"I will never take you on my broomstick, Stan."

"Was that meant to be suggestive? It came across as suggestive."

"It was meant to be a rule. Take it how you will." She paused and muttered to herself and added, "You have thumbs. Wiggle them. How do they feel?"

Stan looked at his thumbs. They were, to be honest, barely larger than an ordinary cat's toe, just placed slightly differently. He picked up a spoon, then a twig, then her wineglass. "Hmm. Maybe just a little bit bigger? So my grasp can exceed my reach?"

"I don't think that's the right–"

"It doesn't matter; just do it."

Despite his attitude, she did. He pranced around a little and decided he was satisfied. "Well, good," he said. "I'm glad we're ending on such a happy note. I'm off to the palace now. If you ever need to reach me, that's where I'll be."

"I don't expect that I will, ever," she said pleasantly. "So farewell."

The cat took off and the evening started to lower, her favorite time of day.

Monica came out with her own glass of wine and sat beside her. "Well done," she said. "That cat's a piece of work, isn't he?" She took a sip. "Have you decided what you're going to do?"

"Do?"

"You could come back to New York, or you could stay. Dolores is actually a very good teacher. She's been under a spell, remember, so you haven't seen her at her best. It might be wise to keep an eye on Stan and see if he needs correcting." She winked. "Gentle correcting. Maybe even a little magical correcting. Dolores could guide you on that. The fact is, you're needed here. Daria destroyed the coven, but you could start rebuilding it, with Dolores. I can feel that there are others here who would be interested, and I can pass them along to you. You'd be part of something new and maybe even important." She patted Eleanor's arm. "If you think the Craft is important."

"I do."

"And if you're interested in, I don't know how to say it without sounding silly – but if you're interested in helping one place in the world heal."

"I am." Eleanor surprised herself; she really did feel that she wanted it, a chance to do significant work. A chance to *want* to do something good. With the coven, with the particular balance a group of women with strengths and differences provided, she was sure she could grow into someone better than she had been.

She hadn't known that was what she wanted, but it was.

ACKNOWLEDGMENTS

In the past decade, I've met a wonderful bunch of people who have become my community. Thank you to my friends and fellow writers, Chandler Klang Smith, Nicholas Kaufmann, John C. Foster, Yume Kitasei, Gloria Lim, Miriam Zivkov, and Alan Cafferkey, and to my great good friends Ellen Datlow and Shawna McCarthy. And to Christine Cohen, exemplary agent and serial raccoonist. Thank you also to my editor, Gemma Creffield, who made this a better book.

WHY, LUDGER SYLBARIS, WHY?

May 8, 1902. Martinique.

It was here, on this island in the West Indies, that the most violent and powerful volcanic eruption of the last century occurred. When the eruption began, lava and fragments of volcanic rock were launched into the air at 200 kilometers per hour from the crater of Mount Pelée, which towered 1463 meters above the sea. Shortly following the explosion – which resulted from the buildup of high-pressured volcanic gases inside the volcano – the earth and rock that had once constituted the ash-covered summit of Mount Pelée began to fall on the southwestern face of the mountain, enveloping the beautiful city of Saint-Pierre, which stood only eight kilometers from the summit.

For the people of Saint-Pierre, the whole event was over in a blink of an eye. They didn't even have the time to identify the source of the sound. Nor did they have the time to say in warning, "Papa, this is not time to be in the bathroom. Pelée just erupted!" They didn't have the time to make tear-filled farewells such as the ones a grandma might say to her old and decrepit husband: "I know we had to live together out of necessity in this world, but in the afterlife let's go our separate ways." Nor did they have the time to gather their clothes hanging in the yard or jump out of the tub naked and throw on a robe before running for their lives. Sitting on the toilet or lying in the bathtub, unable to fulfill their promises, with perplexed eyes wide open – that's how the people of Saint-Pierre were buried alive.

There had been several eruptions in the past, and there was always volcanic activity in the crater, but it never bothered the people of Saint-Pierre. In fact, because they held the absurd belief that the volcano was their protector, they looked at the smoke coming from the crater like a beautiful landscape painting. Every time a rumbling came from the faraway mountain, the grandmothers of Saint-Pierre would place their terrified granddaughters on their laps and rub them on the back, just as their grandmothers had done for them.

"My child, do not worry. The volcano will not harm us. In fact, it protects our town from the evil spirits. They say having a volcano next door is good fortune."

But nothing fortunate came from the 1902 eruption of Mount Pelée. Nearly all of the town's 28,000 inhabitants died, including the tourists who had come from afar to see Martinique's beautiful crater lake. Numerous flocks of sheep, and the dogs that chased those flocks of sheep, and lactating cows, and birds who couldn't fly away fast enough, and wagons carrying milk, and the fountain in the town square that gave free droplets of water, and streets paved with fine rocks, and the church tower that rang its beautiful bells every hour – all of these were buried in ash, desperately hanging on to their last breath.

The thick, heavy lava marched down the mountain blanketing all of their possessions, and, as it dried, it transformed all of the memories, jealousy, joy, anger, and passion of the people of Saint-Pierre into a giant heap of stone.

But amidst this pandemonium, there was one person who miraculously survived: the prisoner Ludger Sylbaris. This sole survivor's good fortune was thanks to a curious prison located in the middle of Saint-Pierre. Usually prisons that house vile inmates are located on the outskirts of a city or in some dark and damp underground pit. But not in Saint-Pierre; for some odd reason, they decided to erect a tower in the middle of the city, and at the very top of this tower, they put the most despicable prisoner in all of the town. Ironically, it seems that Ludger Sylbaris was saved by being a vile criminal.

The prison tower of Saint-Pierre was very tall. It soared forty-eight meters into the sky, and this dizzying height was enough that there was no need for iron bars on the prison windows, something all other prison windows needed. Indeed, for the last several hundred years, there wasn't a single prisoner who was able to escape from that tower, despite it not having any bars. Of course, that's not to say there weren't escape attempts. In 1864, Andre Droppa the sailor, who was as brave as he was stupid, attempted to escape the prison. Droppa used bed sheets, prison clothes, underwear, belts, socks, and several towels to fashion a rope long and sturdy enough (or so he thought) to reach all the way to the base of the tower. A rope, in other words, that was at least forty-eight meters in length. In order to get materials for his foolish plan, he tore up all of the fabric he could find in his cell. And because he had torn up everything that had even a bit of fabric on it – that is, his pants, drawers, prison clothes, bed sheets, and blankets – he was forced to sit naked on the cold stone floor as he wove the rope. At night, a chilling sea breeze blew through the tower. Butt naked, Droppa endured the cold sea breeze and lonely night, thinking of the rosy future in which he would be sitting next to a beautiful woman as he ate hot beef soup and drank rum. Finally, when not a single thread of cloth was left in the cell and the rope had been finished, Droppa was so excited he was moved to tears.

It goes without saying that Droppa's rope did not reach the ground. But with no more fabric to increase the length of the rope, Droppa naïvely thought to himself, "How short could it be? If I get to the end of the rope and I still haven't reached the ground, I'll just jump the remaining height!" and decided to go through with it anyway. Who knows? Such a plan might have even seemed feasible when he looked down from the top of the tower. But deciding to risk it all was the most foolish decision of the many foolish decisions Andre Droppa had made throughout his life. Sure enough, when Droppa got to the end of his rope, he realized that it wasn't even half the length of the tower. And because of the layers upon layers of moss that had grown on the stone, there was no way he could climb back up the tower wall. As Droppa hung from his rope and struggled to not let go, he realized something.

"So this is why they don't have bars on the windows!"

In the morning, it was the old shepherd taking his flock of sheep out to the mountains who discovered the prisoner wrapped up in his rope like a cocoon and hanging on for dear life. Looking at the spectacle, the old shepherd called out to Droppa.

"Andre! What are you doing up there? And why are you butt naked?"

Droppa tried to give the old shepherd a polite answer, but because he had been hanging on to the rope all night, not a single word was able to escape his throat. Instead, the only thing left his mouth before he plummeted to the ground and died was two grunts. Perhaps they were grunts of lament or resentment or regret. Indeed, what could he have said just before dying? I like to think he might have said something like this:

"You old coot! What kind of question is that in a time like this?"

After that incident, bars were installed in the windows of the prison tower of Saint-Pierre. But it wasn't to prevent prison escapes; rather, it was to prevent the foolish conclusions that prisoners often came to when they were bored and stared at things for too long. In other words, it was to remind prisoners both that any rope they could fashion from their sheets and drawers wasn't going to be long enough, and that things were much farther than they appeared.

French prisons treated prisoners like fine wine. Just as wine is aged in dark, damp cellars, criminals are aged in dark, damp cells until they become sweet and tart. But in Saint-Pierre, they treated prisoners like wet laundry or fish to be dried. They hung criminals up in high places where there was good sunlight and plenty of wind so that the dampness of their crimes would evaporate in the warmth of the sun and be blown away by the breeze.

Thanks to this, the people of Saint-Pierre were able to look up at the prison tower and see the town's most vile and despicable human being every time they took a break from work and straightened their back or laughed so hard from a joke that they had to grab their stomach. Each time they did this, they would take turns saying mean things: "Even if you stabbed that man in the ass with a harpoon it wouldn't be enough"; "They should castrate him and leave his balls out to dry so that he won't be able to spread his bad seed"; "Why stop at that? You should cut off his dick while you're at it and feed it to your dog Wally"; "Don't say that about my dog. What did he ever to do deserve such a thing?"

To the people of Saint-Pierre, the prison tower was a symbol of evil, an object of scorn and resentment. It was also the source of all their misfortunes, both natural and manmade. If your pig ran away, you looked to the tower; if your daughter got pregnant, you looked to the tower; if you lost a wager, you looked to the tower. The people of Saint-Pierre blamed everything on the prisoner at the top of the tower – everything from the largest of natural disasters to the smallest of inconveniences. Whatever the reason, regardless of whether it was reasonable or not, all of the evil and bad things that happened in the town were hung on that one prisoner. The town's priest would even say, "Why curse your neighbors, your lovely wife, your beautiful children? If you really want to curse something, just look to the tower!"

The cell at the top of the prison tower was almost never empty. And that was because if there was no prisoner in the tower, the entire town's moral law would collapse – at least, that's what the town's elders thought. Not to mention the fact that people would become exceedingly bored. So, if there was no suitable successor for the current tenant, that inmate would sometimes have to spend a much longer sentence than he or she deserved – and this was despite the fact that they had probably already turned crispy from years of hanging on the windowsill to dry in the sun.

Now let's return to the story of Ludger Sylbaris, the sole survivor of Saint-Pierre. Ludger Sylbaris was locked away in the prison tower for twenty-four long years. He was put in prison at the age of sixteen, and it wasn't until he turned forty that he was able to leave its confines. In fact, he was only able to escape with the help of the volcano, and not because he had served out his sentence.

The charges against Ludger Sylbaris were for raping nuns and insulting a priest. They claimed that Ludger Sylbaris had snuck into the convent each night to rape several nuns and that he had insulted a priest in a public place. Despite admitting to the second charge, he denied to the end ever raping any nuns. But before Ludger Sylbaris had time to defend himself, the judge had already sentenced him to eighty years in prison.

In truth, the claims of rape against Ludger Sylbaris were dubious at best. The accusation of blasphemy also did not make much sense. Although insulting and shaking your fist at a priest in a public space was worthy of punishment, it wasn't the type of thing for which you would lock up a sixteen-year-old for eighty years.

In spite of the charges' ambiguous and nonsensical nature, Ludger Sylbaris was locked away in the prison tower for a total of twenty-four years. Then on May 8, 1902, Mount Pelée erupted. A mountain's worth of volcanic ejecta and ash were spewed into the air, and Saint-Pierre was razed to the ground in a matter of seconds. Sticking his head through the iron bars of the tower, Ludger Sylbaris watched as the pyroclastic material from the summit of Mount Pelée engulfed all of Saint-Pierre's 28,000 inhabitants. From that tower in the center of the carnage, he saw all of the city's death and tragedy. And just before the tower was swallowed up by the poisonous steam from the lava, Ludger Sylbaris was saved in dramatic fashion.

How it was that the tower was able to survive the countless number of large and small pyroclastic projectiles that were flung across the sky, and how it was that Ludger Sylbaris was not suffocated by the volcanic gas, remains a mystery. For whatever reason, Ludger Sylbaris, who endured everyone's hatred and ridicule from the top of that lonesome tower, was able to survive with the power granted to him by that very same hatred and ridicule. Because both the laws and customs that had defined his crimes and the people who remembered those crimes were all buried in lava and turned to stone, and because Ludger Sylbaris' crimes were in turn also buried in lava and turned to stone, Ludger Sylbaris was now a free man.

Many journalists wanted to interview him, but Ludger Sylbaris would say nothing of what had occurred. Instead, quietly escaping through the disordered crevices created by the disaster, he disappeared into the night. From time to time, you could hear rumors about a miraculous survivor, but as with all things that garner the interest of the world, the existence of Ludger Sylbaris was soon forgotten.

* * *

Saint-Pierre was frozen in time. But Ludger Sylbaris' watch kept ticking. He crossed over to Mexico. And there at the edge of a desert where no one lived, he lived in seclusion for thirty long years. By then, no one was even slightly interested in who Ludger Sylbaris was or what he had endured. But then, some ten years after his death, a book was published in his name in the state of Louisiana. The book – which was five hundred pages long, written in miniscule font, and titled *The People of Saint-Pierre* – recounted in detailed, calm prose from a relatively objective perspective the history of Saint-Pierre, the lives of its people, and the eruption of Mount Pelée. Ludger Sylbaris probably wrote the manuscript one section at a time, day by day over the duration of his thirty years in isolation. But in the pages of this book, there are several questionable sections. You could call them somewhat preposterous, or even illogical. Let's take a look at one such section:

Father Cleore had a badger tail on his ass. Bishop Desmond also had a badger tail on his ass. Bishop Desmond's tail was slightly larger and longer than Father Cleore's. Because I only saw it from a distance, I couldn't be sure whether they were really badger tails. They could have been flying squirrel tails or fox tails. Actually, so much time has passed that I now wonder if they weren't wolf tails or hound tails. But regardless of what kind of tails they were, people should never have tails on their asses. I was only sixteen at the time, but I knew enough to know that badger tails only belong on the asses of badgers.

As Father Cleore and Bishop Desmond were standing in front of the holy cross, they rubbed their asses together and stuck their faces in each other's butts and made grunting sounds as they took large whiffs, and when they got tired of that, they lay down and started fiddling with each other's tails. It looked just like how monkeys pick at each other's fur. As Bishop Desmond started petting Father Cleore's tail, Father

Cleore looked pleased and wagged his erect tail several times.

At that moment, the railing I was standing on lurched forward and let out a loud creak. Bishop Desmond looked my way. I was so scared I didn't look back even once as I started to run out of the church. From behind me I could hear Bishop Desmond shouting at me. But I didn't stop. I ran and ran until I reached the Zelkova tree on the hill. Shaking with fear, I waited there for my lover Alisa until night came. But when darkness fell, it wasn't Alisa who came for me, but the police.

This wasn't the only odd thing that Ludger Sylbaris wrote. He also wrote that the town butcher, Mr Billy, had four testes and two penises, and that because he was unable to suppress his huge sexual appetite, he used one penis for his wife and the other for the pig. There was also mention of the Daley family who, every other generation, gave birth to a child with talons. According to Ludger Sylbaris, to hide this fact from the world, the family cut off the toes when it was a boy and killed the baby when it was a girl, secretly burying the body in the family graveyard. These are just a few examples of the many stories about the eccentricities of the people of Saint-Pierre, each one being depicted in shockingly graphic detail.

Was this Ludger Sylbaris' revenge? Was it his way of getting back at the people of Saint-Pierre who had ridiculed him and locked him away in a tower for twenty-four years for having done nothing?

Many believe so. They say it was Ludger Sylbaris' pettiness and deranged desire for vengeance that wrote these stories. But I have a different opinion. After all, is this really how a man who spent thirty years as a recluse at the edge of world would think about the people from his hometown – people who were so tragically obliterated in a volcanic eruption?

"You locked me in a tower and spat at me. Good riddance! Now you'll get a taste of your own medicine. I'm the only survivor of Saint-Pierre, so I'm going to pin badger tails on all of your asses.

With this record of mine, you will all be remembered for eternity as priests who had badger tails stuck to their asses. Hahaha!"

Honestly, wouldn't that be a little childish even for a man in his position?

I sometimes go into my study and take out *The People of Saint-Pierre* to read a few pages. Each time I do this I think about those thirty years Ludger Sylbaris spent away from people and what a lonesome life it must have been. A life in which all the people and places he knew had disappeared. A life in which there were never any visitors, nor anyone to ever visit. A life in which you grew corn and potatoes in a vegetable garden, cooked dinner by yourself, and ate alone by candlelight. A miserably quiet life.

Ludger Sylbaris never once left Saint-Pierre before the disaster. Saint-Pierre was where he was born, the home to everything he ever knew. He couldn't have known how to live in any other place that wasn't Saint-Pierre and he had never imagined leaving Saint-Pierre. So, every day, from the time he woke to the time he went to sleep, there was no way he couldn't have thought about Saint-Pierre and the way it disappeared into the smoldering lava. He would have constantly gone over the memories of Saint-Pierre: beautiful Alisa, and the women who stared and hooted at him; the town at night, when he could hear the ringing of bright bells; the rhythmic beating of the wheels on a horse-drawn wagon carrying milk; the sight of the market with its boisterous and lively patrons; and, of course, the last moments as the town was transformed into a pile of ash. "What was it like down there?" he must have wondered. "And why was I the only one spared to be exiled in this foreign land?"

Ludger Sylbaris had to write about Saint-Pierre. Not out of some sense of duty, but because it was the only thing he *could* do. Each time he wrote about Saint-Pierre, the city that had been turned to stone would come back to life with paved streets and wagons filled with milk. The flower beds would be filled with flowers in full bloom, people would be chatting in the market again, the meek sheep would be bumping up against each other's butts as they followed the shepherd boy. And, most importantly, beautiful Alisa would be waving her hand in the distance and smiling.

"Ludger! Meet me tonight at the Zelkova tree on the hill."

Then why, I wonder, after thirty years had the people of Saint-Pierre changed into monsters? What happened as Ludger Sylbaris walked endlessly through the labyrinth of his imagination? Why, Ludger Sylbaris, why?

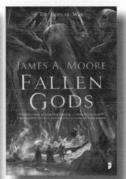
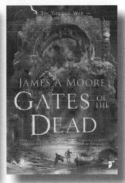

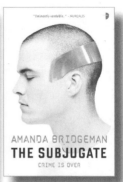

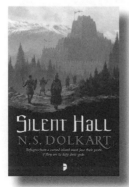

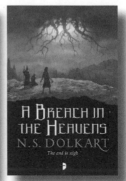

Science Fiction, Fantasy and WTF?!

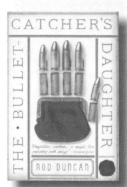

@angryrobotbooks

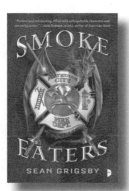

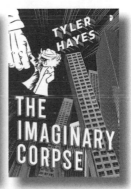

We are Angry Robot

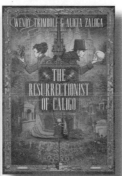

angryrobotbooks.com

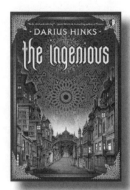

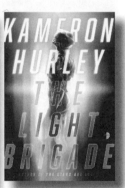

Science Fiction, Fantasy and WTF?!

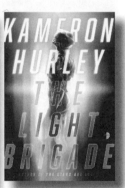

@angryrobotbooks 📷 🐦 📘

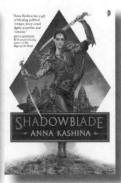